MY DESTINY

MEN OF NEW YORK BOOK TWO

SAMANTHA SKYE

Copyright © 2022 by Samantha Skye

ISBN 978-0-6452730-3-8 (ebook)
ISBN 978-0-6452730-5-2 (paperback)

Cover Design: Angela Haddon
www.angelahaddon.com

Editor: Nice Girl Naughty Edits
www.nicegirlnaughtyedits.com

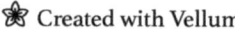 Created with Vellum

CONTENT DISCOVERY

If you are not familiar with my writing I am going to be honest and let you know a few things.

In this book there is spice, lots of spice. There is also violence, the kind that is descriptive in nature and most certainly on the page. Did I mention there is a lot of spice?

This book in particular deals with some medical themes around breast cancer and mutism - both of which carry through the entire book. There is also touch points on drug addiction.

Finally it is a good book. Like really good. Like hard to put it down kind of good.

You have been warned. Enjoy.

To all the girls who want an adventure...

1

DANTE LUCIANO

My eyes flick to Carter, as the stench of smoke and sex filter through my nose. We are both on high alert as we scour the room for movement. Coming to Allure at this early morning hour may not have been my best plan, but with Sebastian in Sicily for another few weeks, he has left New York for me to manage, and this is the call I made.

Allure is smaller than I remember, scummier. With every step I take, my boots stick to the carpet, the sound making us less inconspicuous than I would like. As my team and I move around the furniture, I don't miss seeing the ripped vinyl seats and the chipped dance floor. My reflection is clouded in the dirty mirrors, and the tables look about as clean as the floor. It has been a while since I've entered this strip club in Queens, and as I walk slowly through the space, flashes of memory fill my brain of seeing my ex-wife dancing on one of these poles. My shoulders stiffen at the thought, and already I want to get the hell out of here.

Ever since Sebastian's girl Goldie was taken last year by Riccardo Baldo, Sebastian has made each member of the family disclose every business, property, and asset on a monthly basis. All families have been happily obliging to the new terms because as head family, we offer benefits to do so. Increased men, additional security, a direct line to the head of the NYPD. You give us your details, we give you bonuses; our generosity knows no bounds.

But a month ago, we noticed something off here with the Russo family in Queens. A small outfit, the two brothers do the sneaky jobs for us, like filtering drugs through obscure avenues. We pay them handsomely, supporting them, and I know that Sebastian has given them more than one opportunity to be further up the chain than they deserve. They have several properties, this strip club being one of them, but from the looks of it, there is no money here and any money made here is obviously being moved into something else. Or to someone else.

At 5am, I expected to see people here. Patrons drinking liquor, smoking cigarettes, and watching scantily clad girls wrap their long legs around the shiny silver poles, all the while getting dollar bills thrown their way. But it is empty. Quiet. Another thing that doesn't sit well with me.

The front door was unlocked and had no security, so we walked straight in. But there are no bar staff or waitresses, no dancers, no music. Not even a cleaner, even though they desperately need one.

My hand tightens on the cold metal of my gun, as we

continue through the main room, toward the faint light we see coming from under the door at the back.

Our team is small, but here with Carter by my side, I hope I can get this done and buried. Our getaway car is parked down the street, waiting for us if needed. I don't desire bloodshed this morning; I am merely here to ask questions and demand answers. But I don't mind seeing grown men cry, and if the color red ends up across this grimy floor, then I would say I have earned my keep today.

We are halfway to the back door when it opens. My team spreads quickly as I remain at the front to meet whoever comes through the door head on. Dominic Russo walks through with five of his men behind him and the minute they see us, everyone stiffens. His men don't reach for their guns. They are not that stupid. They know who I am. The minute they raise a gun at me, they know that they have a death sentence.

"Dominic, I love what you have done with the place," I say sarcastically as I saunter toward him. I raise my hands, showcasing the shithole of the place, but keep my gun firmly wrapped in my right hand, while I raise my eyebrows at him in mock delight.

"Dante. I wasn't expecting a visit today," he says, sounding a bit out of breath, clearly surprised by our appearance. I see a bead of sweat travel down the side of his pocket-scarred face.

Dominic Russo and his brother Federico may be gangsters, but that is their only appealing quality. And that's saying something. Italian with dark hair and brown eyes, they are skinny with large pointy noses, bad teeth, and carry an air of arrogance that has yet to be earned. I often observe people and wonder what type of animal they look like. These Russo men are a year apart in age and both look like rats.

Filthy, pathetic rats.

"I am full of surprises, Dominic, and it appears that so are you." I stalk closer. My eyes don't leave his, waiting for a tell, and I get it. His right eye twitches, and I know whatever he is about to say is a lie.

"We are renovating the place, Dante. Plans are being drawn up as we speak!" He puffs out his chest slightly and a smile peppers his face, thinking he has the perfect cover. The mere look of him makes me want to put my knife in him, to cut him from belly to throat. I hate liars. I hate people who keep things from me. Again, flashes of my ex-wife flick in my memory; of her being the biggest liar and disappointment of my thirty-five years on this earth.

I stop a few feet away from him and chuckle, low and threatening. He obviously takes me for a complete moron and has severely underestimated who I am and what I am capable of. A problem I am happy to rectify.

"Try again," I grit out, shaking my head to feign disappointment as I see Carter and my team move strategically around me, knowing what is about to happen. Dominic's men stay still, their eyes roaming the movement, and the smile falls from Dominic's face.

He looks at me, his face becoming red with fury. The man doesn't like being talked down to. None of us do, but he is so slimy, he belongs down in the hole he crawled out of. If it wasn't for him, then my now ex-wife wouldn't be addicted to drugs, wouldn't be dancing on a pole, and would be the mother my son deserves instead of the sad excuse for a life that she now is.

"Perhaps we can meet later this week. I can get the building plans for you then, show you what we have in store for the place," he says, almost threateningly, and I tilt my head, not liking the tone he is taking with me.

His men start to move around the room, sensing the change in their leader's demeanor, positioning themselves near my team. We are equal numbers, but they have nothing on us. I rub my chin and tilt my head while I pretend to mull over his offer, as my men position themselves better, edging backwards to the front door. He is a complete fool for thinking that we will just walk away, but I will use that to my advantage.

Sebastian will be annoyed if we can't put this to bed and get our money back, so as Dominic looks around at his team, I lift my gun. The warm metal presses firmly in my palm, and by the time he looks back at me, the barrel is pointing directly at his face.

"Now, what makes you think I have time to see you this week, Dominic? I am a very busy man, surely you know this?" At my taunting, his eyes drill into me. To anyone else, he would be intimidating, but to me, he is nothing.

"What do you want, Dante?" he asks, acting like we didn't loan him one million dollars for the refurbishment of this place and his repayment is now overdue. He knows that his date for full repayment was yesterday, yet he continues to goad me, trying to showcase his power, of which he has none. I watch as his men reach for their guns, some of them shaking, because they already know that their end might be near. It appears that Dominic is the only one in this room that is disillusioned enough to think anything else.

I cackle at that, the smile not reaching my eyes. I want to shoot him, I do. Then I want to hang his body from the top of the stripper pole and leave him for his brother to find.

But that can't happen today.

"You know what, Dominic? I'm sure we can talk later this week," I say as I relax my stance, and I see his visible relief. "Boys, let's go!" I call out to my team, my eyes not leaving Dominic's. He begins to smile, thinking he has won.

His men keep their guns out and ready, as my team and I walk backwards, making our way slowly to the front door, one of my men already outside signaling to my backup team.

As we reach the entrance, I see his men start to relax, and like a cobra, I strike.

I fire my gun at Dominic's thigh, the bullet piercing his muscle and coming out the other side, embedding itself on the stage nearby.

"Fuuuuucckkkk!" he roars, clutching his leg, falling to the ground. "Well, don't just stand there! Shoot him!" Screaming to his team, he waves his arms about, and only a blink later do bullets start flying.

My team fires to harm because we came here as a warning, not to start a war. Sebastian won't be happy, but it appears that Dominic is taking that decision right out of my hands as his team shoots to kill. After all that

Dominic has done to me in the past, I wouldn't mind seeing his blood splattered all across the room, so my team and I rush out the door, dodging shots until we're outside on the sidewalk.

We have mere seconds before the onslaught continues. Bullets fly through the air one after another, as each of his team race outside, clawing for the accolade of being the person that kills Dante Luciano, Sebastian Romano's right-hand man. But their aim is as straight as their business, and they miss every attempt at making me their target.

I see two of his men each take a bullet to the chest, their bodies flying backwards, slumping against the brick wall behind them. Red now coats their white shirts, and I know this isn't going to look good, but there was no way I was going to back down. Not this time. We have given him more than enough chances, yet he still thought it was better for him to start firing than for him to tell the truth and leave the bloodshed to another day.

I look left and right and see all my team still upright as we wait for the rest of the party to join us outside. Inside would have been a better option for bloodshed this morning, but I will take it out here on the footpath just the same. The door to the club flies open, and gunfire rages again, as the remainder of his men stalk out shooting, with no consideration for the outside world. Glass shatters from the broken windows of the cars nearby where stray bullets have found their surface. The sidewalk is beginning to be coated in red as another one of his team falls to the ground.

My gun is constantly firing, while I also keep an eye

on each of my team, making sure crimson doesn't coat their frames. I am not losing anyone in this shitshow. No one is getting injured on my watch. My frustrations rise more and more as the popping sound encasing us all. We came to ruffle feathers, not to kill the entire goose.

Just as his team storms closer, I catch a movement to my left and I see her. She is like a rabbit caught in headlights, and I don't even think, I just do.

2

ANNIE PETERSON

My feet slap against the pavement in perfect rhythm as I move through the quiet dark streets, lost in my own thoughts. Running has always been my savior, my north star, the one thing that calms and soothes me. I need a moment to center myself after taking a terrifying speeding cab through the city after jumping off the red eye into New York this morning.

After I got to the safety of my room, I had little time to rest my beating heart. Although the room looks like the photos from the website, it was clear that they took creative license with the photography. It is much smaller than I thought it would be. The bathroom has mold, the TV doesn't work, there is no internet, and I am reasonably sure that I need to place the broken armchair in front of the door when I sleep to ensure I don't get stabbed in the middle of the night.

It was hard to miss the peeling paint on the walls, and although the bed is large, it is fully made up with shiny black linen, making me think that they rent the rooms by the hour. And after skimming through the paperwork this morning when I arrived, I felt like an idiot as I realized that they do just that. Lovely.

The damp smell of my new dingy room still lingers in my nostrils as I try to take deep breaths into my lungs, pushing my legs to go faster, only the waft of garbage from the streetscape around me makes me nearly stop and gag.

I am a country girl in the city for the first time, so my expectations may have been a little high considering my accommodation choice was limited. It is my own fault, really. I didn't research this trip at all, and this was one of the only hotels in New York I could afford. I'm already stretching my dollars far enough.

So, I decided not to stick around in the shabby room for any longer than I had to. I left my small duffle bag that contains my entire life in the small wardrobe, then quickly changed into my active wear, and now I am running my stress and fears away down the streets of the Big Apple.

I look down at my emerald-green crop top and matching leggings, proud of the look I pulled from the top of my bag. They were a generous gift from my old neighbor Lilly. They were a Christmas gift she didn't like, so she passed them over the fence to me. She has watched me go running every morning for the past five years, usually in baggy sweats and old, beaten shoes. She said green wasn't her color, but that it would suit my flaming red hair and pale complexion, which I thought was really sweet. I thanked her eagerly, always wanting such an outfit but never having the money to spend on such frivolous things.

Aside from this outfit and a few other tops and pairs of jeans, there really is nothing else. After mom died two months ago, I sold everything, and by the time I paid all our debts, there wasn't much left over.

I slow my pace to catch my breath, my hand involuntarily resting on my chest, rubbing the small lump in my breast. My fate is no doubt going to be the same as my mother's, but unlike her, I have decided to live the rest of my life to the fullest instead of in a drug haze. No matter how short that life now may be.

Looking around, I realize that I only have a little time left of the darkness before the morning breaks, and although my body is weary, my mind is alert.

I pick up my pace, passing a few shops, many of which are boarded up. A convenience store and a few more by-the-hour hotels come into view before I'm crossing the road and guessing my way through the maze of streets, hoping that I am heading toward the water. It will be nice to watch the sunrise from the edge of Queens, even with the planes flying in and out of JFK Airport scattering across the sky.

I make it exactly two blocks before I realize that I am lost. Stopping, I wander down the street to try and catch my breath. Running is the only thing that has gotten me through the past few years, but my stamina is not what it used to be, so the walk is a welcome reprieve. Glancing left, then right, I curse myself for not bringing a map or my phone, or even looking at one before I left. I will definitely need to think more clearly from now on, living in the city.

With the faint glow of the morning sun, I begin down the street, on a mission to find a shop that may be open to ask for directions. Sunrise is certainly different here than back home in Oklahoma. I can't really see much through the buildings. But I wanted an adventure; that is the whole point of being here, and after only an hour in this place, I realize that's most certainly what I have got.

I spot some people gathered down the street and decide I'll ask them for directions. Sprinting off with renewed enthusiasm, I pay little attention to what they are doing, but as I get closer, I see that they are all men. My step falters, and I begin to slow my pace, as they look aggressive even at a distance. But I have nowhere to turn without it looking suspicious, my red hair high in a pony-tail swishing back and forth as I come to a stop. I'm unsure of what my next move should be. Maybe I could still ask for directions and then just keep running... a lot faster?

As I open my mouth, about to speak, I hear a popping sound, along with screams of terror as gunfire goes off all around us.

I stand rooted to the ground, too scared to move. My feet feel like they are encased in cement, and my heart thumps right out of my chest. Is this the way I am going to meet my maker? Is this it? Right here on the streets of New York, is this how it will end for me? My mind is telling me to move, but my body is so stiff, I can't; my legs won't budge, and my glazed eyes don't leave the mess of men and blood. This can't be happening...

In the next breath, the air completely leaves my lungs as a tall, dark-haired man grabs me, literally sweeping my feet from under me. The panic slows, the noise a mere blur as his hands wrap around my body, pulling me to him before we land hard on my back onto the sidewalk. My head is protected by his hand, his strong body covering mine. I can barely breathe as his weight sandwiches me between him and the sidewalk, protecting me. The noise of the gunfire rushes back into my senses as soon as my shock settles, and I bury my head against him, my face firmly planted into his chest.

Popping noises continue, alongside the overwhelming sound of multiple people yelling orders, including my savior, who is still on top of me. I have no idea what they are saying, though, and that only makes me more nervous. I grip onto his shirt even tighter, squeezing my eyes, the feeling of his body the only comforting sense I have to give me hope of surviving.

Then, everything stops. Things go silent, eerily so, and he moves his head until his lips meet my ears.

"You're okay. Everything is okay," he says in a deep baritone voice, with a hint of accent that feels like honey poured down my body, soothing me instantly from the inside out.

My grip on him remains white-knuckled, my eyes still squeezed shut, as I hear him shouting again, his hands firmly around my body, keeping me wrapped in his arms. Before I know what is happening, he lifts me effortlessly, and is standing on the sidewalk. I have no idea what is happening or who he even is, but I decide to trust him.

"Hold on, Little Red. I need to make sure you are

safe." My legs circle his waist, my arms wind around his neck, and as I rest my head against his solid chest, his masculine aroma calms me.

But then I lift my head for a moment and immediately wish I hadn't. The first dead body I ever saw was my mother's and that was two months ago. I can now add another five or so to that list, although the sight of these men is much more disturbing. I bury my head into the crook of his neck, the image of what I just saw now burned into my brain, almost making me retch.

His arm around my lower waist keeps me with him, while he yells some more, and I try to think of anything other than what could possibly be happening right now. What I've been witness to.

The squeal of tires has me jolting upright, looking at the road as a black Escalade pulls up and we are moving towards it with haste. I begin to panic, but I am paralyzed by it. Not getting into cars with strangers is something that is drilled into us from a young age, yet here I am, glued to man who is stepping into the car like we are one person. My savior sits in the back seat, and I remain wrapped around him, my body still not able to move. Straddling his waist, with my head still buried in his neck, his hand rubs up and down my back, and it is only then I realize I am shaking.

My body trembles uncontrollably, the shock at what just happened seeping into my body, and I internally curse myself. I need to be stronger than this. I am in New York now; things like this happen in the big city, don't they? I need to grow thicker skin.

"You're okay. Everything is okay," he repeats in my ear,

continuing to rub my back in slow and soothing motions. His touch is somehow making me feel safe and secure, when I have a feeling that I really should be running in the other direction.

"Take some deep breaths," he says, and I do. I don't need to have a panic attack, that's for sure. I try to slow my breathing as the car we're in speeds down the street. To where, I have no idea. I have never had anyone look after me in this manner and certainly not a man. At this thought, I bolt upright and look the man in the face.

His dark hair falls across his forehead, his brown eyes piercing mine like they're trying to decipher my thoughts. His square jaw is tightly clenched, and his dark blue top stretches across his muscles. He is without a doubt the most attractive man I have ever seen. Not that there were many boys to look at back in my small town. But he is not a boy. He is all man. The tall, dark kind, and he's older by at least a decade, maybe more. There's an air of power around him; he is in control.

I tentatively look around the car and notice another four men in here, including the driver, all busy talking to each other in another language. Italian, I think, but I really have no idea.

As I bring my gaze back to the man in front of me, I see what looks like red paint across my shoulder. "Oh my God," I whisper as I touch my crop top that is now tainted with bright red blood. *Am I bleeding? Have I been shot?* My breath quickens, and I start to panic all over again.

"You're okay. It's mine." My wide eyes flick back to his top this time, and I see red blood seeping through his shirt at his shoulder.

"You've been shot?" I ask urgently, my hands leaving his neck and covering his wound without another thought. I have no idea what I am doing, but in all the movies I watch, they try to stop the blood flow by applying pressure. So that is what I do. I don't miss the definition of muscle on his arm as I squeeze his shoulder firmly with my tiny hands.

He chuckles, bringing my attention back to his face. "I am alright, Little Red. Just a graze. I will live to see another day." His eyes seem to sparkle in delight at my concern for him.

I don't reply, slowly releasing my hands, becoming suddenly very aware of how I am sitting on him. I blush slightly at our position and go to move, but there is nowhere else to sit. All the other men are huge, not leaving a spare space. His hands travel up my thighs and grip onto my waist, and at the unexpected touch, a shiver runs through me, my eyes flicking to his. He leans his head back against the seat, openly admiring me as his hands rest on my hips.

"We are nearly there, Little Red. Stay put." I nod mindlessly, amazed that he is so calm and in tune to how I am feeling, yet he doesn't even know my name. Though, I haven't missed the nickname he's bestowed upon me.

The grip of his hands is warm, firm yet gentle, and I'm surprised by how easily my body relaxes into him. Looking out the window, I try to see if I can make out any landmarks or signs that would tell me where I am or where we are going, but as the buildings rush by, I come to accept that I have absolutely no idea. All I know is that I am in a car with four men I don't know, all with guns at their sides and blood on their clothing. An air of danger lingers around me, and I know deep down I should be frightened, but I am simply not.

I came to New York for an adventure... and it looks like I found it.

3

DANTE

I don't know who this tiny redhead is, but she is nearly weightless as she sits on my lap. I can't say I mind the vision I now have, of her perfect tiny body on top of mine, and if I didn't just fuck shit up by shooting Dominic and killing all his men, I might actually be able to enjoy it. She walked straight into the line of fire, and I had little time to think about what I was doing. Talk about being in the wrong place at the wrong time.

Even though her face is still gripped by fear, her body tells me she is slowly calming down. That is, until she realized I had been shot. It is just a graze, but it fucking kills. I'm pushing out the pain with every shallow exhale, before I take a long, deep breath in. But that's the wrong move, because I become overwhelmed by her scent almost immediately. Citrus fills my lungs, the kind that reminds me of warm summer days in Italy, while playing with my son Leo in the Mediterranean. The one and only scent that makes me feel at ease, in my bliss, the scent of the life I want to have someday.

She is beautiful. I don't think I have ever seen a woman so breathtaking. And young. Probably much too young for me. I am not entirely sure she is even of legal age, and I feel like a dirty old man keeping her secured to my lap.

I can't stop taking her in, though. I try to avert my eyes, but they keep coming back to rest on her. Her flaming red hair is long and tied up, her ponytail tickling my fingers as she looks around out the windows, wondering where she's going. My grip on her hips remains, not only because Tony is driving like an absolute maniac, but because if she continues to move and wriggle around on my lap, I think she might find something solid underneath her that she may not necessarily appreciate. Not in a moment like this, at least.

Thinking back to my meeting, I can't believe Dominic pulled that stunt. He knew what he was going to do the minute he saw me in his club. He has no fucking respect and now all five of his men lay dead on the sidewalk.

He won't like that. Both him and his brother Federico will seek revenge, and I have no doubt they will come after me and my team in time.

I didn't miss the opportunity to pull my gun on him, though. I couldn't kill him, not yet. But I will kill him. I will take great pleasure in doing so as well. We have a long history with each other, and I want him gone. And now, that desire is only amplified.

I'm only injured because a stray bullet skimmed my shoulder before I slammed Little Red into the pavement.

As Carter disarmed Dominic, I didn't miss his eyes as they honed in on the beauty in my arms, my hand under her cute little ass as I brought her with me to safety. She clung to me like I was her last breath, and I nearly was.

Unfortunately for Little Red, her life has just become endangered, and although scared, I am sure she has no fucking idea what she has walked into. Dominic got a good look at her, and with her small stature, long red locks, and glowing pale skin, she is quite easily identifiable. While I don't need another person to look after, the urge to protect runs strongly through my blood.

We reach our neighborhood and all us boys start to settle down. Carter is still on high-alert in the front seat, looking at every car that passes, as Tony continues to weave through the traffic. Luckily, the streets are still quiet, giving us a clear run. As we get close to our city compound, my cell phone rings.

Sebastian's name lights up the screen. Although it is just after midnight in Sicily, I am not surprised he is awake and wanting an update. As I answer, my eyes flick to the camera in the car. We have eyes everywhere and even from Sicily, I know he's watching.

"What happened?" he asks, his tone harsh with no pleasantries.

I have known Sebastian all my life. We have been best friends since we were three years old. My father was his father's right-hand man, and now, over three decades later, we both have stepped up into the same roles with each other. I would take a bullet for him any day of the week. Not because it is my job, but because he is the closest I have to a brother. We are family. After finding the love of his life Goldie, they are currently in Sicily on vacation. I'm sure, since he never really takes a break, he's also building relationships and making deals while he is over there.

"Dominic is what happened," I spit out, and Little Red looks at me wide-eyed. I see her chest rise and fall in renewed panic, and my thumb automatically rubs her hip to reassure her. I hear her gasp at the movement, her skin prickling with goosebumps, and my eyes bounce right up to hers because it is an act that has caught us both off guard.

What the fuck am I doing?

"You had to kill his men? Dante, this will start a war." He sighs, and I can feel his frustration through the line. We both hate Dominic, and we always knew a war was looming. But my actions have just brought it closer to the present.

"Allure is a fucking pigsty; they have taken our money and have no intention of giving it back or providing any return on our investment."

"Look, we all know Dominic and Frederico are the lowest of the low. I know they had a hand in Angelina's demise, but fuck, Dante! You killed five of his men!"

"And I should have killed him too," I say with a smirk as Little Red gapes at me, going pale and beginning to shake again. My move is automatic, the caress against her skin to bring her comfort.

I hate Dominic and Federico for many reasons, but mostly because of what they have done to my ex-wife and mother of my son.

Angelina and I had an arranged marriage; there was

certainly no love between us, and while she was a pretty, blonde Italian girl, I still had to get drunk to fuck her. But arranged marriages are part of our life, and for a while, it was fine. I didn't spend a lot of time around her. I kept busy with Sebastian, building our team, readying ourselves to take on the new roles of head of the New York mob. She got pregnant in the meantime and had little Leo, who is still the only shining light in my dark world.

Only, things changed after he was born. She was often seen drunk at Allure at all hours of the day, leaving my son at home on his own on more than one occasion. Even thinking about it now makes me furious.

Her role was to be at home. Be a mother to my heir and fucking get into line like the rest of us. Like me when I married her.

She didn't want that role, though. And she made sure I knew that.

While I was in Sicily for business, she plied my men with drugs and participated in what ended up being a full-blown sex party. But that was the least of my worries, because she took little Leo with her. He was only five at the time, but he saw and heard things no five-year-old should have. It impacted him so severely, he hasn't been the same since. My blood still boils whenever I think about it.

Afterwards, it became clear that she was hooked on drugs, and when her suppliers started coming to me, demanding payments, I locked her up and tried to get her clean. But nothing worked, so I had to let her go. She was banished from mine and Leo's life, and for the past three years, I have raised Leo myself. She sees him annually at most and never unsupervised, as the drugs still hold on to her, her life barely hanging on by a thread.

Sebastian interrupts my thoughts. "Well, now you get your chance. They have already called me to threaten me, you, and our family, fucking imbeciles. He has assured me that you are a dead man walking, so watch your back. Kill them, get our money, and don't get hurt."

"No problem," I say simply as I watch Little Red blink rapidly. I'm not hiding my side of the conversation, and she's clearly listening in. But surprisingly, she doesn't scurry off my body or lean away from me in disgust or terror. She may well be in shock because any other woman would be screeching at me right about now, I am sure. Regardless, my fingers continue to move against her skin, in the silent assurance that she will be fine, and her body listens as I can see her quick breaths slowing.

"And who the fuck is the redhead sitting on your lap?" Sebastian asks, and I smile slyly.

"I think she might be mine."

4

ANNIE

Mine. I may not be able to hear the entire conversation, but I am pretty sure the man underneath me just claimed me as his. In the midst of my internal alarm blaring back to life, the light outside goes dark as the car drives off the side street and down into an underground parking lot. My breathing quickens as I realize the time for me to escape has well and truly passed. I trusted this man and now I have no idea where the hell I am or how the hell I am going to get away.

Aside from the handsome stranger who I am still straddling, none of the other men have spoken to me, all ignoring my existence as they remain focused. Even before we pull to a stop, they are out of the car and running in all different directions.

I remain in his arms, and he lifts us out of the car slowly, lowering me to stand. My feet hit the cement ground, but he doesn't let me go. Instead, he waits, his hands encasing my waist to ensure I don't fall, or faint – either option totally possible at this point.

Looking up at him, I ask with my eyes if this is the moment that I get taken into a dungeon and killed for being witness to a crime this morning? But his firm hands on my body don't feel like they would harm me, and I hope like hell my instincts are right. My hands shake as we stand side by side, and it is almost comical how small I am next to him. He is even taller than I thought, and broad, his eyes dark as they watch me. His open shirt shows me a large black tattoo that licks up his neck, making him look scarier than I believe him to be. He saved me once, so surely, he won't hurt me now...

Removing my eyes from his, I assess where I am. The underground lot houses a wide range of vehicles from sports cars to large trucks and vans. The cement beneath my feet is lacquered in clear gloss, with markings where vehicles park and large bright lights hanging above us. The entire lot is bigger than my old high school basketball stadium—not that it is hard, it was a small school and underfunded. I have never seen anything like it, and it certainly doesn't look like a place where wild killers bring young out-of-towners to end their life. Regardless, I stay standing close to the man, not wanting to leave his side, where I have been safely residing for the past 30 minutes.

I was tired before, but now I'm wide awake as he takes my hand and pulls me toward one of the many doors that line the perimeter. My small hand grips his, not wanting to let go, and my little legs struggle to keep up to his long, purposeful strides. I continue to observe my new surroundings, watching as men dressed in black scurry around the place, moving cars, emptying guns and cleaning them, then stocking them in the many storage units. All of them armed, all of them looking lethal.

Like the obedient woman I am, I follow my handsome stranger through the door, and without letting go of my hand, he leads me down concrete hallways. Turning right, then left, the hallways begin to turn into more decorative corridors before we come to a large, black glossy door with a brass knocker. It looks just like a front door of a house, only this one is inside the depths of this building, only accessible via the maze of hallways we just walked through.

Looking behind me, I realize that I have no idea how to get out, my sense of direction nonexistent as we made numerous twists and turns that have left me slightly dizzy. Or is that my low blood pressure? It is too hard to know for sure as my body has changed so much lately.

He pauses at the door and looks down at me, his other hand coming up and pushing a flyaway hair that's strewn across my face. My lips part at the gentle touch, and I don't miss his eyes as they flick down, before he gives me a small nod and opens the large door via a small keypad on the side. I follow him through, in awe as he moves behind me and locks it, the click of the lock sinking into my chest and making me feel like I won't ever be able to leave this place.

My eyes sweep the room, and I gasp at the pure opulence before me. Looking at the grandeur, I am not sure I will ever even want to leave. My shoulders slowly leave my ears, knowing that I didn't walk into a dudgeon of death but rather a modern-day palace.

It is *huge*. Tall ceilings, polished concrete floors, and vivid white walls with modern chrome, glass, and black fittings throughout. It is like nothing I have ever seen before. Artwork hangs from the walls, and luxurious soft rugs and cushions give a homely feel to what would otherwise seem like an untouched space.

He takes my hand again, the warmth radiating up my arm, and pulls me along the hallway until it opens up to a living room featuring a white leather sofa, grey rugs, a large flatscreen TV, and floor-to-ceiling windows along one side that overlooks an internal courtyard. I spot the kitchen off to the side, with a long breakfast bar, stainless steel appliances, and what I am sure are marble countertops—although I wouldn't really know, having not ever seen marble in real life before. The kitchen alone looks like it is bigger than my entire trailer where I lived back in Oklahoma. I take a breath in, smelling a delicious aroma of herbs, and I watch a plump older woman, with dark hair, draped in an apron, preparing food. The smell makes my stomach rumble. She lifts her head and gives me a beaming but surprised smile, one which I find myself returning.

There is clearly no time for niceties as the man pulls me through the living space and down another small hallway. He does not let me linger to see the entire place, but rather leads me to some stairs. Following him up, I am breathless for a moment, as when I reach the top, I am met with a bright and airy space, with oversized black, arched framed windows and furnishings of soft cream and charcoal.

Whoever this man is, he is clearly very wealthy, because I didn't even know places like this actually existed. Sure, I saw them in movies, but you can't believe everything you see on TV.

We continue down the hallway, passing numerous closed doors until we reach a door at the end, which he opens for us to step inside. Understanding washes over me as I look at the bed in the center of the room, which looks as soft as a cloud, dressed in light grey linens with large pillows and a soft charcoal throw. There is also a large armchair, a closet that looks as big as Lilly's trailer next door (hers was the biggest in the lot, and we all envied her), and then another open door that leads into a bathroom.

"Stay here," he says, his voice rough. That is the first thing he has said to me since the car stopped. I only nod because where the hell am I going to go? I'm not sure I know how to find my way back downstairs, let alone actually leave the house.

He sits me on the bed and goes into the bathroom, and I watch him as he takes off his shirt, which is wet with blood. I hear him turn on the tap, the gush of water rinsing his hands before he wets a cloth. I get up then and stand at the doorway, noticing him dabbing his arm.

I begin to step into the bathroom, and he stops what he is doing, the wet cloth midway between the basin and his bare chest as I enter his space. Am I crazy? Probably. But I nursed my mother for many months and have an empathetic nature, so the need to help people runs strongly through my veins.

He doesn't say anything, his ongoing silence making me nervous. I stand next to him and grab the cool cloth out of his hands, reaching up to wipe his arm. He remains still, his eyes not leaving my face, his jaw set. I try to be gentle as I clean all the dried blood off his skin, needing to rinse the cloth before starting again.

As I wipe his chest, I can feel his heart beating hard, matching mine, and I see a sheen of water now covering his tattoos where I have cleaned the red away. We remain silent as I take in his body, muscles, scars, and tattoos. He is like nothing I have ever seen before, so I'm finding it difficult to concentrate on the task at hand.

Taking a fresh cloth, I grab the antiseptic that he already had on the vanity and begin to dab some onto the wound. I know the antiseptic stings, so I blow on his skin a little, something that the school nurse always did to me every time I went to her with a graze or cut. From my peripheral, I can see his face, and I note every subtle change. His nostrils flare, but his expression doesn't wavier, his eyes still remaining fixed on me. His jaw clenches slightly each time I touch him, so I know that he is human at least.

When I shift on my tiptoes, his eyes drop to my body, and as I follow his gaze, I gasp. I forgot that my chest is covered in blood. Whose, I am not sure, most likely his. I panic a little at the sight, trying to tell myself that it isn't mine and I don't need to worry, but my nerves are on a knife's edge today and any little thing is now triggering me.

He steps out of the bathroom, around my now rigid form, and comes back with a pile of clean clothes. Leaning across me, he pulls a fresh, fluffy white towel down from the rack and places it near the clothes before opening the shower and turning it on.

"Clean up," he says abruptly, then walks away, out the door, closing it behind him. The click of the door startles me from my shock and my eyes rise to meet the mirror, and I take in my appearance. My porcelain white skin is splattered with red, along with my beautiful green activewear. I take big breaths to calm myself, before I explore his bathroom. The tiles are polished, not a mark on them, a bathtub that looks like I could swim in it is along one wall, and the shower is big enough for a party of five. The glass so clean and clear it is hard to distinguish where it starts and ends. Water pours from the tall rainfall showerhead, steam enveloping the space.

I can smell him here, his woodsy scent that brings me a wave of peace. And it dawns on me that I'm still not sure whether I'm safe here. Whether I'm going to live or die... Only, I'm not scared about what's coming. As terrifying as the events of this morning have been, dying doesn't matter to me. It is going to happen sooner rather than later anyway, something I have known for a long time and have come to terms with it. I have never been diagnosed, but I know the statistics. Breast cancer affects 1 in 7 women during their lifetime, and if it runs in your family, then the risk is higher.

With that thought, it's like I'm free to just lean into whatever this crazy circumstance has provided me. And right now, it looks like it's brought me to a beautiful home with an exceptionally tempting shower. Much nicer than the one waiting for me back at my hotel.

I slowly peel off my activewear and then step into the warm shower. This is what I would imagine a five-star hotel to be like, or even six star if there was such a thing. This level of luxury is not something I ever imagined experiencing in my simple life, and a small grin comes to my face as I lather myself in his soap.

The water runs red down the drain as I wash off the events of this morning, and I grab his shampoo to scrub my long hair next. I have always loved my hair. The red color is striking, and it is one of the many reasons why I have said nothing about my lump in my breast. I don't want to lose the color with medication I would need to take. I wouldn't feel like *me* anymore.

Fresh and clean, I turn off the water and dry myself before looking at the clothes he has given me. The shirt will be fine; it is big, but I can wear it as a dress. But the sleep shorts fall right off me, so I don't even bother with those.

Once covered, I open the bathroom door and step out to an empty bedroom. I can't help but feel slight disappointment that the man isn't here. I should be glad he has left me alone—he could be a highly trained killer for all I know—but I can't deny that he brings me a sense security by just being near him. I walk toward the bedroom door and open it, poking my head out and glancing down the empty hallway. With no idea where I am or who I am with, I decide to stay put. Sighing, I close the door and lean against it, admiring the bed. I didn't even know they made beds this big.

His bed.

There is no doubt that this is his room. The bathroom is full of his personal items, the closet full of suits. His masculine smell is constant, like sandalwood and musk, and I feel like it follows me wherever I go.

All the adrenalin of the morning is starting to wear off, and combined with the warm shower and comfortable clothes, my body begins to falter. I know I need to rest, having not slept for nearly 20 hours since before my flight. Lying on his bed, immediately my head sinks into the pillow, and my body melts into his comforter. I don't even have to count to ten before my eyes close and I fall asleep.

5

DANTE

I left her in my bathroom, my fingers itching to touch what I know I shouldn't. I couldn't trust myself anymore. Her hands on my body were delicate, yet powerful enough to hit me right in the chest. No one has ever done that to me before. Though it unsettled me, I liked it. Too damn much. I have no idea who she is. I don't even know her fucking name.

We have rules in our family, and they are very clear. We don't hurt women or children, ever. I wasn't sure about bringing her here. She was certainly scared, and I don't blame her. I didn't know how she would react about coming with me, but she came willingly, not kicking or screaming like most would. Instead, she gripped onto my hand so tight, her trust in me palpable, and I didn't want to ever fucking let her go.

Dropping her off back into the city would only result in her death now that the Russo brothers will stop at nothing to prove a point. So now I need to figure out who she is and keep her safe, and the safest place for her to be at the moment is here in my house, in our compound. I just need to wait until she finishes cleaning up and then I can tell her how things are going to be moving forward. Maybe that is when she will snap, yell, scream, or try to make an escape.

I stand by my bedroom window and take a breath as I hear the shower going. The image of her naked body runs through my mind, so I quickly grab my supply of bandages and patch up my wound before I rummage through my closet and change clothes. I am out the door in under five minutes, ready to go down to our lower levels to meet my team for a debrief on this morning's activities.

On my way out the door, I stop in the kitchen, seeing my son Leo perched up at the bench eating breakfast, looking sleepy in his favorite Lego pajamas. His hair stands on end as he slurps up what looks like a bowl of cheerios while Maria is nearby, standing at the oven, busy making sugo.

"Hey, buddy," I say to Leo, kissing his head and ruffling his hair. He smiles, his eyes wide with happiness at seeing me, but he remains silent.

Words have not left his lips in over three years, since that goddam sex party his mother took him to without any consideration for him or me. All these years later, I still don't know how to get him to talk. I have spent hundreds of thousands of dollars on teachers, tutors, shrinks, and doctors, both here in New York and in Italy, who all tell me the same thing. He will talk once he is ready. Once he feels safe again. Until that time, we burn through homeschool teachers because no one can get through to him, and he buries himself in books and Legos, sticking to his room and Maria like glue.

Maria and I share a look over the steaming pot of sauce. She has been my housekeeper for over a decade and loves Leo as much as I do. She cooks, she cleans, she babysits, and both Leo and I love her like she is our Nonna. The only problem is that she is over 60 and getting too old to do all the work we need—even if her traditional cooking is unsurpassed. I lost both my parents years ago, so she fills that void in me. I will do anything for her, including letting her retire back in Italy if that is what she wants to do. Although, I hope I can keep her for a little while longer.

"Maria. I have a houseguest in my room who will be staying for a while. Can you please take up some breakfast for her and ensure she has everything she needs?" I ask, and she smiles at me broadly with a glint in her eye that I rarely see.

"Of course, darling. Leave the pretty young thing to me," she says cheerfully, and I sigh. Little Red is the first woman who has been in this house since I kicked my ex-wife out years ago. That's not to say I haven't had other women, because I have. Many, in fact. But I never bring them here. They never get close to Leo or my space. Looking at Maria now, her smile a mile wide, I get the feeling that she and Little Red will become firm friends in a matter of hours. She has been dying for another woman to be in this house, and it appears she thinks this one will be staying.

I don't have time to explain things to her, so leaving Maria to manage the houseguest situation, I shake my head and kiss Leo again before I walk out the door and down the maze of corridors to our meeting rooms. With Little Red front and center in my mind, I wonder how old she is and where she came from. Her face shows a world of innocence, purity, and all these possessive thoughts I have of her need to stop.

I pace through the corridors, frustrated that within a few hours, things can turn to shit. Walking into the meeting room, I slam the door behind me, making all the team who are patiently waiting for me to turn silent. I am furious. I wanted blood this morning, that I can't deny, but I also wanted answers and they were not forthcoming.

Now we have five men who were part of the fold dead, and other families are going to start asking questions. Until I have the proof and answers I need, it is not going to look favorable for us.

"Carter," I bark out to my brother from another mother, who, along with Sebastian, is one of my closest confidants. "Give us an overview."

"We fucked up. They had trigger fingers. Five dead, including Stefano the Russo's second in command." His eyes flick to me, and I clench my jaw. I'm glad the fucker's dead, but truth be told, I probably shouldn't have killed him.

He continues. "Their paperwork has been audited. They have taken a one-million-dollar loan from us over six months ago for improvements for Allure, with the understanding that the building would be extended and renovated. They have given a six-month sales projection of over two million, with a full payback date of Sunday, the 12th, which was yesterday."

Carter can kill a man with his bare hands, but he is smart as a whip too. Everything that comes out of his mouth is always 100% accurate. Where Sebastian and I are in our thirties, Carter is still in his mid-twenties, and although he is with us today, his gym business in Philly is growing and requiring him there more and more. I know that his move to Philly is near, especially since we could use an insider in that location anyway.

I survey the room, my eyes roaming over all our men. They are focused, determined and eager. Just the way I like them.

"So we have nothing new, then?" I grit out, unhappy that we didn't manage to get our money back and created a war in the process. "Well, the heat is on us now, so we need to find the money and get proof that Dominic and Frederico are slimy bastards, who no longer deserve a seat at the table. Otherwise, the rest of the families will not be looking at us favorably. Let's get to work."

AFTER SPENDING the day looking through paperwork, video footage, and talking to our contacts, we are still no closer to finding what we need. Leaving ten new fresh-eyed men to go through it all again overnight, as well as a team monitoring Allure and any known associates of the Russo brothers, I bid farewell to Carter and head back to my place.

The lights are low as I enter, so I know Maria has retired to her room. I go upstairs to my private wing to check on Leo. Peeking in, I see Leo curled up asleep, gripping onto a new Lego Darth Vader that he made today. I slowly peel it from his hands and place it on his bedside table to join the many others, before lifting his blanket and kissing his head. Out of all the pain and trouble of the past decade, he is worth it all.

Turning off his lamp, I decide to check on Little Red as well. Putting my ear to the door, I can't hear the TV or any other noise, so I slowly open the door and am surprised to see her sleeping. The curtains are still wide open, her small body hardly wrapped in my covers, wearing my shirt that I left for her. I walk into the room, stopping at the end of the bed, and I stand there watching her sleep. Looking at the small rise and fall of her chest, I take her in once again.

Her vibrant, long red hair is sprawled out around her head, like flames licking up my pillow. She's on her side, cuddling my other pillow close, her legs bare, showing me her porcelain skin as it glows in the moonlight. Tiny puffs of air leave her pouty lips as she sleeps soundly.

I look around the room and notice the untouched tray of food that Maria must have bought up this morning, and it is then I come to the conclusion that Little Red has slept all day. Walking across the room quietly, I take a seat in my armchair and continue to watch her sleep. It's been a long time since there was a woman in my bed, but for some odd reason, I am not upset by it.

The peacefulness of the house and this room is soothing after a challenging day, and I rest my head on the back of the armchair as my eyes stay on her. Her dainty toes and fingers are painted in light pink, her long black lashes casting shadows on her cheeks. My gaze lowers as I take in the dip and curves of her body that I can make out underneath my white shirt that encases her. I have never been more jealous of anything in my life as I am of that damn shirt.

Pondering this situation, I can't take my eyes off her. I should have brought her to our safehouse. I should have taken her somewhere else, anywhere else, at least that way my mind wouldn't be this distracted.

But who she is remains a mystery. Does she have a family looking for her? Parents, siblings, a boyfriend? If she does, then they should be scared that she is sleeping in my bed, because I am not a man that parents want their kids to end up with. I am not the dream; I am the nightmare, and Little Red has stepped right into my arms.

6

ANNIE

I wake up and stretch my legs out along the smooth cool comfort of the expensive sheets underneath me. Slowly opening my eyes, I look out the window and see the dim morning light starting to peek out. I become aware very quickly that I have slept for all of yesterday and all of last night. A new record for me. It takes a while for me to get my senses, but when I do, I bolt upright. My head flicks around the room, until they land on him.

I can barely breathe as I take him in. A soft glow paints the room in orange, draping over him like a light shield. He is almost majestic as he sits in the large armchair like a king on his throne, staring with intense dark eyes and a menacing scowl. Wearing dark jeans, black boots, and a tight black top with the sleeves pushed up to his elbows, his body stays taut, his shoulders stiff, his jaw clenched. I notice his tattoos again, both on his forearms and his neck, and I wonder what they are and if they mean anything. His leg is crossed over his knee, his hands grip onto the arms of the chair, and his eyes are firmly set on me.

I swallow as my breath quickens, my heart thumps in my chest, and my eyes bug out of my head. Not in fear, because for some reason, I cannot begin to understand, I am still not afraid, but I am not sure what to expect, and that makes me feel unsettled. I pull my legs up to my chest for protection and wrap my arms around them. Making myself small, shielding from what may come, I peek over the tops of my knees, waiting for him to talk first.

"What's your name?" he barks out, and I flinch. He was soft and gentle yesterday, and now he seems angry. I didn't grow up with a father and being an only child, I had no brothers that pushed me around. All the kids at school stayed away from me because I was the poor kid that wore the same clothes every day, so I never had friends. It was always just Mom and me, and now just me. I am not used to rough and grumpy men, so his tone is startling.

"Annie," I whisper to him, not sure how much to tell him and what to keep to myself.

His eyebrows raise at my answer, and I assume it is because my accent gives away that I am not a New York native. My twang is not easy to hide, but it's possible with the craziness of yesterday that he didn't catch on to that.

"Not from New York?" His tone softens and his shoulders relax somewhat.

"No," I reply with an uneasy shake of my head.

His nostrils flair at my one-word answer, obviously wanting more from me, but I am not yet willing to give it.

Clearly, this guy is used to getting things his own way and not at all used to people not being forthcoming. So, I try to make amends.

"Thank you so much for helping me yesterday. I apologize for falling asleep, but if I can call a taxi, I can get back to my hotel and out of your hair," I say as I start to move off the bed.

"No," he replies firmly, and I stop still again, my bare legs halfway out of the blankets.

"What do you mean, no?" I whisper in disbelief, my eyes narrowing.

"It isn't safe for you. Those men from back at the club have security camera footage of what happened. They will be looking for you just as hard as they are trying to get to me. You are safer here." He leaves no room for questions, and I just about balk. *Not safe for me? Staying here is safer?* I can't believe that being here with him is the safest option for me, but with nothing and no one else, what choice do I have?

And as my eyes dart around the room, I can't help but think, if I am captive anywhere, then this luxurious bedroom is not a bad place to be.

"What hotel are you staying in?" he asks, and I look at him again.

"Happy Holidays in Ozone Park." His face scrunches up. Apparently, he knows the place and has just cemented to me that it is, in fact, a dive.

"I will get my men to go and get your things today, so you have everything." I notice his jaw ticking and a sour look on his face. Why do I frustrate him so much? Maybe

I am putting him out by being here. Maybe I should demand he take me somewhere else.

"Where am I?" I ask quietly.

"My private residence. You can sleep and rest here. There is food here, so eat." He gestures toward a tray full of food on his buffet.

"So I can't leave?" I ask again, needing to be completely sure I understand this situation. He stands to his full height and shakes his head, staring at me for a moment, before he walks out of the room and closes the door behind him without a second glance.

What the hell have I got myself into?

I take some deep breaths, feeling like I am getting air into my lungs for the first time since I woke up. His overpowering presence sucked up all the air in the room. I look around again and catch a glimpse of the time. 5:30am, the same time it was yesterday when I decided to go for a run. A run that appears to have changed my entire life.

Sighing, I slide the rest of the way off the bed and nearly topple over as I feel the thick carpet underneath my feet. Walking over to the dark buffet, I look at the tray of food. It is all fresh, pastries and breads, both of which make my stomach curl into itself. I no longer have the appetite I once did, so I grab the small bowl of fruit and take it to the armchair. Sitting down, I pull my legs underneath me and pick at the fresh fruit. I can't remember the last time I had fresh fruit like this, every piece juicier and more flavorful than the last.

As I take another deep breath, trying to relax and ease

the stress that is building within me, I smell him. I don't know how long he sat here waiting for me to wake up, but his scent is stronger in this seat he just occupied. Having a man watch me while I sleep makes my skin prickle a little, but in a good way. It is his room, he can do what he likes, but the fact that he lets me sleep in his bed and watches over me brings an entirely new feeling to settle in my chest. I spent many nights watching over Mom, making sure she was okay, but never once has anyone watched over me. He may be ensuring I don't run, don't go to the police, or break his expensive furnishings in his room. But like the daydreamer I am, I'd like to think that he was being protective.

Surprisingly, I finish the bowl of fruit and feel extremely full, and for lack of anything else to do, I decide to go to the bathroom and shower. I want to be prepared for the day, even though I am not sure what the day will have ahead of me.

I coat myself in his soap again, the lathers and scent making me feel a sense of comfort, like the large grumpy man himself is here. I finish up and once I am out and dry, I put on the same white shirt I slept in because I have no other clothes. Brushing my hair with my fingers, I decide to braid it to keep it off my face. I love doing my hair in two braids; it makes me look like Lara Croft, and I feel invincible... even though I am anything but.

My body is flushed, and I realize I must have had the shower too hot because I can't cool down. Just as I tie the last braid, my vision starts to go. I grip onto the vanity as I fall, but I don't feel the pain of my landing, as I am out before my body even slaps onto the floor.

COMING TO, my head pulsates in pain, and I wince as I start to get up from the hard tiles. The sun is now streaming through the bathroom window, and as I sit and try to steady myself, I wonder how long I was out for. Fainting spells are not new; I know I don't eat enough and having the shower too hot never helps my already weakening state. I run my hands over my body and feel nothing new, the lump in my breast still the constant reminder that my life is on a timeline.

Early breast cancer is still very treatable, but if you are like me, with no money, no family, and no medical insurance or support, the options for treatment are pretty nonexistent. That coupled with the fact that I saw what the drugs did to my Mom, and I never want to have them in my body. Ever. So, fainting is just something I have to deal with in the interim.

I stand up slowly and rub my hip, which is sore. As I look in the mirror, I pull up the shirt and see a big blue bruise starting to appear. I already know that it is not going to look good in a few hours. Likewise, it looks like my head took the brunt of the fall as well because my temple and eye are going purple and a headache is thumping through my forehead. I sigh in frustration.

I hate feeling weak. I feel pitiful.

Taking a cloth, I run it under cold water and apply the compress to my head and neck for a few minutes before I open the bathroom door and step into the bedroom. As I make my way out, I notice there's a variety of freshly pressed and folded clothes on the bed, all in my size. The breakfast tray has been cleared and replaced with a lunch tray, and the bed is fully made. It is just like a hotel, only better.

I gingerly walk to the bed and sit down, still not confident on my legs. My eyes find the clock, seeing that it is now nearly midday, so I was out for hours. That has only happened once before. I need to make sure I eat more and have cooler showers if I want any chance of enjoying the time I have left. After putting on the fresh underwear that is on the bed for me, I place a pillow under my feet and lie back.

As I stare at the ceiling, I think about the man whose bed I am in. Who is he? He is heavily armed, has a large team of men, and appears to be the boss of them all. Obviously, he is a criminal of some kind, but not being a native New Yorker, I have no idea.

He is extremely handsome and strong, all man, and he seems somewhat protective and gentle in an unexpected way—all attractive qualities in my book. Not to mention that I saw him half naked yesterday in the bathroom, and I didn't miss his chiseled chest or patchwork of tattoos, which any woman would be a fool not to find sexy.

But all these romantic thoughts that begin to enter my mind are nothing but the makings of a young girl's fantasy. He is much older than me and probably has a supermodel girlfriend. He probably thinks I am nothing but a young, naive girl, and to be honest, he wouldn't be wrong. I have had a full life, of that I am sure, but it has been full of heartache, pain, and I have had to grow up fast, never having experienced sleepovers or girls' shopping trips or prom. I haven't even been on a real date.

Given that I don't know who he is or what he is capable of, I need to rid my mind of him and erase any loved up thoughts I am having. Immediately.

7

DANTE

I adjust my dick in my pants as I walk away from her, down the hall to my office. Why she has such an effect on me, I have no fucking idea. She is too young, too innocent, and after the debacle I had with my ex-wife, I don't ever want to be involved with another woman. They only end up lying to you and fucking other men anyway. I wish my cock would get the same memo.

Little Red didn't say much this morning, appearing to be a little shy and reserved, but I can confirm my original thoughts that she was in the wrong place at the wrong time.

I push my office door open and see Carter already here, coffee in hand, leaning back in my leather armchair which overlooks the courtyard below. I spot an extra coffee for me on the side table and grab it before I join him. It was a late night and I sigh as my body molds into the soft leather, enjoying the five minutes of peace we have with each other.

After checking on Leo and Little Red last night, I spent some time in my office before grabbing a few hours of sleep in my spare room. But I didn't stay away any longer, since as soon as I opened my eyes, my feet were moving back to my room on their own accord, not stopping until I was sitting in the armchair, watching her. Watching the rise and fall of her chest, the outline of her small curves underneath the linen. Why, I have no idea. There is something about her that has me on edge, and I seem to like torturing myself with the pretty young thing sleeping in my bed. When I brought her home yesterday, I could have put her in any one of the spare bedrooms, but like the fool I am, I brought her to mine. The look of her in my sheets, her scent in my bed, her hair splayed out across the pillow, is now permanently etched into my memory, and I don't want her anywhere else. The itch to touch her but knowing I shouldn't festers on the surface of my skin, making me itch. My fingers twitch just thinking about it.

"We've got to get this shit sorted," Carter says, and by the look of him, he hasn't had any sleep either. We have worked together for the past ten years, ever since Carter was 15 and Sebastian and I caught him pickpocketing. We offered him a job, and he has been with us ever since. He isn't Italian, but learnt the rules quickly, and although he can never be second in command or head of the family, his role is no less important, and we consider him a brother. Like me, he has no living parents, but at least I have Leo.

My eyes flick to the clock on my wall, and I remember

I must go down and have breakfast with him when he wakes in an hour or so.

"I know. Fucking Dominic is already shooting his mouth off about it to anyone who will listen. Of course, he doesn't tell anyone who matters that he owes us money. Fucking rat," I spit out. My hatred for the man goes deep, probably as deep as his cock was in my wife all those years ago.

He has no respect. None. And while I know many of the other families in the fold feel the same way, if he can cover his tracks as well as he thinks he can and say we acted without necessity yesterday, then it is not going to be well received in our wider circle. I already know Sebastian's phone is running hot.

My cell rings then, and it was like I conjured him, because Sebastian's name lights up the screen. "Sebastian." I put him on speakerphone for Carter to hear.

"Boys, give me an update. Everyone has been calling, and I need some fucking answers," he says wearily.

Carter and I run through what we know, which is not much at this point. The Russo brothers have taken our money and very sneakily made it appear that they didn't even receive it in the first place. It is currently our word against theirs, and while our word will always win, the fact that they are now out for revenge for the deaths of his men plants a small seed of doubt in the other families' minds. It's enough to topple us if others jump on board, which they undoubtedly will, because when you are at the top, there are many people waiting in the wings for their opportunity. The constant battle to remain the head family is tiresome at times.

We talk at length, and together the three of us decide to visit every venue and property they own, put a tail on the rest of their family, and do a forensic accounting audit on their files—the ones we have, anyway. All their phones will be bugged by the end of today, and we have already planted some of our girls into their other strip joints to see if we can get their girls to talk, all the while keeping our ear to the ground.

With Sebastian away for a while longer, it is decided that I will start local talks with our contacts on his behalf. A job that I have done before and one that I have no problem with. It will take me out of the compound which, given they want my head is not the smartest, but I will take Carter and a large team with me wherever I go.

After discussing things for close to an hour, we end the call.

"Carter, get the team to go to the Happy Holidays Hotel at Ozone Park and grab Little Red's things, would you? She checked in yesterday before the shooting, so she hasn't been there even a night."

"Little Red?" he fires back in question, his eyebrow raised and a smirk forming on his face. "She's still here, then?" He already knows the answer.

"Yes, she is still here," I say, offering him nothing else in reply, pretending to busy myself with paperwork on my desk.

"Perhaps I should take her off your hands?" Before I even realize it, a deep rumble leaves my chest at his prodding.

"Okay, okay..." A full grin takes over his face, palms up in surrender, as he steps backwards through the door. "I will leave the pretty little thing with you, then." He promptly steps out of the door as soon as the last word leaves his mouth, so as not to get his head bitten off.

I shake my head and slam the papers onto my desk. *What the hell am I doing?* She has been here a day. *One fucking day!* I don't know anything about her, yet I am jealous of another man wanting her. Carter is no threat; he doesn't get close to women. He has too much on his plate to begin with.

I run my hands through my hair and walk out of my office. Pausing at the door, I look down the corridor toward my room, thinking about checking on Little Red again. I decide against it and follow my nose to the kitchen, where Leo is having waffles, and Maria is busy making lasagne for dinner.

"Morning, buddy." I kiss his head in greeting, ruffling his hair.

He smiles as I sit next to him up at the kitchen bench, and have another coffee while watching Maria place the pasta sheets one by one, followed by the meat and the cheese in perfect layers.

"I just went up and put fresh clothes on her bed. She was already up and in the shower. She didn't eat much, such a little thing. I think she needs a good bowl of Bolognese," Maria states, her eyes not leaving her masterpiece.

"What did she eat?" I ask, wanting to know given that she hasn't eaten in the 24 hours since she has been here.

"The small fruit bowl, and that is it. She didn't touch the pastries or bread." Maria sounds astounded, and I know from her healthy roundness that skipping carbs is not something she can fathom.

I nod in acknowledgement, and then notice Leo looking up at me.

"She is just a houseguest, Leo. She won't be here long, but I'm keeping her here safe with us for now. You don't need to worry." I answer the question I think he is asking me with his eyes. It must do the trick, because he nods and looks back to his waffles, dribbling more maple syrup over them and eating with gusto.

This is what I don't understand. Leo looks and acts perfectly fine. He is smart, he eats well, and sleeps without issue. He reads and plays. Sure, he lacks confidence and doesn't make friends easily. Hell, he won't leave the house to make any. But otherwise, he is 100% healthy, so why he doesn't talk is an absolute mystery to me. Traumatic Mutism is the terminology that has been thrown around by the various doctors and specialists we have seen.

I leave Leo to finish his waffles and go back to my office to work through some paperwork. We are bringing in new blood, most of which are fresh soldiers from Italy that Sebastian and I spotted when we were there a year ago. New York is new for them, so their onboarding and training has to be thorough before we let them out in the field. Nico is also a new member of our team and currently shadowing Sebastian while he is in Sicily. He is a great addition, and we hope by broadening our search for quality soldiers throughout Italy that we find more men like him.

We have high expectations, and get the fittest and

fastest men we can. They also need to be trained in not only family dynamics and all the players both in New York and Sicily, but they need to know every street, every building, every sidewalk of New York and who owns them before they start their first day with us. They will begin with me in the coming weeks, their first posting here at the compound, where they will shadow our teams before doing solo days to get their bearings.

Sitting back in my office chair, I crack my neck and lean my head back against the cool leather, my mind once again wandering to Little Red down the hall. What the hell am I going to do with her?

My cell rings, startling me from my thoughts, and I see my ex-wife's name on the screen. If I thought I was stressed before, my stress levels increase tenfold the minute I see her name. It has been a few months since she's last called, so it is unexpected, to say the least. Last I spoke with her, she was still high as a kite, full of a toxic mixture of alcohol and drugs, slurring her words about wanting to see my son.

"Angelina," I grit out as I answer. My blood boils at the very mention of her name passing my lips. She is not worthy of the air I exhale while talking to her.

"Dante." I am surprised to hear her sounding clear for a change, but I know the truth of her current state will become more apparent the longer she speaks.

"What do you want?"

"I want to see Leo," she says simply, like she has a right to see him. Like she has forgotten that she gave up that right years ago.

"No."

"He is my son. You cannot keep him from me." As predicted, I can hear the tremor in her voice and the slight slur of her words, telling me that drugs or alcohol are still in her system, which only infuriates me further.

"The last fucking time you saw him, he had nightmares for a week and wet the bed for a month. You are not going near him," I grit out to her, trying to rein myself in, the memory of that time permanently burnt into my brain. I pull at my hair. The frustrations I feel just from hearing her fucking voice grate my insides like rubbing an open wound against rough cement.

"Fuck you, Dante. You can't stop me from seeing my son!" she screams at me, sounding out of her mind.

"You're unfit to be a parent. I gave you chances, I sent you to rehab, and you didn't comply," I reply steadily.

"Fuck you and your need for obedience. He is my son!" I wish she felt this passionately about him while he watched her fuck numerous men.

"Don't call me again until you have been clean for a year. Then we can talk," I say before ending the call. I don't want to be a monster, but nothing will harm my son, not even his own poor excuse for a mother.

I stand up abruptly from my desk and grab my coffee cup, throwing it against the wall. The cup smashes into a million tiny snowflake-like pieces as I seethe in anger. Running my hands through my hair, I take some deep breaths, trying to get myself under control. My eyes flick up to my door when I hear a tap.

"What?" I bark, not in the mood for visitors.

It's my men, back from Ozone Park, where they grabbed all of Little Red's things from her hotel. I watch two of them as they walk into my office, and I look down at their hands.

"That's it?" I ask in question. She has a handbag and a small duffle bag. That can't be right. I can't believe that a woman such as Little Red would travel lightly. No woman does.

"That's it, boss. We spoke with the clerk. She checked in an hour before she went for her run yesterday, so she hadn't even fully unpacked."

"Bring it to me." I take a seat in one of my leather armchairs by the window. The duffle bag is cheap, and as he lays it on the floor, I lean over and unzip it.

I find three tops, two pairs of jeans, a few dresses, and underwear, all perfectly folded neatly in little piles. She has two pairs of shoes and her toiletries as well, but that's it. Zipping it back up, I pass it back to them.

"Give it to Maria. She will know what to do."

"This is her handbag, sir," my other man says, giving me the fake black leather bag.

I open it and rummage through. Gum, hair clips, tissues, lip gloss, and an old, cheap cell phone. It is flat, so I can't access it. I pull out a slip of paper. It is her boarding pass. One-way economy airfare to New York from Oklahoma, arriving yesterday at 4am. She took the red eye; no wonder she was exhausted.

I grab her wallet. Looking through it, I notice she doesn't have much. Only about $200 in cash, which would last her less than a week here in the city, a bank card, and a driver's license

I look at her ID. Annie Peterson. You can't get more American than that. She looks to have just turned 21 and is from a small town in Oklahoma, which explains her sweet, southern accent. A quick search online, and I see her residential address is a trailer park just outside of the main town.

My boys leave, and I call Carter and ask him to run an ID check to get more information on her. Then I take her wallet and the rest of her handbag down to my room. It is close to 2pm now, so I am startled when I open the bedroom door and see her back on the bed, asleep. I stop midstride and look around the room, noticing her food tray is once again untouched and nothing else has been moved. I place her handbag on the dresser and quietly walk over to the bed.

Standing over her, I look over her sleeping body. She must have had a shower because her hair is damp and now braided in two perfect plaits running down her back. The need to grab them is near stifling. My eyes wander her face, and my heart stops as I see a bruise on her cheekbone around her eye.

"What the fuck?" I whisper to myself as my fingers reach out and softly caress the discoloration, feeling the lump underneath. My eyes drift down her body, checking for anything else amiss, and I clench my teeth, as the white shirt she is wearing, my shirt, has ridden up and is around her waist. Her perfect ass and curves are on full display, along with some black cotton briefs. But I have little time to enjoy the view as my eyes get stuck on her hip, where a massive black bruise has formed. It looks painful, and I wish I knew what the hell had happened.

Glancing around the room again, I don't see any clues as to what may have caused this. Everything looks just as

I left it. I quietly step away from her and back out the door, heading down to see Maria. I need her to leave pain relief for her and some arnica cream. She is going to be sore when she wakes up, and then we will have a little talk.

8

ANNIE

I sit on the edge of the king-sized bed, swallowing the bile that has risen in my throat as I stare at the pain medication on the bedside table with disgust. I hate drugs. In the end, my mother was addicted to them. They were prescriptions, but when someone becomes reliant on medications like that, it doesn't matter if they are legal or illegal, the effects are the same. They are not the people they first were. They change. They become sicker, both physically and mentally. They become withdrawn whilst also cunning in their quest for the next hit.

For Mom, the pain relief medication from her cancer diagnosis kept her in a permanent state of near-comatose for the better part of her final months. As a young woman, working three jobs to keep us afloat, worrying about how Mom was doing, I have spent the last year of my life permanently on edge, walking on eggshells each time I went home, wondering if the next day was going to be her last. Wondering if she would die from a drug overdose before the cancer got her. I didn't like that version of my mother. I didn't like that version of a human.

He must have been here. The man. I still don't know his name, but now I'll be thinking of him as my wolfman. When I fell asleep earlier, I dreamt that I was *Little Red* Riding Hood, and he was The Big Bad *Wolf*. Except, he wasn't bad at all. He saved me, brought me to his home, took care of me and kept me warm. Kept me happy. It seems fitting, considering real life isn't so far off from that dream.

Where does he sleep if I am now in his bed? My cheeks heat at the thought of being in his space like this. I keep telling myself it doesn't mean anything, but I haven't been in another man's bed before.

My one and only awkward sexual encounter happened when I was seventeen, with a boy who stayed in the trailer park for only a month. His name was Jimmy, and he came from Kansas. He and his dad were passing through and kept to themselves, but we got chatting the first week he arrived and became fast friends.

One night, we were out looking at the stars and he kissed me. It was my first kiss and every romantic notion I had of what it was like to be kissed immediately flew out the window. It was sloppy, and he tasted like an ashtray and cheap whiskey. I'm not sure how it happened, but within five minutes, his hands were down my pants, touching me where no hand had ever touched me before —including my own. Before I understood what was going on, I was bare on the bottom half, and he was putting on a condom. It was consensual; he didn't force himself on me or anything. But I was so incredibly naive. It was all over pretty fast, and I can't say that I understand what all the fuss is about. If that is what sex is like, then I am happy to remain single.

I didn't have time in my life for boys or romantic dates leading up to that experience. I left high school and went straight to work to be the breadwinner for Mom and I. I waitressed at the local diner at night, babysat kids in the afternoons, and cleaned for our neighbors in the trailer park on the weekends. In my free time, I looked after Mom. That was it. There was no time for relationships, hobbies, or even college. That path was never an option for a girl like me, anyway.

I sigh and roll my neck. I slept all day and night again, and now as the bright sunlight of a new morning hits my face, the throbbing pain of my bathroom injuries seep in. Aside from a dull headache and a sore hip, I feel pretty good otherwise.

Ignoring the medication, I take the arnica cream into the bathroom with me. While my face is feeling and looking better, my hip is still hurting, covered by a swirl of purple and black.

Just like yesterday, I take a shower, although this time it is cooler and I don't wash my hair, keeping my braids intact. Drying myself quickly, I step back into the bedroom to see all my clothes. My things from the hotel and my handbag. Everything is freshly washed and pressed, sitting on the dresser. There is also a fresh breakfast tray full of fruit and bread again.

I smell him then. I haven't seen him since the first morning when he quizzed me, but I know he came. His scent is all around the room.

Changing quickly into my jeans and a simple white t-shirt, I grab the fresh bowl of fruit and make fast work of it. I pause as I look at the bread but decide against it. After I put everything back on the tray, I am sitting on the bed, when the door opens and a small head pokes through.

A little boy, with brown hair and a cheeky glint in his eye peers around the large timber door. Our gazes meet, both of us wide-eyed, startled to be seeing a new stranger. He looks like he was caught with his hand in the cookie jar, and it makes me smile. Before I can get myself to speak, he backs away and closes the door.

Odd. He obviously isn't meant to be here.

Intrigued about who this cute little boy is, I jump off the bed and slowly open the door, poking my head out. Having been in this room for days now, I am keen to explore. Wolfman didn't say that I couldn't, and I bet the rest of the house is huge. I look up the long hallway in time to see him dart into a room down at the end, so with no other sign of life in the place, and no idea what else I am supposed to do, I slowly walk in that direction.

His door is open, and I see him sitting in his room on the carpeted floor, Lego blocks sprawled all around him. He looks up, but doesn't say anything, before looking back at his Legos and continuing with his build. From the completed formations around his room, clearly this is a talent of his that he enjoys. Right now, it looks like he is building a spacecraft. Continuing to approach him slowly, I am unsure if I am allowed to be here. Not wanting to scare him, I keep my distance but sit down on the floor with him. He is a cute boy, no older than 8 or 9 and I wonder why he isn't in school.

"Can I play too?" I ask, but he ignores me, so I reach down and grab a few pieces of Lego. He doesn't object, so I grab a few more and start building. Building blocks is not my strength, I realize, as I try to follow along with what he's doing, but I enjoy being in a different room with a new face. So while he creates something that looks like it needs to be displayed in a museum, I get busy trying to build a simple square house instead, which looks more like a bad bundle of bricks.

We are both silent in our concentration, but I take in the rest of his bedroom. It is a large room with a bathroom off the side, not dissimilar to where I am sleeping. With the bright blue décor and selection of toys, it is most certainly a little boy's room. One wall is covered in floating shelves, each one full of different Lego models; some spaceships, others are cars, and even a castle, which I think might be something from a movie.

Watching him, I can see a resemblance to the man who brought me here, so it could be his son. Does that mean he is married? Am I sleeping in a married couple's bed? I didn't see any female products in the bathroom, but maybe she isn't here right now...

I feel sick thinking about it, realizing that I may have been romanticizing about a married man.

The little boy remains silent, so I begin to talk. I talk about everything and nothing. His eyes flick to me and he nods at times, but no sounds come from his mouth. Because I babysat a lot back home, I know it takes some kids a long time to open up to strangers. And since I don't want to make him uncomfortable, I just continue on. Not asking him questions, not requiring him to talk in return.

"You are so lucky to have this many Legos. I didn't have anything like this when I was your age. I used to play moms and dads, except I didn't really have any friends either, so I played both the mom and the dad. I wasn't very good at it, though. I only ever had a mom, so I wasn't sure what the dad was even supposed to do! But I copied what I saw on TV."

He doesn't say anything, so I continue.

"My favorite show was the Simpsons, but Homer... although he was funny, I can't really remember him doing much around the house. That was always Marge. Oh, and I loved her hair! I always wanted to dress up as Marge for Halloween." I glance over at him as he's assembling a new part of the spaceship, still quiet as can be. "I never got to do Halloween. My mom used to say the candy would rot my teeth and that I had beautiful teeth." He looks at me then, so I smile wide to show him my teeth, and he nods before looking back down at his masterpiece.

"But I had a really nice neighbor. Her name was Lilly, and sometimes she would sneak me some candy. My all-time favorite are Peanut Butter Cups. They are sooo good. I wish we had some of those right about now." I hum as I briefly dream of the peanut butter and chocolate hitting my tongue. They are my favorite, but I haven't had them in a very long time.

He looks up at me and smiles, before giving me a sly nod so I know he likes them too.

"Aside from the Simpsons, I didn't watch a lot of TV,

but Lilly used to have the radio on all the time. I love music and dancing, even though I am not very good at either of them." I laugh, the memories filling my brain. As bad as things were, especially toward the end, Lilly was really my guardian angel. "My mom also used to play Dolly Parton a lot when I was growing up. So when I hear Dolly, it reminds me of my mom." I look down at my hands and pretend I am concentrating on the Lego pieces as I try to push the tears back down that threaten to spill over my cheeks. His little hand comes out and touches mine, and I still.

"I'm okay, thanks," I whisper with a smile, trying to get my emotions in check as I see the concern on his face.

I am by no means a teacher or a specialist with kids, but I have babysat a lot of them over the years, from all walks of life. I can tell when kids need extra support. This little guy sitting next to me can certainly hear me, and by the look of his Lego skills, both his gross and fine motor skills are perfect. From seeing his bookshelf, he can probably read, and his acknowledgement of my tears means he can sense others emotions and show empathy.

Yet he doesn't talk.

"Why don't you talk?" I decide to ask. Might as well just get straight to the point.

He just shrugs his shoulders in response.

So he can talk... he just doesn't want to? A little girl back home that I babysat had Mutism, so it may be something similar. At the time, I read every book and watched clips on the web at the local library on the topic. Although I don't have the qualifications, I saw what worked with her, so I will just treat this little boy the same and see what happens.

It can never hurt to try, right?

"There you both are!" a female voice says from behind me, and I turn to see the older lady who I saw in the kitchen when I first arrived.

"Hello, dear. I am Maria." Her accent is thick as she introduces herself, taking a step toward me, and I stand quickly.

"Hi, I'm Annie." I'm still a little startled, but her warm expression puts me at ease.

"Why don't you both come downstairs. I have some snacks ready for morning tea." Even though I am not really hungry, I already know there is absolutely no way to say no to this lady, as her face lights up and her eyes graze over my appearance.

Leo jumps up beside me and is already out the door, so Maria and I follow him.

"I'm the housekeeper and friend of the boys. Let me give you a quick tour. You haven't been outside of the bedroom for days!" She sounds excited, and it makes me smile.

"Down here are a few spare bedrooms, each with their own private bathrooms. I nod as I look in the doors as we pass down the hallway, wondering if this is where wolfman sleeps.

"Downstairs here has all the living spaces, including an office, a small library, gym, and theatre room." We walk down the stairs, her arm sweeping over the array of rooms and hallways that appear to be open for me to explore as I wish.

"It is a lovely home," I say to her, which has her beaming.

"My dear, you have lovely manners."

As we walk into the kitchen, I see the young boy already at the bench, eating the fruit and pastries Maria has prepared. She moves into the kitchen and starts getting busy making something on the stove.

"Can I help?" I ask as I begin to walk toward her. It is only right that I offer; I am staying here after all.

"No, darling, but why don't you sit up at the bench for a while? You can watch and see how I do things?" she offers, and I nod before going and sitting next to the young boy, watching them both with interest.

This is all new, and the reason why I'm here is crazy, yet I feel so at home and welcomed.

"What are you cooking?" I ask her as I perch up onto a stool.

"Osso Buco," She answers, her accent even thicker.

"Osso B..." I try to say.

"Buco, Bella. It is a traditional Italian dish, like a stew."

"Are you Italian?" I ask, already knowing she must be, but trying to make conversation.

"Yes, Bella. Do you know any Italian?" she asks me, smiling.

I shake my head, feeling very sheltered having not traveled or done anything remotely interesting in my life.

"Well, I can teach you!" she says, and I perk right up with interest. I have never had the opportunity to learn another language, but even I know I would be stupid to pass up that offer.

"Really? That would be great!" I swear, my smile is now a mile wide.

As I watch and listen to Maria who starts talking to me and telling me sounds and words in Italian, I periodically look around the house, still not quite believing that I am here.

Who are you wolfman, and why have you brought me to your home for safekeeping?

9

DANTE

The boys and I have been out all day, talking with families, calming their emotions all the while trying to find the Russo brothers before they find us. It has been a long fucking day, which went from bad to worse after Angelina called me again this morning. That makes twice now in a matter of days, demanding things that she has no business demanding of me, and I have barely had time to take a breath. As our car pulls up to another one of the shithole strip clubs in Queens, I crack my knuckles in anticipation. We may not find the Russo brothers, but I sure feel it in the air that we are close.

Carter and I step out of the car and our team follows closely behind, nodding at the two security guys out the front as we step into the dark seedy venue. Our eyes laser focus on everyone and everything around us, trying to assess if we're walking into another shitshow. The music is loud and sultry, and the bar looks busy. It's obviously one of Russo's more lucrative businesses, and I wonder if our money has been poured into this place instead of Allure.

To be honest, I don't really care what business they put it into, we just want our money back. That was the deal.

We get the usual stares from people as we walk in. All of us together is a menacing sight and the patrons that frequent these places enough already know who we are. I don't miss a few men as they skirt around us and out the door, sensing the trouble brewing and wanting no part in it.

I don't blame them because I can feel it too.

I stand at the end of the bar with Carter, and together we canvass the room as our backup team also now enters and positions themselves around the perimeter, waiting for our command.

"Do you think they are here?" Carter asks me as our eyes track the movements of every asshole in this place.

"No," I answer, my tone short, because while the Russo brothers are stupid, they are also sneaky and slip their way out of everything. They want our blood, but I know they are not yet ready to take it. After killing five of their most senior soldiers, they need time to reconnect, to plan and strategize their next move because they want it to be deadly.

That's why we need to find them. We need to get them before they are prepared. We need to take them by surprise. It has already been a few days, and the longer it takes, the harder they will be to find and the more ammunition they will have against us.

"Fuck," Carter mumbles, and I look to where his eyes

are resting and stiffen slightly when I see my ex-wife. She's stripping on stage to a song about regrets, and I bet she has a few. I know I sure do. Marrying her being one of them. I watch her for a moment and realize that I feel nothing. When I first saw her on a pole years ago, I was angry. Livid. But I tried. I tried so hard to help her, to get her better, and now as I see her oily hair in tangles on her shoulders and her black mascara smudged under her eyes, both of which are bloodshot and barely open, understanding washes over me that there is really no hope for her anymore.

I watch as she twists and turns, and my mind briefly goes to the woman in my bed, her perfect soft skin, her bright green eyes, and her long red hair. They couldn't be more opposite, and I am already itching to get back home to watch her sleep some more. It has become my new favorite pastime over the last few days—as creepy as it may be.

I lift my chin to Carter. "Over there," I say, pointing to a hidden door at the back of the room, just to the side of the stage. Carter nods, and we stalk toward it, completely uninvited, but not giving a shit. Out of the corner of my eye, I spot a few burly men from the venue's security team come closer, but one look from me and they stay rooted to the ground, turn their eyes, and pretend they don't even see us.

Carter opens the door to a long corridor, and I walk through quickly, along with our men. There are doors down the hall, on both the right and the left, and my team and I open each and every one as we make our way to the end. The corridor is bare, and aside from the bustling dressing room for the dancers, we find nothing. Frustrated, I push open the exit door at the end of the corridor and what do you know, outside, in the back parking lot, appears to be where all the action is.

"Well, what do we have here..." I say, mocking, as I spot a group of four men, one of whom I know is Benny, a cousin of the Russo boys. My eyes flick to Carter, and I nod to him. Benny and his men reach for their weapons, but they needn't have bothered, because we are faster. Three of the men are shot dead point-blank while I shoot Benny in the hand and relieve him of his gun.

"Fuck, Dante! What the fuck!" he screams as he grabs his hand in pain, his right hand now out of action and short of a few fingers.

"Benny. You know better than to have your guys raise their guns at me." I pocket my gun and put my hands in my pants pocket, walking around his men who are lying on the ground to get a better look at them.

There is no one that I recognize. No doubt they are all petty criminals thinking that working for a family in the mob would be something they should aspire to.

"Where are your cousins, Benny?" I ask as Carter moves toward him and grabs him by the shoulders, keeping him still. I move to stand right in front of him. Benny tries to get out of Carter's hold, thrashing about, but Carter never lets go.

"BENNY!" I shout, now tired of his shit and wanting answers, anger seeping out of my pores. "Where the fuck are your pathetic cousins?"

"I don't know, Dante. I have no idea," he breathes with a shrug, and I know he is lying.

"Wrong answer, Benny." My fist flies out, and I punch him across his face. The sound of my knuckles hitting his flesh is like music to my ears, and so, I do it again, twice, in quick succession, to see if I can make it sound like a symphony.

Benny's head falls back, rolling left, then right on his shoulders like a newborn baby.

"I will ask one more time, Benny. Where are Dominic and Federico?" I snarl and get up close and personal to his face, seeing the blood drip from the broken skin on his nose and lips.

"Fuck you, Dante," he spits out, and all I see is red. It doesn't happen often; I can count on one hand the number of times in my life where I have really lost my mind. Sure, I will fight. But right now, knowing that those two assholes are out there, hatching a plan to come for us makes my blood boil beyond control.

Like a raging bull, I unleash, all my anger and frustrations come out of my body by way of my fists. I am relentless, my vision blackening, and I only stop when Carter says my name.

"Dante!" Carter shouts, looking at me, breaking me from my trance. "He's done. He's dead." He lets go of Benny, throwing his body onto the gravel where it remains lifeless, just like the other three.

Panting, I wipe my hands on my handkerchief and catch my breath, trying to calm my anger. Nodding to Carter, I look at my men. "Let's go." With my emotions once again in check, they follow me back through the club and out the door to the car, like the soldiers they are.

S<small>TRETCHING OUT MY FINGERS</small>, I wrap my hand in a towel with ice, then fix myself a whiskey before heading upstairs. All is quiet as I walk into the bedroom. I need to find these brothers and sort this shit out, because I need Little Red out of my house. When I am not thinking about work, I am thinking about her, and the two are starting to blur. That's a dangerous thing for a man like me. She is a distraction, albeit a very fucking tempting one.

Once Carter searched Little Red's bank records, I learned that she has some money but not a lot. A consistent weekly pay from a local diner was her only income until recently. She has no medical history. None. No police record, not even a parking ticket. There is no car registered in her name and no known living relatives. What I do know is that her mother recently passed away, and when Carter called the trailer park that she has listed as her residential address, they only confirmed that she was living there but recently moved.

But what I am currently too aware of is how she looks like a lazy Sunday morning, all tangled in my sheets, like comfort, desire, and a pool of innocence I want to swim in.

I rub my eyes to erase the thoughts from my mind. I have no plans to keep a woman here. No plans to get involved. The destruction my lying, cheating, drug-addicted ex-wife caused has permanently damaged me too deeply.

Sipping the whiskey, I settle into the armchair, ready for a long night of watching.

"Hey, wolfman," she breathes out sleepily. I'm startled by the sound of her voice at nearly 2am, but also by the name. Wolfman? Is she dreaming, or is she talking to me?

"Buona sera," I say as she slowly scoots up, leaning her back against my headboard.

"Buno what?" she asks, yawning, and I don't miss her legs as they peek out from under the blankets as she gets comfortable again. The sight has me thinking about doing things to her that I have no right to.

"Did you call me Wolfman?" I ask, not responding to her question. I'm too intrigued by why she would call me that.

She blushes a little, catching me off guard, and I decide to let it pass for now.

"Why are you awake?" I ask.

"I think I have had too much sleep these past few days. I am not that tired tonight," she answers honestly, and my eyes stay on her as I take another sip of my whiskey.

"Why are you awake?" I don't generally like people questioning me. I answer to Sebastian and Leo, and I will be considerate of Carter, Goldie, and Maria. That is about it, though. Everyone else I hardly even tolerate, but for some reason, speaking with her feels different.

"I just got in." As her eyes flick to the clock on the wall, her eyebrows raise. She stays quiet for a moment, almost seeming to contemplate her response, but then she surprises me with another question.

"How long will I be trapped in this room?"

"You can leave the room whenever you'd like. You are welcome to use the kitchen, and all living areas. My housekeeper Maria will look after you and can get you anything you need. But I have a team here that secures the place, so you can't leave the premises. If you do and my enemies find you, they will kill you. I don't want that on my conscious, Bella."

The term of endearment leaves my lips before I can stop it. I am having a hard time thinking of anything but her pouty lips showcasing the softest pink and her red hair falling in tendrils around her face.

"How long before it is safe for me to leave the house, then?" she presses, fidgeting with the edge of the blanket by her side.

"Have you got somewhere to be, Little Red?" I ask, tilting my head. We both know she has absolutely nowhere else to be.

Her eyebrows furrow slightly, and she glares at me with clear frustration. It is damn cute.

"The men who we fought with are out to hurt us. I don't suspect that you are a threat, but because you are with me, they will try to hurt you. Until we can fix the situation, you need to stay here." I shrug.

She nods, and I can tell by the distant look in her eyes that she is thinking everything over. She is such a good girl for trusting me like this. I run my hands across my mouth to hide the smirk that is forming.

"What happened to your hands?" She gasps, her eyes now wide as they take in my blood-stained sleeves and my bruised and beaten knuckles.

"Just some business I had to take care of," I reply,

waiting for the moment she runs into the bathroom and locks the door in fear.

"Business?" she questions, before jumping out of the bed and walking over to me. She steps so softly on the carpet, her movement can't be heard. But I can't say I am focused on her steps but rather her legs, her pale bare skin looks like porcelain under the glow of the lamp, and with her wearing nothing but my shirt, she looks like every man's wet dream.

Stopping in front of the armchair, she picks up my large hand in her two small ones and lifts it closer to her face to inspect it.

She drops my hand gently and turns, going into the bathroom, and I watch her ass as she goes. Licking my lips, my cock hardens, and I wait for her to come back, wondering what she is doing. Less than a minute later, she comes back out with a damp cloth, a towel, and the arnica cream that we left for her bruises. Maria told me they were due to her falling over on the tiles in the bathroom, but that's something else I need to get to the bottom of.

"Are you playing nurse again?" I ask, looking up at her small frame as she once again stands in front of me, placing the towel under my hand and dabbing my knuckles with the damp cloth.

"Somebody has to look after you," she mumbles, and I grit my teeth to bite back the smile that threatens to break my steely gaze. "Besides, you have taken care of me since I have been here. I thought I could return the favor." She nibbles on her lip in concentration, and I ache to suck on it.

"Thank you for getting my things..." I nod in acknowledgement.

"He looks like you, you know," she says with a small smile appearing on her face, and I want more of it. Her small lips curve upwards, and she gets a small dimple on one side that makes it difficult for me to sit still with the growing bulge in my pants. Her happiness is starting to turn me on more than her body.

"Who?" I retort as I come back to myself, my eyes narrowing as there's only one person she could be speaking about.

"The little boy who likes Legos," she replies easily. Now she has my full attention. It appears Little Red has met my son.

I lean back in the chair at that, not as concerned with that fact as I thought I would be. I'm also truly enjoying her touch and the way her bare legs graze mine as she repositions herself to wipe my other hand. The fact that there is someone who wants to look after me is unusual. Aside from Maria, I haven't had a woman look after me since my mother died when I was young. It is not something I thought I would have missed until now.

"Leo. He is my son." As the words leave my mouth, her eyes meet mine.

"He is amazing. You must be very proud," she says with a smile that takes up her whole face, her face genuinely lighting up at the thought of him.

I sit shocked for a moment, because yes, he is amazing, and yes, I am very proud of him, but for a boy who doesn't socialize, I wonder how much time she spent with him today. I should be worried about having a strange woman in my house around my kid, but I'm not. If it was anyone else, I would already have thrown them out.

Yawning, she answers my thoughts.

"We spent all day playing with Legos. I don't think I have talked as much as I did today in all my life. My throat is sore." She rubs her throat, and I clench my hand at the gesture, thinking about how pretty her neck would look in my hands. I really have to get ahold of myself.

Happy with the cleaning, she grabs the arnica cream and begins to rub it into my knuckles, so softly I can barely feel her touch.

"What is your name?" she whispers, her attention staying on my injuries.

"Dante," I reply without hesitation, and she smiles in approval.

"How long will I be here, Dante?" she asks again, and I like the sound of my name from her lips. Her twang makes it sound like it's a name just for her to speak.

"Until it is safe enough for you to leave." I repeat what I've already told her, and as her eyes flick to mine, she nods in understanding. Her obedience does something to my insides, and I grit my teeth so hard that I am sure she can hear me grinding them.

She moves her body slightly to grab more arnica cream and her bare legs hit my fingers. I take advantage of the closeness and lift my finger, trailing her thigh slightly, feeling her soft skin, my cock now painfully awake. I hear her intake a breath and my eyes flick to hers as I make a small pattern against her skin. God, she is soft, delicate, small, yet is not begging me to let her go, crying for her friends or family, or screaming in horror at what she has seen. I watch her, completely fascinated by her, as she continues with the cream, not acting offended by my touch. The only change in her demeanor is the quickening of her breath and the slight blush to her cheeks. I should stop. But I can't.

"There," she says, breaking me out of my lust-filled trance. I look down at my hand, which although is still red and raw, looks much healthier than when I first walked into the room. She takes the cream and the towels to the bathroom and then walks back into the bedroom and slips into bed. *Good move, Little Red. Keep your distance.*

"Goodnight, Dante..." she says as she closes her eyes, my name on her lips the sweetest sound in the quiet of the night.

"Goodnight, Little Red," I reply, but I don't think she hears me as she quickly gets lost in slumber again.

I sit sipping my whiskey for the next few hours, only leaving when the sun threatens to peek through the windows to start a new day.

10

ANNIE

My body is weary after a day of building spaceships with Leo and watching Maria cook her traditional Sicilian meals. My mind too is a whirlwind as I continue to quietly practice the few Italian words Maria mentioned to me today. But although I am exhausted, I am currently sitting up in bed, engrossed in a book I chose from Dante's library earlier this morning. I spent hours looking over the selection, then grabbed a few on childhood development. Clearly, he has them for his son, and I have tagged a few pages in them I want to revisit tomorrow. Now, I am cozy in the delicate soft linens as I read all about Sicily, which I've learned is a small island in Southern Italy, and by the look of the photos in this book, it is the most stunning place I have ever seen.

Bright blue water, beautiful pink bougainvillea, all the amazing foods that Maria prepares, and so many stunning historical landmarks. A place I can only fantasize about visiting one day.

"You're still awake, Little Red?" Dante says in surprise as he walks into the room with his nightly glass of whiskey. For a big man, he can be extremely stealth, because I didn't even hear him enter the room. As my eyes flick to his, my lips part at the sight of him, and I feel a flush overtaking my cheeks.

Tall, menacing, dressed all in black, looking exactly like a man who conducts his business at night. He stands at the end of the bed and gazes down at me, his dark eyes roaming over my body with a hunger I'm sure I'm imagining.

"Is it late?" I respond, while my eyes search the clock, noticing that it is after midnight. Late for me, but early for Dante.

"No," Dante sighs, looking worn from his day as he walks a few steps across the room and takes a seat in his chair. He places his whiskey glass on the side table and begins to roll up his sleeves, his posture relaxing.

"Tough day?" I ask, placing the book down on my lap, deciding to start a discussion. I'm excited to see him, to spend more time with him. To learn more about the man who has locked me in his house with no release date in sight. I have been here for a few days now, and with no idea how long I am here for, or what he is going to do with me, I might as well try to get to know the man who watches me sleep every night. He looks at me for a few moments before he answers, and I think back to the way he touched me yesterday, wondering if it will happen again.

"What are you reading?" he asks, expertly dodging

my question, which makes me smile. I don't particularly want to know what he gets up to when he is out, but clearly what he does will only be discussed on a need-to-know basis, and we are not at that base as yet.

"I found this in your library. I hope you don't mind?" I show him the front cover, suddenly not sure if taking one of his books is something I am allowed to do.

"Ahhh... Sicily. Have you been?" His eyes light up at the topic, and he watches me intently, already knowing the answer as he takes a sip of the amber liquid.

"No, but it looks amazing. Tranquil. Colorful. Relaxing..." My voice wanders off as I get lost in the images on the pages again.

"It is all of those things," he says as he leans his body back into what is his usual sitting position, head back, eyes focused on me, shoulders relaxed, legs apart. I wonder what it would feel like if I were to curl up on his lap? The safety, security, and comfort he may offer to a dying small town girl like me...

"Tell me about it?" I put the book to the side and snuggle into the blankets, placing my head on the pillow as I look at him expectantly.

"The blue of the water is unmatched to anything I have ever seen before. The fresh summer breeze has the most delectable scent, and the sound of the water lapping on the cliffs is what lullabies are made of. It is a place that I love. I grew up there." His lips now form a small grin as he reminisces.

"It sounds so beautiful. Do you go back much?" I ask, my eyes growing heavy, but wanting to hear his story.

"Not as much as I would like. I would like to be back there permanently, but my work and family are here," he says, taking another sip of his whiskey, and I nod in understanding.

"Do you fish?" I ask at random, and by the look on his face, he is surprised by my question. However, I was just reading about the amazing seafood and ocean lifestyle, and I can't imagine a man like Dante doing something so domesticated as fishing.

He tilts his head, and his lips form a smile. "I like to take the boat out on the water. Leo and I often spend time fishing when we are there." His eyes glisten at the memories, and I can tell it is a special place for him. I wonder again about Leo's mom, who she is and where she is. Dante hasn't mentioned her, and I don't want to ask.

"Leo is lucky to have you," I say genuinely, and he huffs.

"Did your parents never take you fishing, Little Red?" He sounds playful, and that makes me smile.

"No, I never knew my father, and my mother was sick for a long time before she died. Fishing was not something I ever got to do," I answer honestly, bringing our lighthearted conversation crashing back down into reality with a thud.

"What was wrong with her?" Dante asks, his eyes turning serious, staring right at me.

"Cancer. But to be honest, I am not sure if it was the cancer that killed her or the drugs." I don't miss the slight flinch he makes or the stiffness in his shoulders that reappears. "She wasn't really the mom I remember since she began treatment. She became addicted, and couldn't go a day without something in her system. To start with, it was to ease the pain, but it soon turned into more than that for her. I worked to pay her medical bills, which included her medication. I worked every day for years just for her to get her drugs. In the end, she loved the drugs more than she loved me, and she told me so each and every day of her last few months." I don't catch the tear before it drops from my eye.

I am sad, but also angry. Angry at her, at myself, at the situation. When you grow up poor, it is really, really hard to keep your head above water and working 16-hour days, seven days a week becomes the norm. My life has been tough, and although I never want pity or charity, I need to rest. My body, mind, and soul are weary.

"Drugs change a person, Little Red. They are not the people we thought they were before. They will do anything for their next hit. Lies become their truths, but those lies bury them in the end. They become dangerous to themselves and to others, and if they can't get better, then we need to let them go." I can't help but feel like he is speaking from experience.

"Sounds like you know a lot about it too?" I ask, knowing that I won't get an answer, but prodding anyway.

"I hate liars, Little Red. Even small little white lies fester and grow until all that is left is an explosion of pain and destruction." His hands clench onto the arms of the chair, and I know not to push the topic with him anymore. Looking straight at me, he continues. "We need to let them go, Little Red, otherwise the pain becomes too much for everyone involved."

I nod, letting his words seep into my mind. He is right.

I need to let it go. I can't hang onto the feelings I have, the memories of the past, the hatred for the drugs, the hatred for her or what she became. I am also acutely aware that I haven't told him of my ailments, not that I was planning to, but he does appear to want honesty and that makes me unsettled.

But when does someone broach that subject with a man that is still mostly a stranger? Especially since I don't know what will come of me staying here. Does he really need to know?

When I look back at him, his eyes are still firmly on me. Watching, piercing me, like he is looking for an answer. His deep eyes are nearly hypnotic. Like they are looking into my soul and uncurling me from the inside out.

"Why do you watch me every night? Do you think I will escape?" I ask softly, and I am shocked when he lets out a loud laugh that vibrates around the room. And between my legs.

"Little Red, you can't escape, it is physically impossible. Besides, if you really want to leave, then I will let you leave. But, I prefer you to stay. You are still not safe outside of these walls." He rubs his chin as he looks at me like he wants to eat me whole, and I would probably let him. No, even that's a lie. I would undoubtably let him.

I glance around the room, noting that I probably can't escape, but I am actually okay with that. I have never had this much luxury before, and Leo is a delight. Sure, I would like to look around the city and see some sights since I only just got here, but I am safe, warm, and looked

after here. Those are all things I have never felt before...
and it is nice.

"So why do you watch me every night, then?" I try
again. He grows serious at my persistence, taking a swig
of the remaining whiskey and placing his empty glass
down next to him before he answers me.

"Don't ask me questions that you are not ready to
hear the answer to, Little Red," he states gruffly, leaving
no room for me to counteract. He doesn't like to be questioned, yet I see his nostrils flair and his jaw clench, but
not in anger. There is no doubt that he likes to be in
control and as someone who had to manage a lot of
things since I was younger, letting go and having
someone in charge is somewhat of a relief for me. I no
longer want to make decisions, be the responsible one, or
the one in charge. For years, I have been the nurse, the
breadwinner, the confidant, the worker. Now I have a
chance to rest, not have to make decisions, take each day
as it comes. It is invigorating.

"I like you watching me," I whisper, looking right at
him, not sure if I should be saying the words out loud. My
heart is beating out of my chest, as I see him take a breath
of air, filling his lungs as his eyes continue to devour me
before they meet my own. The tension in the room has
skyrocketed; it is near stifling as my body warms underneath his gaze.

He rests his head in his hand as his fingers brush back
and forth along his chin, assessing me.

"I am a dangerous man, Little Red..." he replies in
warning, and I catch him off guard with a small smile.

"I'm not afraid of you, Dante," I say in another small

whisper, my eyes getting heavier. It is a true statement; I am not afraid. He has done nothing to me to cause me to be frightened. The complete opposite, in fact.

He remains silent for a while, watching me as my body becomes tired enough to close my eyes. It isn't until I am almost asleep that I hear him murmur.

"You should be."

11

DANTE

I watch her eyes close and her face soften as sleep takes her under. I inhale a deep breath and relax my body into my chair, which now fits snugly into the mold I have created in the soft leather. Being in this position every day for the past week or so will do that. I hear her small tufts of breath as they escape from her soft pink lips, and I move in my seat and adjust my pants because what I really want is to have them wrapped around my cock. I have never yearned for a woman's touch so much before as I do for Little Red's, and I bet she would look fucking delectable on her knees.

Her openness about her past is refreshing. It has been a long time since I have had someone in my life who just talks openly and honestly like that, and I find that I enjoy it. I enjoy her. Hearing nothing but excuses and lies from people is common in my world, especially from women, so it is yet another thing I'm starting to admire about her. My eyes wander over the outline of her body under the blankets, and as I do every night, I imagine feeling my way up her legs and how perfect her small, innocent body would feel underneath mine. My hands on her body, touching every inch. The visual I have of undressing her and showing her exactly how to be my good girl is vivid, my cock now painfully pressing against my zipper.

How has this young woman become so intoxicating, engraving herself into me in such a short period of time?

Touching her thigh last night was a mistake. Now in the quiet of the night, I have space to think, and I really need to get my shit together. She is too young for me. Too innocent. Her life is literally in my hands at the moment, and I need to be careful.

The ticking from the clock nearby steadies my heartbeat as the early morning hours creep closer, but my eyes never leave her. I watch her chest rise and fall, and I get lost in her state of peace. She calms me. Her presence, her voice, the way she moves, the way that she is just not afraid. Of me. Of what happened. Of anything.

My eyes flick around the room, and I see that her cell phone hasn't moved from the buffet, and without getting up and looking at it, I already know that she still hasn't charged it. The battery remains dead. She is not expecting any calls. I know she has no family, but friends, a boyfriend or partner? Obviously, no one is looking for her. I wonder how such a beautiful, tough young woman can go so unnoticed. It is astounding because I noticed her from the moment I saw her, and I imagine her in every moment I have had since.

But she needs to go. She can't get comfortable, or more to the point, I can't get comfortable with her here.

Now not only am I invested in her, but it appears that also Leo and Maria have welcomed her with open arms. I don't know why I ever thought keeping her here with me was a good idea. But I need to protect her, of that there is no question.

I feel the stress and anger beginning to well in my spine as I think of our current situation. There is still no word from Dominic or Federico. Fucking slimy bastards. They are laying low, so low, in fact, that we can't flush them out. We have uncovered a few pieces of information but are constantly hitting dead ends, as they still prove elusive. If I could find them and kill them, then she can leave and will be safe. We will all be safe. Leo and Maria have targets on their heads as big as Little Red's now, if not bigger. I know these two brothers won't stop until they end me, and they know that Leo is the gatekeeper to my soul.

It is not only the issue of the money they have stolen —there is no coming back from that—but our personal vendettas against each other, which have been building to this crescendo since Angelina started entertaining them years ago.

At the start, I didn't think anything of it. She met most of our associates, either through business activities or by chance. Although our marriage was arranged and there was never any love from either of us, she did attend dinners and other social engagements where business was conducted. And that's how she met both the brothers at different times during our short poor excuse for a marriage. But Dominic took a particular eye to my ex-wife when they met and whilst at the time, she was stun-

ningly beautiful, I know the only reason he wanted her
was because he wanted to be me. He wanted to be
embedded in the fold. He wanted to be part of the head
family. He wanted Sebastian as not only an ally, but also a
brother. He wanted my life. Jealousy is a curse, and he
was cursed from the moment he met me.

My role is a significant one. I protect, I serve, I make
deals and I break them. I kill, I threaten, I manage a large
task force of soldiers and strategize our war moves, all for
the greater good of the wider family and also our head
family. I follow tradition. I am Italian by blood and a
brother by choice. I chose this life, and I made it my
mission to lead alongside Sebastian and create the wealth
and connections we have that many people are jealous of.

When it became apparent that Angelina and
Dominic were spending too much time together, I had
my team follow her. The reality of the situation called me
back from Italy when it was uncovered that she was
doing serious drugs in front of Leo, and her and Dominic
were fucking behind my back. Again, in front of Leo.

I sent her to rehab, and I nearly ended him. I should
have. I had every right to. But we weren't in charge back
then, Sebastian's father was, and the situation was tense. I
didn't want to add pressure to an already explosive situation. I needed to think of the greater good. Of our future.

Dominic and my need to teach him a lesson had to
wait.

So I bided my time. Watched him from afar and tried
to get her the help she needed, not because I loved her,
far from it. I hated her and still do. But because Leo
deserves a mother and one that is healthy, and I would do

anything for that little boy of mine. His hands hold my heart and if it wasn't for him, I know that my life would be a mere shell of what it is now.

But it is true, the words that Little Red just whispered. They love the drugs more than they love anything else and Angelina loves them more than she does Leo, and she has for years. As his father, the best thing I can do for him is to protect him and keep him safe, and that means keeping her away from him. Unfortunately, her calls are becoming more insistent as the days pass. She never has cared enough before, yet her calls have increased these past weeks, demanding to see him. And I do not take kindly to demands from anyone.

A small snore escapes from Little Red, bringing me back to reality. Perhaps I should move her. Out of sight, out of mind. Then I could concentrate fully on catching these assholes who are threatening me and my family.

I could take her to the safehouse, though I haven't been there in a long time. It was where I took Angelina to dry out years ago. Her screams that bounced around the walls are still sounds that nightmares are made of. I could also offer to send her back to Oklahoma. But with no family or friends, and no assurance that the Russo's wouldn't find her there, I can't in good conscious do that either. Frustration settles in my bones, and I grind my teeth and rub my eyes as I sort through my options.

I look over at Little Red again, and my heart begins to calm once more. The rise and fall of her chest acts like a meditation that soothes me. Leaning back in my chair, my eyes drift over her face, discovering something new, like the little freckle on her chin or the small dimple on one cheek. Her long black lashes as they rest on her cheekbones, or the way she hums softly as she hugs the pillow next to her.

No, there is no doubt that the safest place for her to be is here. With me. She is not going anywhere.

12

ANNIE

I t has been two weeks since I first arrived at Dante's place, and I have fallen into a very domesticated lifestyle. I play with Leo all day, and then I talk to Dante each night, with cooking lessons with Maria and sleep filling the spaces in between. Dante and I talk for hours, me wrapped up in his bed and him in his armchair under the cover of darkness. Our voices soft as I tell him stories of my life and he reciprocates with some of his own.

He tells me more about Italy, a place that I can tell he loves deeply because his face lights up every time he talks about it. It is a place that is vibrant in my mind, and I visualize what he tells me, letting my imagination go wild. Since I'm extremely unlikely to go in my lifetime, it now takes up part of my dreams that help me to sleep sounder.

Along with the dark man himself.

Having never had a boyfriend or a man spend time with me, talk with me, or look after me, I feel oddly at ease in his presence. I almost feel wanted, but I know that is a ridiculous schoolgirl fantasy. I like the way he watches me. The desire I have for him grows with every day that passes, so much so, I often find myself daydreaming about him.

Dante is not a boy; he is a fully fledged man, and a dangerous one at that, who probably has any woman he pleases, whenever he pleases. The sooner I let go of these feelings that are creeping up, the better. Although perhaps heartbreak is something else I should experience before my heart stops.

After sleeping in today, I make quick work of a shower and then decide to venture out to find the others.

"Bella!" Maria chimes upon seeing me walk into the kitchen. She is a lovely woman, very maternal with Leo, and she gives me a warm hug in greeting.

"Buongiorno!" I say happily, and I smile at seeing her eyes light up at me using Italian.

"Perfect, Bella. You're starting to remember the language. Come va?" Maria asks, and since we have been greeting in Italian for the past couple of days, I recognize the words.

"I am doing well, Maria," I reply, while looking over her shoulder.

"Come, come, I am cooking. I will show you the recipe for tonight's dinner." She drapes her arm over my back, escorting me farther into the kitchen while I spot Leo over at the breakfast bar.

"Here, I am making sugo for the parmigiana. Pass me that basil." She begins to stir the large pot that is simmering on the stove. My eyes flick to Leo whose smile is a mile wide as he tucks into a bowl of Cheerios that Maria prepared for him, and he watches me as I take a cooking lesson.

Grabbing the green leafy herb, I walk back to her at the stove and wait for further instruction. This has been our daily ritual for the past week or so; she gets me in the kitchen and shows me how to cook. It's now one of my favorite things.

"Wash the leaves, then pat them dry with the paper towel, carefully. We don't want to bruise them," she instructs as she continues to stir.

"What is in the pot?" I ask, getting busy with the basil.

"I sauteed onions in some oil, then added my chopped tomatoes..." She leans across to grab some sugar. "I am adding some sugar. Dante likes it on the sweet side, Bella. Remember that." She looks at me with raised brows before giving me a wink. My heart pulses at Maria's words, thoughts swirling that maybe I will get to make this dish for Dante myself in the near future. But I shake myself out of it.

"There, basil is ready," I say proudly, and she looks over at my completed task with a surprised grin on her face.

"Good, Bella, very good," she purrs. "Now, let's put in the basil and let it simmer." I pick up the leaves and drop them into the pot, watching her continue to stir the simmering sauce. The aroma in the kitchen is amazing as I take a deep breath in, causing me to nearly salivate.

"Smells delicious," I say, smiling, as she looks at me with glee.

"Come, eat, Bella. You are too skinny, you need to eat.

Then you can help me make the parmigiana." She gestures to the kitchen bench where a large plate of pancakes is waiting for me.

Stepping away from the kitchen, I do as she asks and take a seat next to Leo at the breakfast bar, drenching my pancake in maple syrup. Leo and I both sit in silence as we eat and continue to watch Maria as she moves around the kitchen with ease, like she was born to do it. I decide then and there that I want to learn a new recipe from her every day that I am here. Already she has taught me way more than my mother ever did.

Leo and I pack away our dishes, and he runs off to his room to finish his Lego project while I take my new position in the kitchen next to Maria. Together we make the parmigiana for dinner. She goes through step by step, and I follow her every instruction. Once that is prepared, she teaches me the art of more Italian cooking as we attempt to make fresh pasta. Mine keeps breaking, but I improve throughout the afternoon.

"Dante likes fresh pasta, Bella. Fettuccine is his favorite," she says like a proud mother.

"Well, I don't plan on cooking for Dante. I think I will be able to leave soon. Besides, he has you," I say to her with a small smile, hating the words as they drip from my mouth. But I need to be realistic and pause her thoughts of this being more than it is. Otherwise, I'll get carried away along with her.

"Leave? Why do you leave?" she asks with a wave of her hands, stopping what she is doing. Looking right at me, confused, her eyes quiz me as a frown mars her face.

"Ahh... uhm... because this is not my home?" I offer to

her with a slight shrug, not wanting to upset her. But my answer catches me off guard because it dawns on me then that I don't have a home and have no idea where to go after I leave here.

"Dante has never had a woman here. But you are here, and in his room!" She smiles and shakes her head. "No, Bella, no, you not leave." Her eyes glisten with happiness, and I give her a soft smile in return, not knowing what to say.

"What about Leo's mother?" I ask tentatively, and I still as Maria looks at me sharply. There are no photos of her, no momentos around the house, nothing in Leo's bedroom. It's like she never existed.

"She is not a nice woman, Bella, not a good mother. Dante hasn't let a woman in this house since his ex-wife left. You are the first. But let's not talk about her. Come, we must make tiramisu. Dante loves tiramisu!" She changes to topic so fluidly, there is no more room for questions before we start with the final cooking lesson of the day.

Moving around the kitchen with her, I can't help thinking Dante was referring to his ex-wife as being the liar, and that she's the whole reason he hates liars in his life. My stomach feels like I have swallowed lead, the fear of him uncovering my secret now beginning to crawl up my spine, knowing that I should probably tell him, yet knowing I really don't want things to change. As the days have passed, I have wanted to share that part of myself with him because he doesn't feel like a stranger anymore. Even if whatever we are feels like more in my imagination. But I can't get myself to do it. I hate the thought of him pitying me. I want him to treat me like a woman, *see* me as a woman, not an invalid.

With the finished tiramisu in the refrigerator, I join Leo who is perched back up at the breakfast bar as Maria slides over an afternoon snack. A large platter containing salami, prosciutto, olives, sun-dried tomatoes, bread and oil, and cheeses is front and center. Little Leo looks like he hasn't eaten for days as I watch him devour olive after olive like they will disappear at any moment. I scrunch my nose, not having acquired the taste for them myself.

Glancing back at the platter, I look over the food, which is all very Mediterranean and nothing like I have eaten before. In fact, the amount of food in this house is astounding. I have never eaten this well in my entire life. Back in Oklahoma, our dollars didn't stretch far. I was lucky that the manager of the diner let me take whatever was left over from the day. Sometimes I would save up my tips so I could rummage up some biscuits and gravy. But my meals at home were nothing like this.

"You know I have no idea what half of these things are, but let's see if I can stomach them," I say to Leo, who looks at me with his eyebrows raised.

"No, I haven't eaten any of this before. I remember I tried olives once and I vomited, so here goes..." I say as I pinch my nose and quickly shove an olive into my mouth.

I hear a snort and realize that Leo is laughing at me, and that snort is the first sound from his mouth I have heard since I arrived. Although I am startled, I remain calm and decide to play along and see if I can get a full-blown laugh from him.

"Okay, I think I survived, but what is that?!" I ask in

disgust as I point to a sundried tomato. It is the one thing on the platter that I have eaten before and didn't actually mind, but he doesn't know that.

"Eat! Eat!" Maria waves the kitchen cloth at me as she coos in her thick Italian accent, pushing the plate toward me. I swear I am going to put on weight while staying here. Already my jeans are feeling more snug than normal.

I grab a tomato and put it in my mouth, scrunching my nose up like it is the most disgusting thing I have ever tasted. "OMG, who eats this stuff?" I exaggerate, and I hear a giggle. It is small, but it is there, and so I join him and have a good laugh at myself.

Maria stands in shock at the sound coming from Leo, just as my eyes flick to a shadow behind me.

Dante stands stiff as a board with a look of utter shock and awe on his face, his eyes flicking from me to Leo. It is the first time we have seen each other outside of the bedroom, and I am glad I took the time to brush my hair today.

"Leo? Did you just laugh... out loud?" he asks, the surprise obvious in his tone. He doesn't even sound like himself.

Little Leo nods and gives a small shrug like it is no big deal, before he carries on eating, not wanting to expand on the conversation. I meet Dante's eyes as we acknowledge the moment. It is a milestone, and we both know it.

"Little Red, my office. *Now*," he grits out before he struts away, and I wonder if I have done something wrong. Dante and I have never spoken about Leo's Mutism. But I have been spending a lot of time with Leo, trying to cultivate a safe space for him to feel comfortable enough to talk if he wants to. Now, as I slip off the stool and follow Dante to his office, I am trying to tamper down my excitement in case Dante thinks I stepped too far over the line into his family matters. I quickly run to catch up with him as he makes his way down the hall to his office, of which I have never been in.

When I follow him in, I am immediately greeted by what can only be described as an overwhelming amount of masculine energy that washes over me as I take in his space. His large desk is made of dark wood, the kind you know is expensive, and not the cheap look-alike material that everyone back home has. His large windows are beautifully draped in deep red velvet curtains, with large leather armchairs nearby, along with a side bar full of whiskey and what looks like a large cupboard, storing who knows what. Perhaps guns, perhaps secret documents. I have no idea how he lives and what he has in his possession. To be honest, I am not sure I want to know.

Dante stands by the window in his office, looking at the view below, and I stand there, waiting. He continues to remain silent, but unable to just stand here any longer, I walk toward him. I can only imagine that hearing his son laugh for the first time in many years must be overwhelming. Even for someone like Dante.

Approaching until I'm standing next to him, I look out at the view below of the large courtyard with its majestic gardens. Without really thinking, I reach out and grab his hand, giving it a squeeze. My nerves immediately leave my body as his hand tightens around mine, and we stand connected.

He looks down at me then, and as our eyes meet, my belly flips. The emotion swirling in his eyes is something I haven't yet seen, but his eyebrows pull together as he battles to keep it together. He turns his body and faces me, coming closer, mere inches away, before he brings his other hand up and caresses my cheek so softly, I wonder if I am imagining his touch.

"Tell me, Little Red. Have you ever been kissed?" he asks, and I blush at his question. My heart races, and I swallow hard, unsure of where he is going with this.

"Yes," I say quietly, not sure how much information to tell him.

"Did you like it?" His hands cup my jaw, and my heart begins to beat as I prepare for what he is going to do. Is he going to kiss me? I want him to kiss me, so badly. I want to feel his lips on mine. I want him to teach me how good it can be.

"It wasn't what I thought it would be like," I say honestly with a small shoulder shrug, my eyes still locked onto his.

"Then he wasn't doing it properly." His thumb brushes across my lips, pulling my bottom lip down, my breathing quickening at the feel of him touching me like this.

"Dante..." My body is acting like it has a mind of its own as I step a little closer to him.

He drops his head to mine, his lips grazing my ears. "If you say my name like that again, Little Red, I don't think I will be able to stop myself from showing you how a real man treats a woman." Pulling back slightly, nerves dance around in my stomach, and I can hardly breathe as

I realize that he is going to give me exactly what I've been longing for.

Dante leans in and takes my lips in his, softly at first, his lips massaging mine, before his tongue begins to explore. This is nothing like I experienced before and everything I've ever dreamed of. His hands cup my jaw as he lifts my head to meet his, and I grip onto his wrists, not wanting to let go. He kisses me harder as I hold on to him, like he can't get enough, almost urgently as if I am about to disappear and he needs his fill of me before I vanish.

He tastes like coffee, but subtly so, and his lips are so plush as he kisses me like I never imagined anyone would ever kiss me.

He pulls away slightly, both of us panting, and leans his forehead against mine. I notice a small twinkle in his eye, which makes me think he enjoyed that just as much as I did.

"Was that better than what you had before?" he asks, with a growing smirk on his face.

"Very," I admit quietly, my voice unstable, still trying to gather my thoughts and calm my racing heart. Our eyes are glued to each other, and it is like he is looking right into my soul, before we are startled apart by a clearing throat behind us.

Dante is whip-fast as his head flies up and he immediately pulls me behind him, keeping one hand on me as the other reaches for his gun. But he doesn't need it because the man at the door must be one of his men. He's leaning casually against the door frame, his arms crossed across his chest as he chuckles.

"Asshole," Dante grits out, and my mind slowly reconnects to my body.

What the hell just happened?

"Little Red, this is Carter, my brother," Dante says with a wave of his hand, and I look at the man, already knowing he isn't brother by blood. They look completely different.

"Hi, Annie, pleased to meet you. Sorry to interrupt..." Carter says my real name instead while offering me his hand to shake, a cheeky grin on his face. So, he already knows me, then...

I blush at being caught kissing Dante, our tender moment now all but gone. "Hi, Carter." I shake his hand quickly. "You're just as stealth as he is, I didn't even hear you come in," I say by way of making conversation, because I was too enthralled with Dante to notice anything else.

"Yeah, well, looked like he was sweeping you off your feet there..." Carter says before Dante interrupts, startling us both.

"Little Red, why don't you head back out to Leo and enjoy your lunch. I have some work to do," Dante says to me softly, and I nod and walk past him and his brother. I stop at the door and look back at him, noticing Dante's eyes still firmly on me as he leans back, his hands gripping onto the desk on either side of his body. A mix of admiration, protectiveness, and perhaps a sparkle of something more flashes in his eyes, and I give him a small smile. One that I am surprised he returns before I walk away, back down the hall, to the safety of the antipasto platter with Leo.

13

DANTE

She has been in my house only a few weeks and already Leo is responding to her better than he has anyone else. Even Maria, the same house-keeper I have had since he was born, hasn't been able to sit down for a meal with him, yet when he is with Little Red, he looks... happy.

I don't know what kind of voodoo magic she has, but whatever she is doing is working. She has not only cast her spell on Leo, but me as well, and I am entirely caught up in her orbit. Her sorcery has captured me completely, making my heart beat in a way it has never before. It is unnerving. I feel vulnerable around her, and I have no idea how to get myself out of it before I get in too deep.

She looked so fucking beautiful sitting at my kitchen bench with my son. Like she was always meant to be there. When I heard Leo laugh and saw the delight and sparkle in her eyes, I had to force myself to walk away and not to throw her over my shoulder and take her to bed. I asked her to my office to quiz her, to find out how Leo went from being totally quiet to laughing. I'm no fool; I know they have been spending time together, but the fact he has made such significant progress in a short amount of time can only boil down to one thing. Her.

Once I had her in my office, it became even harder to stay away. Her presence as she walked straight to me, her scent as it wrapped around me, and her fucking innocent eyes as they looked up at me, all nearly put me on my knees in front of this woman, who I am sure has no fucking idea what she is doing to me. All thought of quizzing her about Leo disappeared, and I was overrun with the need to have her. Although I know I shouldn't have touched her, I couldn't stop the urge to put my mouth on hers, and fuck it was worth it. She tasted like everything I don't deserve, and everything I desire. The innocence pouring out of her, the flush of her cheeks at my touch, it was enough to let me know I want to mark her as mine. My desire for her grows every day, and it is getting harder and harder to stay in control.

But I need to stop. Not only because we are like night and day. Me with a load of baggage and many fights left ahead of me, but also because she is so young, so completely innocent, I wonder if she has ever had a man touch her before. In the ways I want to, at least.

I also told myself after Angelina, I would never have anyone close to me like that again. Someone who was meant to be your partner, someone you were meant to trust, but who ended up being the biggest cause for pain in your life. I am no angel, I know that, but I'm loyal and honest to a fault. And maybe that's what draws me to Little Red. She's genuine and honest right down to her bones. I don't think she could lie even if she was paid to do it.

Thinking about her soft skin under my hands and the way she whispered my name, like she was begging me to touch her, is enough to get me hard all over again. I need to adjust myself as my cock begins to throb in my pants at the mere thought.

"Are you listening to me?" Carter asks, and I rub my eyes. I'm tired. I'm tired because we still can't find the Russo brothers and they are really grating on my nerves. But I am also tired as I hardly sleep at night because all I want to do is watch her. She is my addiction, and I need to have my hit.

"Yes, I am listening," I grit out to Carter, as he smirks at me and shakes his head.

"Have you fucked her yet?" he asks bluntly, and my nostrils flare as I glare at him. The urge to punch his smarmy face is strong right now, but I know he is trying to get on my nerves, so I remain calm.

"I am not having that conversation with you today, and don't talk about her like that unless you want my knife in your throat." While I haven't touched Annie, fuck, I want to. I want her underneath me, on top of me, splayed out across my desk. I want her in every position, in every way. I want her begging for me and giving me everything in return.

"Whoa, okay, but I see the way you look at her." Carter shakes his head, a grin on his face because he knows that I am totally and utterly fucked over for this woman.

"How the fuck am I looking at her?" I ask him, playing dumb like I don't know I look at her like I want to bow at her feet.

"Like you want to fuck her, marry her, and make little baby Dantes," Carter says, laughing as I look at him and scowl.

"Been married once and look how that turned out," I huff to him as I shuffle the paperwork in front of me.

"Okay, perhaps you just want to fuck her, then." Carter's trying and succeeding at pushing my buttons.

"Like I said, don't talk about her like that."

"Fine, but if you don't, I might, because she is..." Carter doesn't get to finish his sentence because I have already grabbed him by the collar and pushed him against the wall. He laughs then because he got what he wanted, which was to prove that Little Red was more than just a visitor at this point.

"Fuck," I sigh, letting him go as he continues to chuckle, running my hand through my hair.

"You are wasting time, man. She is a pretty little thing, and you deserve someone new in your life. It has been a long time since Angelina. It will do you good to have someone here for you," Carter says seriously, and it gives me pause.

Is that what I want? Do I want to get closer to the woman who sleeps in my bed every night? I should stay away from her, but like a moth to a flame, I can't seem to distance myself.

Our moment gets interrupted by Carter's cell phone as it shrills from his pocket.

"Yeah?" Carter answers as I walk back around to my desk and take a seat.

"What? When?" I am familiar with that tone, and I sit up, immediately on guard.

"Okay give us ten." He hangs up before looking at me.

"We have found a Russo. Federico was just spotted down near Allure. Our team is following him now. We need to roll. I will go and grab a few things, and I will meet you in the basement," he says before turning and walking swiftly out the door.

I pull out my desk drawer and grab my gun, ensuring it is loaded, then put it in the belt of my pants at my back. Grabbing my jacket from the back of my desk chair, I pull it on before quickly walking down the hall to see Leo, since I may not be back in time to say goodnight. But as I get closer to his room, I stop abruptly at the sound of her voice.

"I seriously wish I could make one like that," I hear her say. Quietly, I take a few more steps and peer around the bedroom door to see her sitting on the floor, cross-legged, playing with Leo.

"How do you get those wings to stay on? Mine always falls off." I watch as he takes her model and fixes the wings on the spaceship before handing it back to her.

"Awesome! Thanks!" she says enthusiastically before continuing.

She might be young, but she's mature. Her face is not stuck in her phone, and I never see her taking selfies like other girls her age. The way she took care of my hands the other night and the way she is with Leo shows her caring nature, which is hard to find these days. From our nighttime talks, I know that she has had a lot to look after in her life; her drug-addicted mother just one of those things. I haven't told her about Angelina yet, and I'm not sure that I will. But I know dealing with that kind of shit from family makes you grow up real quick.

"You know, Leo, you have the best laugh. I can't wait to hear you laugh some more. If I had known how funny it would be to see me eat a sundried tomato, I would have done it sooner!" He smiles back at her, and it's a beautiful sight.

She seems genuinely interested in Leo and spending time with him, as I listen to her babble on for the next few moments before entering the room.

"Hey, buddy," I say as I walk over to where he is sitting and squat next to him. "I need to go to work, and I may not be back before bedtime, so I will check on you later, okay?" He nods and leans toward me, and I give him a small hug. Standing, I turn and walk toward Little Red, looking down at her as she remains crossed-legged on the floor.

"I'll be home late tonight." She smiles, nodding in understanding. Before I realize what I am doing, I bend down and grab her chin, lifting it so I can capture her lips. The move surprises both of us. I kiss her quickly before I walk out of the room and back down the hall, not waiting for her to reply.

Feeling settled at home for the first time in years, I feel like a weight has been lifted from my shoulders as I push out the front door and make my way to the basement. As I walk down the corridors, my stride builds in momentum and my anger starts to grow as my thoughts refocus on what awaits me today. As I put my game face on, the adrenalin rises through my veins.

Federico will meet his maker tonight, of that there is no doubt.

14

DANTE

Carter and I have been sitting in the car outside Allure all fucking afternoon. My ass is numb, my teeth are sore from my grinding, and my mind has been a mix of capturing these assholes and dreaming about Little Red in my bed. Now as the clock ticks close to ten, and the pitch-black of the evening covers us, we make the decision to go inside.

We have watched people walk in and out all day, doing a headcount, taking photos, looking for familiar faces, watching to see if Federico comes out so we can follow him, but he hasn't shown. Not once. That doesn't bode well with me. The feeling that they are all waiting inside for us to show up slivers through my mind, but Carter and I are not cowards. So with our guns prepped and our team positioned, we walk swiftly across the road to face this fucker head on.

As we walk through the door, the business is quiet, as I expected. There are a few patrons around the bar, many of our boys, and there are a few dancers on the stage. I don't miss the ladies' eyes as they roam over Carter and I as we walk past them and go straight to the bar to take a look around the room.

I lean against the bar for less than five seconds before her voice hits my ears, and I snarl.

"Dante!" Angelina screams at me, obviously trying to get everyone's attention. To say that she is walking a very fine line with me at the moment is an understatement.

"Not now, Angelina," I grit out to her, as I ignore her look of disgust.

"You're a fucking asshole. I want to see Leo!" she yells again, and I look at her with murderous eyes, only to see her disheveled and wobbling on her feet. Her eyes are barely open, her hair looks like it hasn't been washed in days, and the outfit she is wearing barely covers anything.

"I said, not now, Angelina!" I growl at her, and she grabs onto the bar next to me to steady herself. I see Carter out the corner of my eyes, lifting his chin at the security man who promptly walks over.

"Come on, Angie. Let's get you back out to the dressing rooms and get you a drink," he murmurs to her before gripping her elbow and marching her swaying body to the back door to the private office spaces.

I grab the glass of whiskey that Carter ordered us and down it all, washing the anger away, not quite believing that she thinks she is in any state to look after an 8-year-old boy. I don't even know where she is living at the moment, no doubt couch surfing. I don't like the idea of the mother of my child not having a home, but after trying to set her up in an apartment, I realized that she was selling all the furnishings for money to shoot up her arms and constantly trashing the place until it was unlivable. No, Leo most certainly cannot go anywhere near his mother.

"I think we need to just wait and watch. They will come," Carter says, as he leans against the bar and orders us another drink.

"Something doesn't feel right. Something feels off," I grumble to him, my eyes piercing every patron. A few who can't handle the heat in my gaze, simply stand and walk out. It makes it easier for me to see where my team is positioned undercover and which ones are truly there for entertainment.

We sit and watch for another ten minutes, and I begin to wonder if I need to go out the back. Perhaps Federico will be down there? I have a team at the rear entrance, so he can't have escaped through the back door, and by now I am sure his security team would have told him I am here.

"Over there." Carter nods over to a small booth table in the far corner of the room. It is dark, but I can clearly see Federico sitting, surrounded by his men, who are all looking at me. Looking like a king presiding over his kingdom. His casual demeanor does nothing to settle my nerves. I feel like he is the bait, and I glance quickly around the room for anything that may be amiss.

Seeing nothing out of place, I bring my attention back to him, as he relaxes into the corner booth like he's on a holiday, his arms up behind his head and a smirk on his face. Suddenly, his face changes, though. He bites his bottom lip and his hands come down between his legs, which are covered by the table. His eyes leave mine for a moment as they focus on the ground in front of him before his body slumps back again, his hands against the top of the booth seats. And that's when he gives me a big, shit-eating grin.

I have no idea what the fuck he is doing until I see my ex-wife get out from under the table, wiping her mouth, and he squeezes her breast before she stumbles away. If that had happened a month or more ago, I would be livid, but now, with a new woman on my mind, I feel nothing but sadness for Angelina. Federico is so blind to think that my drug-addicted ex-wife sucking his dick would rile me up to the point I would start something.

I won't be starting this fight. But I will be ending it.

I push off the bar and walk over, Carter right beside me. We both stop in front of the booth, peering down at the men that surround him. They are young, inexperienced, and from the looks on their faces as I gaze at them with murder on my mind, their confidence is waning.

"Federico, where have you been, my dear friend? I have been looking for your skinny ass for weeks!" A chill takes hold of my tone, and I see one of his men fumble under the table. I know he was reaching for his gun. Fucking imbeciles.

"I have been enjoying the excellent skills your wife can offer me, my friend. And enjoying the opulence that I now live in thanks to your money." He's trying to goad me, but I still can't see how he is going to win this. It is then I realize that he has nothing. Nothing but his pure arrogance and false sense of power. He baited us here tonight to kill us with this measly team of adolescents.

It would be almost laughable if I wasn't out for his blood.

"Well, I am glad you can enjoy her, I certainly no longer do. She is all yours, my friend... at least for the next few hours, as you will be dead before morning breaks." His nostrils flair and his jaw clenches, the thought of him not winning this war dawning on him as he becomes visibly uneasy.

"It is the two of you against the eight of us. Simple math tells me that you are on the losing side, Dante, not me," he retorts with another shit-eating grin, and I still can't believe how stupid this guy is.

I say nothing back to him and tilt my head in curiosity. He stands then and leans toward me to whisper, "But I will be the one to take your life." There's a flash of silver as a knife appears. I lean away from him just in time and it slices the top of my shoulder.

"You worthless piece of shit. You can't even kill me from a few inches away!" I mock, laughing before nodding to the booths on either side of Federico's. My men stand up, guns already pulled and pointed at the back of everyone's head.

"Fuck," Federico mutters.

"16 to eight Federico. Simple math would say you are outnumbered," I grit out to him, the pain in my shoulder now burning, but my anger at him cannot be deterred.

"Do it," I say to my team, and one by one, each man is taken out of the club. His men are guided out the back, where they get a swift and painless end to their mafia life. Two of my soldiers, along with Carter and I, take

Federico with us, back to the compound. Because I need some answers.

An hour later, with my shirt soaked in blood and Federico chained by his hands to the ceiling, Carter and I stand before him, demanding information. His skinny frame dangles, his feet unable to touch the floor, and he knows his time is up. There is no way out of this for him.

"Where is our money, Federico?" I ask him again, for the second time tonight.

"I'm not telling you shit," he spits out, and Carter punches him across the jaw. Federico's head flies back and blood pours from his nose. I have never been punched by Carter, and I have no plans to be, because he is an exceptionally strong man, a fighter who knows exactly where and how to hit a person to inflict the most amount of pain.

"Where is your brother?" I ask him, my patience wearing thin. He has no plans to tell us anything. Even now, in his final moments. While I would love to drag this out all night, I know Little Red is upstairs in my bed and I want to see her.

He laughs. "Oh, Dante, you still don't know do you. After all these years, you know my brother was fucking your wife from the moment you married her, right?" He takes joy in telling me this, and I stiffen for a moment because I had no fucking idea that happened. I didn't think it started until after Leo was born. I stand then, walking closer to him.

"That's right. They have been fucking for years and she has been spilling all your secrets. Until you kicked her out, at least. Hell, Leo may not even be your son!" He cackles. I seethe as I look at him, Leo is most certainly my son, there is no question to his heritage.

In that moment I see red.

I grab the nearby steel rod and slam it across his torso. He gasps for breath, but I don't wait, doing it over and over and over again until I hear his ribs break. I move places, then and I do the same to the other side. He is barely breathing by the end of it, but I don't want to kill him yet.

"Where is your fucking brother.?" I seethe. He is barely conscious, with no air in his lungs, so he certainly can't talk.

"Where is our fucking money!" I'm sick of his fucking antics and ready to take the life from his body.

He raises his head slightly and looks at me in the eyes. "Coming for you," he wheezes.

I don't hesitate for a moment longer, grabbing my knife and slicing it across his throat. Then I walk out of the room, leaving him to bleed out on the concrete floor.

My shoulder needs a doctor, and I need Little Red.

15

ANNIE

I am relaxing in Dante's big bed. It is late, but my head is propped up on his soft headboard as I think back to his lips on mine. It is a memory that I have been reliving all day, and so as I devour yet another book about Italy, I can't help but wonder what he feels about me. Engrossed in a page about Sicilian cooking, I jump when the bedroom door flies open, watching open-mouthed as he struts through the room and into the bathroom, his face hard, and his eyes angry.

My heart pounds and adrenaline pumps through my body as I scramble off the bed, rushing to follow him. I stop suddenly, speechless as I stand in silence at the bathroom door. He peels his now red, wet shirt off his body, surveying his torso in the mirror.

There is so much blood. My eyes roam him from top to bottom, looking for wounds or gashes, but I can't see anything but blood. He looks at me then, eyeing me, watching to see what my next move is.

After a moment, I position my small body in between

his and the bathroom vanity and turn on the tap, filling the basin with water and wetting a cloth. His attention stays on me, his jaw is clenched, his eyes searching my face, his nostrils flaring. I say nothing. I don't ask questions, because I know he won't answer me anyway.

I begin to wipe his bare chest with the wet cloth, clearing the blood and searching for any sign of damage. The bathroom light shines down on us from above, and I can now clearly see the array of black ink covering his body. His muscles are carved, built broad and strong, and he has scatterings of scars that make him even sexier. His battle wounds of sorts. My hands shake a little as I touch his skin, setting my own on fire in the process.

He is tall, so I reach up on my tiptoes to wipe down his shoulders, his chest glistening in the lights from the blood and water. My hands move gently over his hot skin as I try to concentrate on ensuring he is okay and not the fact that I am now touching his bare chest.

His hands close around my waist, and before I know it my feet are off the ground as he sits me on the vanity. It brings me high enough that we are now nearly face to face. He doesn't drop his hands, instead they remain warm against my waist, and he steps forward, even closer to me, his hips spreading my legs apart and positioning his body flush with mine.

I look up at him and stop mid-wipe as his hand comes up to my neck, tilting my head back slightly, and he pushes my hair off my shoulders. As it falls down my back, he leans in. My heart thumps out of my chest as my hands rest near his shoulders. I can feel my nipples peaking against his chest as his lips barely skim across the sensitive skin of my neck, and I am sure he can feel them too. He growls then, a low, deep growl that vibrates down my spine. My sex begins to throb in response, and I can't help the small whimper that leaves my mouth, my body now completely reacting to his desire.

I don't dare move, but my hands tremble on his shoulders, and I want so badly to dig them into his hair as his head remains buried in my neck. I feel him take deep breaths, like he is drowning in my scent, and I am grateful that I had a shower before bed tonight. Without thinking, I tilt my head farther, giving him more access, and his nose drags from behind my ear to my shoulder, making me shiver.

"Dante," I whisper, the effect he has on me stifling. I try not to moan his name because just this small act of attention has me undeniably aroused.

"What did I tell you about saying my name like that, Little Red?" he growls into my ear, as he continues brushing his nose and lips against my neck. My mind has turned to mush, but understanding washes over me from one of our previous conversations about kissing me like a man should.

His other hand travels up my torso, feeling every curve and dip before it lands on the other side of my face, and he pulls back slightly, cupping my face in his large hands. His eyes look deep into mine, and I hold my breath as I stare back at him.

"Say my name like that again, Little Red..." he says to me in his baritone voice, and my lips part on a breath.

"Dante," I breathe out, and barely have time to complete the word before his lips are on mine.

He is dominating, demanding, and I get lost in the passion as his tongue delves into my mouth and begins to tangle with mine. It is like nothing I have ever experienced before. I feel his need, his want for me through every touch. It is like we are drowning and neither one of us wants to come up for air.

His grip on my face remains solid, and he lifts my face farther to meet his. I hang onto his wrists tight, still not sure what part of his body is injured, so I don't know where to touch. Even though I want to touch every inch.

He pulls away then, both of us panting, my eyes searching his.

"Fuck," he says before bowing his head a little. I watch him as he steps away from me and turns on the shower, letting the bathroom fill with steam. He doesn't talk, but has a permanent scowl on his face, and I am left sitting on the vanity, my body in his white shirt, now also tarnished with red.

My eyes widen as he strips naked in front of me, throwing his stained clothes into a messy pile on the floor. I need to grip onto the vanity to ensure I don't fall at the vision of all-man before me. I have never seen a fully naked man before, and Dante is huge. Everywhere is huge. His brown eyes remain on me, yet my eyes travel downwards. I take in his very aroused state, before I quickly avert my eyes, and no doubt my red cheeks do very little to hide my ogling.

His nostrils flare as he watches me looking at him, and then he steps into the shower. I look at him as he runs his hands over his body, washing away the blood, before he starts to touch himself. I watch him pump his cock slowly, all the while his eyes remain on me. I swallow hard, my nerves now totally overtaking my body as I wipe my sweating palms on my thighs, unable to look away. My body begins to tingle, my underwear becomes wetter, my nipples peak, my heart races. I haven't felt like this before, and I am at war with myself because I want to join him. I want to strip down and get naked in the shower with him. But I am not sure how. I don't know what to do. Should I stay here in the bathroom with him, or should I go back to bed? I want to stay, but am I woman enough for him?

He continues to watch me, and I want to be near him. I want my hand to be on his body. I want to grip onto him and give him pleasure. My eyes continue to flick between his and his movement. I'm still as I wage war in my mind on whether to continue to sit and watch or go to him. He remains where he is, waiting, watching me, letting me make my own decision.

I promised myself that I would live my life to the fullest and take every opportunity life brings me while I still can. Now, sitting here watching Dante, I want him more than anything, so I slowly slip off the vanity, not trusting my legs to catch me, and walk over to him, opening the glass shower door. "Show me?" I say to him, and his dark eyes darken further. "Show me how?" My voice is only a whimper, filled with want. He looks down at me, like he is having an internal debate on whether to let me touch him, and then he stops. Lifting his arms above his head, he leans them against the top of the shower frame, his full naked body now open to me as he stands before me in all his glory.

"Wrap your hand around me, Annie," he grits out, and as the steam billows behind him, I reach toward him and wrap my hand around his cock. He is hot, heavy, and very hard.

He hisses as I start to move, so I go to pull away, scared I have done something wrong.

"No, keep it there," he says in a commanding tone. I stop dead in my tracks, my hand still firmly wrapped around him, and I can feel him throbbing underneath my fingers. My eyes flick to his, waiting for his next command.

"Now move it up and down, slowly. Like I was before." His wet hair falls across his forehead, and water drips down his face as his body leans into my touch but doesn't move farther. He's leaving me to explore and make the decisions on how far I want this to go.

Along with the red stains on the white shirt of his I've been wearing to bed, the water is beginning to drench on it, causing it to stick to my body, but I don't care.

I begin to move my hand up and down slowly, just like he asked. He is hard, *really* hard. His veins pop along the length of him, and I move my thumb slightly so I can feel his tip on each stroke. He is large, smooth, and beautiful.

"Just like that, Annie. Good girl," he says on an exhale, and as I look up, I see him looking down at me, his eyes hooded and full of desire. My confidence grows. He seems to be enjoying what I am doing and so am I. All I want to do is please this man.

I increase my speed slightly, gripping a little harder as I do.

"Fuck, Bella, you like having my hard cock in your hand, don't you?" he asks, smiling down at me.

"Yes, I love it..." I barely whisper, a faint smile appearing on my face, and I hear him groan in response. It makes me feel good to know that he wants me touching him, that he wants my hands on his body, just as much as I do.

I don't miss his eyes as they look over my body, at the white shirt now see-through and clinging to my naked breasts. Even though I'm clothed, visually, he can see everything.

I increase my pace and his breath hitches. Without losing my rhythm, I decide to explore him a bit more. I use my other hand and cup his balls, feeling them, large and heavy in my hand. As I move them slowly, I see his torso muscles tense.

"Do you know how perfect you look right now? Holding me in your hands... Fuuucckkk..." He groans, long and deep, and I know he must be close. I shiver at his words. I like him complimenting me, wanting me, needing me.

He lowers one of his hands from the shower frame and brings it to the collar of my shirt, opening the first few buttons, showing him my bare breasts, and his lips part in wonder.

"Keep moving your hands, Bella. I want to come on your chest. I want to mark you as mine." He's barely hanging on, and I speed up my pace, wanting to please him, wanting to feel him come undone by my hands, feeling powerful that I can make a man like Dante weak at the knees with my touch.

His hands rest back up on the shower frame as his eyes pin me in place. His hips begin to move a little, pushing his hard cock into my hand, and a slow growl rumbles up his throat as he explodes, his need for me painting my bare chest. My soaked white shirt hangs heavily from my shoulders as he brands me, my skin now warm where he covers me with his orgasm. He looks directly into my eyes, his stare penetrating, his nostrils flaring, and I grip onto him until there is nothing left.

16

DANTE

I feel light-headed as the hot water from the shower drills into my back. The steam rises around me, and this beautiful woman stands in front of me, coated in my desire. Panting, her chest moves up and down, her bare breasts glistening, even more so now that I have branded her. Her cheeks are flushed, her body covered in my wet white shirt, hiding nothing but everything at the same time. She looks fucking perfect. I know she is innocent, that she has not experienced anything like that before, and the fact that I am the first man she has ever touched, ever marked her, it is enough to make me fucking hard all over again. My grip on the shower frame is solid, but I don't dare let go because I am afraid of what I will do next. Grabbing her and ripping my shirt from her petite frame is extremely appealing right now.

She releases her hold on me and runs her hands up my torso, looking at my scarred and tattooed body, investigating the story that it tells from years of war, near misses, and chaos. She stands close to me now, the water falling on both of us as it continues to run pink, blood now mixed with water. I lower my hands slowly, moving them around her neck, admiring how good she feels in my grip. I squeeze my hands a little, and her eyes widen slightly. There is no fright in her stare as her lips part, and I hear her breath hitch, but from arousal.

Anyone else would be begging me to let go already, knowing that with a simple twist, I could make their life leave their body. But not her. Little Red is almost inquisitive as she continues to explore my naked body with her hands, hers still draped in my wet white shirt. It's the same one she has been wearing to bed each night, and I would be lying if I said that wasn't a massive turn on. It is too big for her, perfect nightwear, yet I am itching to rip it off her and show her exactly what I have been thinking of doing since I jumped on her during the gunfire at Allure weeks ago.

She steps into the flowing water a little more, and I watch her as she washes her chest, and *Goddamnit*, what she does to me should be illegal.

Her hands reach my shoulders and then stop abruptly. She has found the knife wound. The one that needs at least ten stitches, yet feels numb due to the fire that heats my body from her touch.

Her fingers brush closer to it, and her brows furrow. "You're hurt," she says, her eyes big and round as she looks up at me. "You need stitches." She comes to the correct conclusion, and although I would rather just take her up against the shower wall, I know from the light headedness I am feeling that it may not end well.

I nod stiffly, my eyes never leaving hers, and she nods

in reply before stepping out of my grip and grabbing two towels. She hangs one next to the shower for me as I rinse the blood from the rest of my body, my eyes not once leaving her as I watch her remove the wet white shirt and quickly wrap a towel around her, giving me a sneak peek at her petite body. She is not at all the shy little thing I thought she was, but it's also cementing that the fun we just started needs to be moved to another time.

She leaves the bathroom then, and I groan into the water as I wash my face, the vision of her naked body now etched into my brain. The feel of her hand gripping me, all too vivid. I want her now more than ever. I'm barely able to rein it in, my cock already twitching, ready for round two.

I turn off the shower and dry my body, the blood now dripping slowly from my wound, Frederico's blood all washed from me. Any remnants of him are long gone, following his soul down the drain to hell where he belongs. I move my head from left to right, cracking my neck to relieve the tension as I think back to the mess I just caused, but not regretting it for even a moment.

Dominic will be murderous now, more so than he was before. He was angry and wanting revenge, but now that his brother is mere mush after the beating I gave him, I know his need for payback will be ferocious.

I walk out to my bedroom, spotting Little Red now back in my bed, and I smirk at her as she looks all cozy, because that is exactly where I want her to be. In my bed. Preferably underneath me, screaming my name as I teach her and show her everything that she needs to know. I want to cherish her, make her come with my fingers, my tongue, and my cock, before doing it over and over again. But I'm not sure she is ready for a man like me yet, so I will bide my time.

Strutting across the room naked, I grab a clean pair of jeans and put on my timberland boots before walking over to the bed.

"I'll be back later...." I say as I look down at her.

"Okay..." she whispers. I raise my hand and cup her cheek, pulling her bottom lip down with my thumb, and then bending down, I kiss her lips. Quickly, but deliberately, before I leave her. As I get to the door, I look back at her briefly, and I don't miss the smile that has now appeared on her face, which I return before walking straight out the door and closing it firmly behind me.

I stalk with purpose down the hall. I need to meet the doctor down in our medic room, as I'm already about half an hour later than promised.

As I walk out of my front door and make my way through the maze of corridors, I nod at a few of our new men who are starting their patrols in our compound. Many of them will get lost over the course of the next week or so as they find their footing in what is a new world here in New York—worlds apart from their Sicilian upbringing.

I walk farther down the hall until I reach our surgery.

Sebastian and I have built up our compound bit by bit over the years. First, purchasing all the properties around the entire block, building secure housing, basement levels that go deep underground, along with meeting rooms, surveillance rooms, a doctor's surgery, and many panic rooms and supply rooms.

Sebastian and Goldie have their residence next door to mine, Carter has a smaller apartment across the way, and the whole building runs the perimeter of the entire square of the block. Our large garden is enclosed in the middle, where our friends and family play and where we have our social gatherings. Leo plays with his soccer balls and our men do their daily fitness. It is our peace in the mayhem. Our secure compound is impenetrable; no one can come in or out without either massive fire power or stealth knowledge.

I sigh as I walk around the next corner and then into our infirmary. The doctor and nurse are there waiting for me, having been called in to assess the damage from today's activities. They are some of the top surgeons from the nearby hospital. We have them on our payroll, and while they don't always like to come to help us and get in the middle of our messes, we pay them handsomely and they are good associates of ours. I nod to them in greeting, and I can see they have everything ready to stitch me up and send me on my way. Plonking down in the chair, I remain silent as I let them get to work, before my head snaps up at a voice coming from the doorway.

"I leave you for a few weeks and you already need stitches?" Sebastian laughs as he waltzes through the door with Carter. The two of them with smirks on their faces as I jump up from the chair and greet him. I love Sebastian like a brother; our bond could never be broken. We hug one another with solid back slaps and laugh.

"Good to see you back in town. When did you get in?" I ask, knowing that he mustn't have been in town long, since he was only in Sicily yesterday.

"An hour ago. Goldie is resting, and then I walked into Carter on my way to your place, and he filled me in on what happened," Sebastian says, his eyebrows raised in question as he takes in my nasty gash.

Goldie has tamed him a little. He is still lethal, of that there is no doubt, but he is happier, almost joyful, and I know she has had a positive impact on him.

"Yeah, we got Federico tonight, but Dominic is still proving to be elusive," I grit out, still not thrilled that we only got one brother. To be honest, I expected him to be more forthcoming, but he remained tight-lipped. Even when pushed, he still doesn't know how to kill a man, which is apparent from the slice in my shoulder just now. I took pleasure in using his own knife to slice it across his throat merely an hour ago. Unfortunately, most of his blood went directly onto my torso, kindly washed off by Little Red, and as I sit back down in the chair for our doctor to continue stitching me up, the thought of Little Red's hands on my body is enough for me to adjust myself.

Fuck, I need to get a grip.

Sebastian's eyes narrow at my sudden change in demeanor, and Carter stifles a laugh, at which I scowl.

"What am I missing?" Sebastian asks, looking back and forth between Carter and me.

"Nothing," I say at the same time as Carter.

"Fucking spill it," Sebastian says, and I sigh, looking at him in the eye.

Sebastian's eyes drill into mine, and a small smile appears on his lips.

"Ahh, the little redhead is still here, isn't she?" Of

course he hits the nail on the head. A sly grin turns to pure joy across his face at the fact that I am now the one with a woman on my mind. Something he battled with not long ago after meeting Goldie.

I look down at the doctor's hands as he takes the small needle and threads my skin together. Carter passes me a glass of whiskey, which I make quick work of to help dull the throbbing.

"So where is Dominic?" Sebastian asks as he types something into his cell phone, changing the topic and getting us all back on track.

"No idea. He is hiding like the rat he is," I spit out, and Sebastian looks back up at me.

"He is filth, Dante. What he did to Angelina is unforgivable, but we need to remain focused. I need our money back and then we kill him."

"I have some men monitoring his local haunts. We are watching his cell activity as well. We will find him soon," Carter adds, and I watch Sebastian as his attention goes back to his phone.

"He will make a mistake, and when he does, we will pounce," I add. He won't let the death of his brother go too long before seeking revenge. I watch as Sebastian continues to look at his cell, typing out messages, his behavior unusual. He is always focused on work, so I wonder what he is doing.

"Who are you texting?" I ask, and his eyes flick to me. Carter and I are the only ones who can question him and even then, he barely tolerates it. But he smirks at me again.

"Goldie. I told her about your little redhead, so she is

going to come to your place to meet her tomorrow. You know, girl shit." He winks, and I groan. This is Sebastian's way of finding out more about her, ensuring she is someone who should stick around. He is as protective of me as I am of him and after the debacle of my arranged marriage, even more so. The fact that I haven't ever had a woman in my life for more than one night since my ex-wife, and now Little Red has been in my bed for weeks obviously gives him reason to investigate.

Sebastian will also want to see if she is someone who can remain in the fold. Goldie is a pretty good judge of character. I am not concerned, although I prefer to keep Little Red to myself while I sort out what to do with her, not yet wanting to ever let her go, but knowing I need to at some point. I can't keep her locked in my place forever, no matter how much I want to.

"She got Leo to laugh out loud," I say to him, and both he and Carter stop dead still, looking at me in astonishment.

"What the fuck?" Sebastian asks, pure shock on his face. As Leo's godfather, he has a special connection with my son, and would protect him with his life, Carter too. So I know they understand the breakthrough that has happened.

"How did she do that?" Carter asks in awe.

"I have no fucking idea, but it was the best sound I have heard in a long time," I say, pausing to get my thoughts together before they leave. "We need to find Dominic. We need to get our money, and then I need to kill him, because he will be out for blood, and he knows the way to get me is through Leo. Now Little Red is also on his radar." I look between the two of them, anger starting to well inside my body. "And I will die before either one of them gets hurt."

"War has started, brother," Sebastian says to me, nodding slightly, his face and tone now both serious.

"It's time we ended it," I state, leaving no room for questions.

17

ANNIE

I haven't seen Dante all week since our tryst in the bathroom, and I feel a little uneasy about it. For weeks since I arrived, he and I have spoken every night, and now I miss our nighttime chats. Did I do something wrong? Is his life just extremely busy right now, finding the men from his gunfight? I don't know what to think. But I know he still comes. I may be asleep, but I still smell him the moment I wake. Sometimes I spot his empty whiskey glass too.

However, I have kept busy here in his house. Leo and I are firm friends, my Lego skills now improving each day, and I actually finished a rocket, which he proudly displays on his shelf next to his castles and spaceships.

A few days ago, I met Maddison, who I have learnt is the wife of Dante's friend Sebastian. She's a glamorous woman who I have a lot in common with, both of us growing up in small towns, now caught up in this insane lifestyle. She is an art gallery owner, something I don't know too much about, but it sounds amazing. After meeting her, I wish that I had the opportunity to go to college. I always wanted to become a teacher. I love kids. It is probably why I was in such demand as a babysitter back home, and why I get along so well with Leo.

I do a lot of the cooking with Maria now, learning many authentic recipes and some I make just as well as she does. I like the way she looks at me proudly each time I complete a dish. However, today she wasn't feeling well, so she retired to her room.

I have just put Leo to bed, cleaned up the kitchen, and tidied up the house. It is the least I can do after being here for so long, and I hate how Maria cleans up after everyone—even if it is her job.

With a sigh, I turn off the light, dimming the now sparkling clean kitchen into darkness, and decide to go to bed and read, such is my nightly routine. On the way through the house, I stop at the library to see if I can grab a new book, spotting a few more on childhood development.

As I do, I spot Dante's office light on, and thinking he isn't home, I move toward the doorway to turn it off before seeing him at his desk, sipping whiskey all alone. I stop in the doorway, like a deer caught in the headlights, not sure what to do or say. His eyes flick up, and he looks at me intently, a small smirk appearing, even though his face looks tired and dark circles run underneath each eye.

"Come here, Little Red," he commands as he swivels on his chair a little. I do as I am told, excited to see him and happy that he wants to see me. I walk into his office and around his desk to stand next to him. He leans back in his chair and watches me, his head resting against the high back, his whiskey now all but forgotten on his desk.

Standing in front of him, he looks me up and down, taking in my appearance. My flaming red hair is out and wavy around my shoulders, and I am barefoot, wearing a simple airy day dress. Casual, but cute.

"You're a sight for sore eyes, Little Red," he says with a sigh, as he sits forward a little, and his hands meet my legs before they skim up my thighs, so softly I can barely feel him, yet I tremble underneath his touch. My face heats under his gaze as he moves forward, leaning his head against my stomach. I wonder if he can hear my butterflies, which only appeared the moment I laid eyes on him. He is exhausted. I feel bad that I haven't been able to look after him this week. I lift my hands and bury my fingers in his hair, moving them against his scalp, massaging his head as his hands skim up and down my thighs. "Mmmmmmm," Dante moans, and I smile because I like to make him feel good. I want him to relax, especially when he is home.

He sits back up, my hands falling slightly and resting on his shoulders. My eyes flick to his shoulder where his wound was, but I can't see anything underneath his black shirt.

"How is your shoulder?" I ask, running my fingers across the area gently.

"It was better the moment you stepped into the bathroom with me," he replies with a grin, one which I return as a slight blush colors my cheeks.

"I like how you blush when you think about us. Did

you like what we did?" he asks as his hands pause on my hips, watching me with a small smile.

"Yes," I whisper, unsure of my voice, my heart beginning to race as I see his eyes darken.

"Yes, what?" he asks in return and at first, I am not sure what he is asking me, but then it dawns on me.

"Yes, *Dante*," I breathe out, and I hear his chest growl in approval, making my sex throb.

"You know I like it when you say my name like that."

"Yes... Dante.." I say again, teasing him a little.

"This is a pretty dress, Little Red, but I think you would look better without it?" As he removes his hands from me and sits back, my body stills, my skin still tickling from his touch and aching to have it back. He's once again leaving it up to me to either answer his question with action or walk out the door. It is like he wants to touch me, but is afraid to, as I see his hands clench like he is trying very hard to not reach out to me when it is all I want him to do. I have never been in this position before. Never wanted something so much and for it to be offered up for me to take. Because I want Dante. All of him. I want his hands on my body, his lips on mine, I want to please him, and I want to learn everything from only him. I dream about him daily, and every time I am around him, my heart races.

I look down at my dress, knowing that I am not going anywhere. He has already seen my body, but this feels more deliberate. In the shower, he took control; he was fully naked and I stayed in my shirt. But now, the tides have turned, and I will be undressing for him. It feels different, yet I still feel in complete control of the moment. I swallow as my eyes flick back to his, seeing pure lust in his gaze. Then I pull the cord that ties my dress together, undoing a few buttons at the top near the neckline. I let the thin fabric slip off my shoulders and then shimmy it down my arms before it falls like a feather down my body, skimming my small curves and landing in a puddle at my feet.

My skin prickles as I see his fingers dig into his thighs. I am nearly bare, standing right in front of him with just my bra and underwear remaining. I have no idea what I am doing, but I am confident that he likes what he sees. My breath quickens as I wait for him to make the next move. His eyes slowly lower down my frame, like he is committing every inch of me to memory. Wearing basic black cotton underwear, with no lace or pretty details, I don't move an inch, my breasts heavy as I pant in arousal.

As his eyes move back up my body, I decide not to wait for his next command. I want to make it obvious to him that I ache to have his hands all over me. I move my hands to my back and unclip my bra, letting it fall down my shoulders, following my dress to the floor. This move surprises him because I hear him intake a sharp breath, as his eyes hood, looking at my chest, my pink nipples now hard.

"Is this better?" I ask timidly, holding my breath for his answer. I let my hands fall down my shoulders, and my fingers trail down my chest, almost seductively, my skin is covered in goosebumps.

"Are you wet for me, Annie?" he asks, his voice deep and raspy, vibrating right to my core.

"Yes, Dante... very," I reply in a whisper, again my

cheeks blushing as his eyes blaze, scorching my skin, clearly enjoying my response.

He leans forward, and I feel his hands touch the backs of my thighs, his fingers trailing upwards, but this time, they don't stop. He looks me in the eye, his face close to my chest, as his fingers reach my underwear and he grabs onto the waist band, before slowly pulling them down my legs. I move my hands and grip onto his desk on either side of my body as he pulls them all the way down, leaving me entirely naked in front of him. And he remains seated and fully dressed.

"Show me how wet you are," he commands as his eyes pierce mine, and he leans back in his chair again. His jaw is clenching, and his nostrils flare as he waits for me to move. He still leaves the decision up to me to make. But I have no hesitation.

"Yes, Dante..." I say, this time with more confidence, and his eyes widen slightly as he raises his hand and rubs his jaw like I am a tasty meal being placed right in front of him.

I move back slightly until my bare ass hits the edge of his dark timber desk, and I lift onto my tiptoes and perch myself on it. Leaning back, I move my hands behind me so that my body is tilted backwards, and I look at him to see his hands fisting as he struggles to restrain himself. It is good to know I am affecting him and once again the power I feel at making this dangerous man weak for me is addictive.

Once comfortable, I move my legs. Slowly widening them, my bare body now totally open to Dante, my wet desire front and center. My long red hair falls back over my shoulders, as I arch and open myself to him completely.

"Fuck, Annie, you are beautiful," he grits out.

"Dante, please..." I whisper, nearly begging for him already. I have never felt like this before, never ached for a man, never needed a man so much as I do Dante. I just want him to touch me before I implode. I don't even realize I have said his name until I hear him growl again, and he sits forward, bringing his chair closer to me.

"I am going to touch you, Bella. I will try to be gentle, but I am not a gentle man," he says, looking up at me, his eyes asking for permission.

"I want you to touch me...You don't need to be gentle," I reply, my body nearly vibrating off the desk such is my desire to have his hands on me.

"Oh, but I do, Bella. I want to take my time with you." He lifts his hands again, placing them on each ankle, skimming them up and down my legs before he grabs them and lifts, placing my feet on the armrests of his chair. His body positioned in between them.

His hands then skim up my legs, and warmth spreads through my body with his touch as his hands run over my bent knees to my thighs. He grabs my thigh, needing the muscle before he leans forward and presses a kiss on the inside of my knee.

"You're dripping for me, Annie..." he says between his kisses as he continues to place his lips farther up the inside of my thigh.

I let my head fall back. "Dante... please..." I exhale, and I hear him groan as he moves closer and closer to my center.

My heart is beating out of my chest, as I feel his hands glide down the outside of my thighs and rest on my ass just as he nudges my core.

"Tell me to stop, Bella. God, tell me to stop," I hear him say, almost pleading as his lips brush against me and I shudder.

"Don't stop, Dante, please don't stop." At that, a switch must flip, because his tongue lands on my flesh and delves into my heat as he begins to devour me. The breath leaves my lungs for a moment as his lips and tongue become tools of magic. He licks, sucks, and explores my center, creating a pleasure like nothing I have ever experienced.

"Ahhhh, Dante, God, shit, please don't stop," I pant out, my words free-flowing, my strong desire overpowering all my senses.

I fall back more, leaning on my elbows as my hair sweeps across his desk, his face remaining firmly between my legs. I can barely breathe as the sensation runs wild through my body. His grip on my ass remains firm, and I start to move my hips a little, wanting the friction.

"You taste fucking delicious, Annie. Do you like fucking my face like a good girl?" he asks me, before plunging his tongue back inside, my body wriggling at his touch. But he holds my hips down, pushing his face into me farther, licking me, kissing and sucking a place no man has ever explored before.

"Oh God, Dante." I have never felt like this. Never felt this heat flowing through my body, the tremble in my legs, or the slight tickle and pulsating happening down below.

"Oh my God... yes." My mind is no longer connected to my body as I feel myself reacting in ways I never knew it could. His chest rumbles, and I feel the vibration on my flesh. I begin to feel hot all over from my head to my toes as they curl.

"Has anyone ever touched you like this, Annie? Has anyone ever had their mouth on your perfect fucking pussy?" Dante grits out, before taking a long, languid lick and making me tremble.

"No, Dante," I all but whimper, my body starting to feel like absolute putty in his hands.

"Has anyone made your body feel like this, Annie? Has anyone had you naked, your body trembling, needy, and wet for them?" I feel his hot breath touch my skin, as his hands continue to grip onto my waist.

"No...Dante..." I moan out, and he groans in response. I wriggle in his grip, but he continues to hold me down. And being at his mercy is turning me on even more. My back arches, wanting him closer, needing more.

"Are you going to let me fuck your pussy with my tongue until you can't stand it. Are you going to let me be the first man to make you come, Bella?" Dante asks but doesn't wait for a response before he dives back into my center with renewed vigor.

"Dante... I'm... I'm..." is all I can get out in between my panting and moaning, but he is relentless, going faster and deeper with his tongue. And I let go. My light scream leaves my lips, but he doesn't stop. He continues until I am left an exhausted heap on his desk. My arms give way as I lay on my back on his expensive timber desk. My hand splays across my chest as I try to catch my breath and close my eyes to steady myself. I'm completely void of energy and in shock at what I just experienced.

He kisses my thighs, letting me just be for a moment. It was my first time a man has ever made me come, and I can safely say that I now understand what all the fuss is about.

18

DANTE

I sit back and admire her. She is hot as fuck, naked and splayed out on my desk, looking like every man's wet dream, yet she is my reality. I know that was her first orgasm from a man, and damn if I don't feel like a king making her experience that for the first time. I lick my lips, her flavor still present, and she tastes exactly how she looks. Pure heaven, a place I never thought I would ever experience, yet here she is, giving me exactly what I want but do not deserve.

I run my hands up and down her bare legs, the feeling of her soft skin soothing my soul, then I stand up and look down at her. Fucking perfection right here in front of me. I'm not sure anyone else will even come close to comparing.

My cock is hard as a rock, but I need to take my time with Little Red. Her innocence is not something that can be played with. I wasn't sure after the other night in the bathroom whether to go near her again. I knew if I did, it would be game over for me. One time, I can live with. I have tried to ignore the constant pull I have toward her, forced myself to stay away, not to be tempted. I drowned myself in work, even though it has been hard keeping a distance. I thought that was the right thing to do. But having a week away from her was torture. I missed her, missed our nightly chats, I missed hearing her banter with Leo, I missed seeing her sexy body parade around me. And now, the gloves are off, because after tasting her, there is no way I can stay away and no way I can ignore her. She was in full control tonight and she wants me. The pull we have toward each other is now extremely evident, and I am not fucking standing back anymore.

She opens her eyes, and a blush creeps up her cheeks when she finds me staring.

"That was..." Her whispering voice trails off, lost for words.

"Fucking addictive," I finish for her, and she grins.

"Yeah, addictive, Dante," she says, and I grin. My name on her lips is everything, and I lean in and kiss her. Tenderly, appreciating her, showing her that she is a fucking masterpiece and perfect for me in every way.

She looks up at me from where she is lying on top of my desk, my paperwork and trinkets now pushed to the side. I run my fingers from her shoulders down her body, tracing patterns and feeling her soft skin. Pinching her nipple, my hands explore down her middle, down her sides, her clear, fresh skin not tainted like mine. My body tells a story, a dangerous story, yet hers is only just starting. I will be damned if anyone is going to touch her and mark her in any way. She will stay clean. Perfect, flawless. I will make sure of that.

I stand in between her legs and lean my hips into hers, and although still fully dressed, my cock is aching to be released as I push it against her warm wet pussy and hear her gasp a little. I run my hand back up her bare chest before grabbing her around the throat and pulling her up off the desk. Leaning down to meet her halfway, I smash my lips into hers. Sweeping my tongue into her mouth, I show her how much I want her in case there is still any doubt.

Pulling back a little, our noses nearly touching, I look at her. Her lips are red and swollen, her eyes wide, and her perfect breasts push against my chest. I am aching to be inside of her. I tighten my grip on her throat a little more and instead of being fearful, she actually leans into my touch, submitting to me. With that trust from her, I need to grip onto my desk to prevent me from just taking her hard right here, right now, on the edge of my desk.

She deserves better.

"Come," I say to her, as my hands reach around her bare ass, and I cup her cheeks, pulling her body to mine lifting her off the desk. Leaving her clothes on the floor, I stand as she wraps her legs around my waist, and I grind her hips into my cock, again letting her feel how hard I am for her. I press her body close and walk with her out of my office and down the hallway.

Her arms circle around my neck, and she buries her head into my shoulders. As I run one hand up and down her bare back, I tell myself it is to keep her warm, but it is because I just want to feel her under my fingertips.

Reaching the bedroom, I walk in the door and kick it closed behind me as I take her inside.

I place her onto the bed, and she immediately sits up on her knees and looks up at me. "I want to taste you now," she says, quietly but confidently. I am jarred for a moment because she was nearly asleep in her lethargy a moment ago, and now, after weeks of looking at her perky pink lips and imagining them around my cock, my dreams may become reality.

"Little Red, you don't—" I begin to say, but she cuts me off.

"I want to, Dante. Show me how..." There is not a red-blooded man on this earth who could deny such a request, especially when it comes from someone as sweet and perfect and naked as Little Red.

If she wants me to show her, then I will. I nod to her in response, and she sits back on her heels, waiting for me to tell her what to do.

Standing next to the bed, I grab the bottom of my top and lift it over my head, throwing it across the room. Her eyes lower, taking in my bare chest. I begin to undo my belt, all the while watching her, waiting to see if I see any hesitation. I don't. The opposite happens, in fact, when her hands come up and take over from me, lowering my zipper. I cup her face with my hands, rubbing her jaw with my thumb, watching as she pulls down my pants. They fall to the floor, and I step out of them, now completely naked alongside her. Her eyes run down my body, and I am trying very hard to contain myself as I palm my length, feeling myself hot, solid, and heavy in my hand.

I pump my cock a few times, watching her as her eyes widen slightly before flicking back to me.

"You still want to taste me, Bella?" I ask her, my voice rough. "Do you want my cock in your pretty little mouth?"

She nods slowly. "Yes, Dante." I don't miss the small glint in her eye, because she knows when she says my name what it does to me, and I am positive she now enjoys teasing me with it.

"Open your mouth, Annie, nice and wide," I say as I grab the back of her head in one hand and my cock in the other. As her mouth comes closer, she licks her lips, and it is a fucking sight that I will now have engraved in my brain forever. Holding my shaft, I feed her my throbbing cock, and she takes in a little, swirling her tongue instinctively around the tip, and then backs away.

"Mmmmm," I hear her murmur in appreciation, and I almost lose my load right there and then.

"Fuck, Bella, you like that?" I grit out. This woman has me right on the edge and doesn't even know it.

"Mmmmhmmm," she hums as my hand on the back of her head remains, although I let her set the pace as she begins to explore.

She grabs the base of my shaft with her hand and starts licking my cock like an ice cream without asking for any more direction. Her flaming red hair falls down her back, her mouth's open and hungry, and her tongue licks me so slowly I think I might explode.

"Touch yourself, Annie. I want to see your fingers on your clit while I have my cock in your mouth," I grit out, loving the visual I have as she moves her hand across her body, down her hips until they find her center.

"Good girl," I purr out to her, and her eyes light up. I

have noticed she loves my praise, and fuck do I love to give it. I love her trusting me like this, being my good, obedient girl.

Taking me by surprise, she takes me deeper into her mouth, eager to please me, and my other hand rests on the side of her face, massaging her jaw a little, encouraging her to open even wider. I am a big man, and she is petite, but fuck, her wet, warm mouth feels good.

"That's it, Bella. Fuck, that feels so good." I see her hips moving so I know she is enjoying herself too. I begin to match her movements, my hips beginning to move, pushing my cock into her mouth as my grip around the back of her head tightens. My fingers weave into her hair, and I pull it a little, lifting her head back even more, opening her throat wider because I am not going to last much longer.

Her nipples are peaked and she is making little moans, which vibrate around my cock, and my balls tighten. "Fuck, Annie, I am going to come. Fucking take me." I grit my teeth and see my perfect obedient little girl nod as I start to fuck her face.

I am trying to be gentle, but I can barely hang on, the need to fill her mouth suffocating me as I push in and out of her. All the while, I notice her hand is still moving on her clit, her moans and pants increasing.

"Come for me, Bella. Fucking come for me, Annie," I say to her, and as I do, she lets go, her body convulsing, her jaw slacking even more, giving me more room to push inside her. While her body orgasms, I push her to the brink, my cock sliding down her throat. I start to pull out of her mouth because I am about to explode, but she knows what I am doing and grips me tighter to pull me back in. "Fuuuucckk," I growl, my orgasm ripping through me as Annie sucks me, taking it all, before pulling back and gasping in a big breath. We are both panting, yet she moves forward and licks me, again holding my shaft and slowly dragging her tongue along me like she would an ice cream.

I chuckle as I notice she licks her lips, ensuring she gets every drop of me. That was the best fucking blow job I have ever had, and I have had many. And now she is still on her knees, licking me, even though she has pleased me more tonight than any other woman has in my lifetime.

"Good girl, Bella," I say to her, cupping her face before I pull her up and kiss her. Hard.

My hands settle back on her ass, and I squeeze her cheeks, wanting to feel her muscles between my hands. Lifting her up, I wrap her legs around my waist, her body gluing to my front and I kiss the ever-loving fuck out of her.

My tongue explores, and my grip around her tightens. Our naked bodies are pressed up against each other, not leaving an inch of space between us. Her body clings to mine, and she feels amazing. I kiss her more, not slowly, not stopping, not able to get enough, and she matches me in strength and ferocity. I want to show her how a real man kisses his woman.

His woman. The thought surprises me so much I stop and pull back. Her eyes look drunk from her two orgasms, and her perfect bare body is flushed with heat.

"You tired, Bella?" I ask her, my lips now peppering her bare neck.

"Hmmmm," is all she replies, and I know that she is. She has been doing a lot more around the house lately because Maria has been unwell, and I know Leo tires her out with all the games they play.

She leans her head against my chest, her arms wrapping around me. "Sleep with me tonight, Dante?" she asks, and my body stills. I haven't slept with a woman since my ex-wife and even then, I had to be at least five glasses of whiskey deep. Tonight, I had one glass and already the thought of staying in this bed with Little Red naked next to me for an entire night is getting me hard again.

But I can't.

"Sorry, Bella, I've got to go out. I have some work to do, but I will be back soon. You sleep." I kiss her temple and lower her into the bed, putting her bare legs under the blankets and pulling them up around her shoulders.

"What do you do, Dante? What keeps you out all night every night?" she asks innocently, as she snuggles into the blankets.

I pause, not sure what or how much to tell her, but wanting to tell her everything. "I'm Italian, Little Red, and I work with the Italian mob." I watch her face as she looks at me with an unflinching expression.

"I don't really want to know exactly what that entails, do I?" she asks, her eyes never leaving mine. "But you will keep me safe, won't you?" She is placing her trust in me fully, and that feels significant.

"You're safe with me, Bella."

"Please be careful," she murmurs, her eyes already closed, and I kiss her lips softly before I back away. Grabbing some fresh clothes, I have renewed energy in my bones, the need to find and kill Dominic now stronger than ever. Because one night with Little Red is not going to be enough. No. I think I will keep her forever.

19

ANNIE

I wake with a start, my body wracked with cold shivers, which happens from time to time. I curl myself into the thick, soft bedding and move my legs up and down on the mattress to try and generate some warmth, but it does little to help. My limbs tremble a little and my teeth soon follow with their chattering. My mom deteriorated the same way, so I know what to expect. Her circulation got worse and worse throughout her last six months to the point that hot water bottles were a constant. Not able to warm up, I decide, even though it is pitch-black and late, to get up and take a hot bath. Hot showers always helped my mom in the early days, so I hope that it is the same for me.

I sit up slowly and dangle my feet out of the bed, ensuring I am fully awake before I slip out onto the carpet and make my way to the bathroom. My nakedness is a reminder of how I filled in my time earlier tonight, and I smile while touching my lips, already wanting to kiss Dante again and explore his body further. He is so gentle, so patient, teaching me how to do things and what he likes. I enjoy it. I enjoy him.

My thoughts keep me company in the quiet house as I fill the massive tub, adding a splash of his scent for extra comfort. I grab a fresh towel and place it nearby before I immerse myself into the deep water, letting the warmth envelop my body like a warm hug.

I run my hands over my body, thinking about Dante and what we did. I have never felt more like a woman than I do with him. I no longer feel like the poor girl from small town Oklahoma. My confidence in myself is rising each and every day. I love the way his large hands run over my body, his mouth and lips on me, making me feel more wanted and desired than I ever have before.

I sigh as I lay my head back and think about my situation.

I should be scared, fearful or worried. I should be panicking that I am locked up here, wondering when I can leave. But I have no family, no friends, no job; I left everything behind in Oklahoma to live what is left of my life to be adventurous, then within hours of being in New York, I see a gang shooting, then move into the most luxurious house I have ever seen, start hanging out with the coolest kid every day, am sleeping on soft sheets, and now even exploring my sexuality with the most handsome yet dangerous man in all of the city.

To anyone else, it may sound odd, scary, and totally immoral, but how can something that feels so right, so fun and safe, be scary? How can a man who treats me as well as Dante be anything other than the right place for me to be? I wiggle my toes in the water as I continue to move through the pros and the cons of my situation, before I begin to feel my body warming enough to relax. I lift my arm and place my hand on my breast. My fingers massage my flesh for a moment until I feel it. It is still there. The small pea size lump that appeared out of nowhere.

I don't really know what my fate will be, but given the situation, I can only think the outcome will be the same as my mother's. I still haven't told Dante, and after a lot of thought, I don't think I will. Despite my feelings toward him and his obvious affection for me, once it is safe for me to leave, I am sure he will pack my bags and send me on my way. After nearly a month here, I don't want to leave. I feel like this is more my home than the trailer park ever was. But I need to face reality, and that reality is that I have no home and that this is all just temporary. It is just me and my duffle bag, with the weight of my decision not to seek medical treatment heavy on my shoulders.

Before too long, I notice my skin is wrinkled and my body is now warm, so I slowly step out of the bath and wrap a towel around myself. I stand in the bathroom for a moment, my body weary now, and I know it is late. The early hours are a ridiculous time to be having a bath, so I am glad no one can hear me. I open the bathroom door, eager to crawl into bed again, but I stop short when I see him sitting in his armchair looking directly at me. A questioning look of concern etched onto his face.

"Everything alright, Bella?" he asks, swirling his whiskey in the crystal glass. My eyes flick to the clock; it is 3am.

"Yes, everything's fine. I was just cold," I say, gripping the towel around my chest, acting as casually as possible. I know he knows something isn't right, but I can't bring myself to tell him. We are just starting to enjoy each other, and until I'm forced to leave, this is how I want it to stay. I feel like a normal woman with him, not the poor girl from the trailer park, not the girl with a sick momma. If I tell him I have a lump in my breast, then he will undoubtably treat me differently. For the first time in my life, I have someone who treats me like a woman, and I don't want that to change.

He stands then, walking slowly across the room toward me. I should tell him; I know I should. He likes honesty, and I can tell from our nighttime talks he appreciates me opening up to him and telling him about my life. But no matter if I want to or not, my lips remain shut.

"You're cold?" he asks as he stands in front of me, and as if on cue, my skin is covered in goosebumps, but not because I am cold. This man has me feeling all kinds of things that I haven't felt before. I have experienced more with Dante since being here than I have in all my 21 years. Not having a boyfriend was not really something I planned or thought about, it is just the way my life has been. I haven't been living in a bubble. I wasn't saving myself or waiting for Mr. Right. I just had other priorities, and myself and boys wasn't one of them. I have never been a priority to myself or anyone else. My life has revolved around working to pay the bills, and then spending all my time looking after my mom. I don't even know who I am outside of that.

"I was," I say softly, and his hands reach out to cup my

cheeks, lifting my face to look him in the eye. My breath hitches, and I see his Adam's apple bob in his throat. He nods as his eyes roam over my face. I can tell he is waiting for more information, like he knows I am hiding something.

"I will be back in five minutes. Get into bed," he says abruptly, clearly unimpressed that I am not offering him any more information. Stepping back from me, he walks out the door, closing it behind him.

I put the towel back into the bathroom and pull my hair up into a top knot, the damp heat just making it a hot mess of waves. I feel better after my bath and sit on the edge of the bed for a moment, trying to balance my body temperature, just as he comes back into the bedroom.

His arms are full of blankets. One smaller white one, which looks soft and dreamy, like velour, although it's probably a hundred times more expensive. And the other is a large gray mohair, big enough to wrap me up twice over.

"Get into bed," he commands.

"Will you join me?" I ask, holding my breath, hoping that he will get in beside me and hold me for a while.

"Not tonight, Bella." I try to hide my disappointment. "Get in, and I will put the blanket on top."

"Yes, Dante," I oblige, too tired to talk, liking the feeling of him taking care of me in this way. I get into his bed, and he places the small white rug around my shoulders, then drapes the larger blanket over my body twice.

"Sleep." he says, his fingers smoothing a few flyaways off my face as I get comfortable. His eyes search mine, still seemingly trying to work out what is wrong. I'm too afraid to look him in the eye as mine grow heavy.

"Dante," I whisper. "Thank you." I see him swallow roughly, giving me a small nod in acceptance as his eyes drink me in with wonder. Then I rest my head and close my eyes, but not before I see him take his nightly position in the armchair to watch me as I sleep.

20

DANTE

I'm in my office, looking over video footage from Allure last night. I need to be concentrating on who is coming and going, but instead, all I can think about is Little Red, and her soft, flushed skin. The way she was splayed out across this very desk last night, open and fucking perfect for me. It is what my dreams are made of. I'm too old to want anyone so perfect, sweet, and innocent, yet I do. I like that she does everything I ask her to. Her obedience is a big turn on, as is her willingness to please me. In return, I would do fucking anything for her. I yearn for her when I don't see her, and at night, I can't move from my fucking armchair, my obsession with this woman growing by the day.

I watched her small snores for a while last night as I wondered what she was keeping from me. She has been honest with me from day one, so it wasn't hard to see her falter. Her hesitation at explaining why she was in the bath at 3am concerns me. Something doesn't sit right with me, and I don't like secrets. Maybe I was too rough with her here in my office, or later when I exploded in her pouty mouth. Her body may have been in a rush of adrenalin or something. Having your first orgasm followed quickly by a second one could have been too much.

She seemed to enjoy our activities, and I was careful not to push her too hard, even though all I wanted to do was slam into her over and over and over again. Maybe she was regretting our encounter? Maybe her body was aching? These questions continue to filter through my mind on repeat as my eyes look over the grainy nighttime vision. Seeing no one of interest, my eyes are glued to the screen as my mind continues to wander to a few weeks ago, the bruise on her face and hip when she fainted after a hot shower. At the time, I put it down to her not eating much, since she was stressed about the new situation she was in. Fuck, I have no fucking idea.

I can hear her now, out in the kitchen with Leo. She is blabbering on, Leo sitting up at the breakfast bar, completely enthralled by her. Although he still remains speechless, he no doubt is reacting to her in his own way. Their connection is amazing, instant, but Little Red has had that effect on us all.

It is a new feeling for me, something I never felt with anyone else, including my ex-wife. Just the thought of her has me bristling. I feel equal parts agitation, disgust, and empathy when I think of her.

Her calls have been constant and unusual. Another thing that doesn't sit well with me. Something doesn't feel right. She is clearly jacked up on something when she calls and makes demands, but this past week, I hear evil in her tone, along with anger and entitlement. It is different. She is different.

My cell phone vibrates and grabbing it makes my anger rise as I see Angelina's name flashing on my screen. Again. I swear to God, this woman is really pushing me to my limits. I think about not answering, but I know that if I don't, she will keep calling. While I could turn my phone off, in my line of work, that is not a luxury I can afford.

I hit the answer button and wait.

I don't talk. I just sit and listen and wait. Standing, I begin to pace my office as I grip the phone and hold it to my ear, my agitation already sky-high.

"Dante!" she shouts like I am 100 yards away from her. "Dante!" I pull the phone away from my ear.

"What!" I bark at her before I can reel myself in. I walk over to close my office door, slamming it a little too hard, probably getting the attention of Little Red and Leo in the other room.

"What the fuck do you want!" I scream back at her, my patience for this woman now all but gone.

"Leo! He is my son. You can't keep him away from me!" She is high as a kite. Her words are slurred, and I can barely make out what she is screaming down the phone. I try to remain calm, as I repeat over and over in my brain, *Do it for Leo, do it for Leo.*

"We have talked about this, Angelina. You are in no state," I say, calmly, before she interrupts me. One of my biggest pet peeves.

"You are a bastard! You think you are so high and mighty. You think that just because you are *Dante Luciano,* you can keep him away from me!" I can barely make out what she is yelling about. Her voice is so slurred. I look at my watch; it is only 2pm.

"It is fucking 2 in the afternoon Angelina. Get your fucking shit together!" I scream at her, totally losing my shit. I know I shouldn't, but I am stressed. Stressed at her constant demands and calls, but more stressed because I can't find fucking Dominic.

"You are not going near him. You are not fit to be a parent. You are not fit for fucking anything!"

She is quiet then. My hands are still in fists. I am ropeable. At her, at myself, at the world. Leo deserves better than this. He deserves a mother who is clean and sober. One who is loving and will cherish him. I grew up without a mother, and I know what it is like to just need that special female in your life to give you those cuddles, read you the stories and kiss your grazed knee. Leo shouldn't have to go through life without that and I am a fucking failure for not providing it for him.

"Get some fucking sleep, Angelina, and stop calling me." I hang up the phone, throwing it across the room, grateful that it hits my soft armchair rather than the wall.

Pissed off, I throw open the door and stalk into the kitchen. Both Little Red and Leo look at me, their bodies are still, eyes wide, not scared but unsure, like they don't know what to say in case I yell at them. I don't unleash my anger at home very much. I like this to be a nice and quiet, loving home for Leo, and a sanctuary for me.

I stop midstride, and look at them, realizing too late that in the rush to see the two people I want the most in my life, I didn't school my features quick enough. Two of the last people I want to scare look hesitant and uneasy, all because of me. Sighing, I run my hand over my face. Understanding washes over me that I was louder than I thought as I yelled at Angelina just now. I have been trying for years to keep myself in check when it comes to Leo's mother, not wanting him to have to be subjected to any of the negativity that will only upset him more. He's been through enough. But, I let it slip just now and feel awful for it.

I walk across to Leo, slowly, my body language now more relaxed, and I ruffle his hair as he looks up at me. His eyes crease and a look of concern flashes across his face, but I give him a small smile of reassurance.

"Don't worry, Leo, she won't take you. She won't touch you. Never again." I mean it. "You are safe, no matter what. You are safe here with me." He nods at me slowly. I see his small body begin to shake slightly; the fear he has of his mother is something that has never left his body. I have no idea what he experienced because he won't talk about it, but it is still blindly clear that it was traumatic for him. I look at Little Red then, and she stares at me with so many questions that will have to wait for another time.

"Here, Leo, eat the tiramisu I made your dad. I know it's his favorite, but I am sure he won't mind you having the last piece," Little Red says to him from the other side of the breakfast bar as she pushes a small bowl of my favorite creamy dessert across the bench. *She made it for me?* She knows it is my favorite, and other than Maria, no one has ever made me anything. I am in awe of her, and my body relaxes even more on the exhale as I watch this woman, all domesticated in my kitchen, looking after my boy. It all fits. She fits.

"Hmmmm, just this once, Leo. Next time, I am not sharing," I say to try and lighten the mood, and I get a brief smile from him. I decide to push him a little more and dip my finger into the cream before he can dig in his spoon, shoving it into my mouth.

"Mmmm, on second thought..." I begin to say as I reach out to grab the bowl, but he is quicker. Tiramisu is also his favorite, so he snatches it away, and I smile, ruffling his hair again. He looks up at me and gives me a big grin, scooping up a big spoonful before I can take anymore from him.

Little Red seems unsure, and I fucking hate that I did that to her. It is the first time I have had to think of anyone aside from Leo, but I defrost a little more as I take her in, the joy in her eyes at watching Leo devour her cooking, the light as it reflects off her bright red hair that flows down her small frame in waves. Looking at her, I am enamored. I am totally and utterly amazed by this woman.

21

ANNIE

I have no idea what just happened, but I get a sick feeling in my stomach as I watch Leo start to scoop up the cream and eat the dessert like it is his last chance to ever eat again. He is shaking slightly, but seems okay now, completely focused on the bowl in front of him, as his father stands by his side. My eyes flick between him and Dante as I try to sort out in my head what the hell is going on.

Dante is angry. Really angry. I heard him yelling in his office, and from what I can gauge, it was at Leo's mother—his ex-wife. Someone we haven't really talked about, and I haven't brought it up since the time I spoke to Maria about it. By Dante's outburst, they don't get along at all. As I look between Leo and Dante, I am angry and equal parts scared. I'm angry because I don't know what she has done to elicit a response from Dante and Leo like this. But I am also fearful because Maria said she wasn't a nice woman, and I wonder what she is capable of if she has such an effect on them both.

What did that woman do to these beautiful boys? My boys! I still at the thought. The feelings I have for both of them are all-encompassing, and I want them in my life more so than on a temporary basis.

Dante runs his hand through his hair, before resting it on Leo's shoulder, providing him the comfort he needs, and I see him visibly calm, clearly needing his dad's support. I haven't seen Dante this angry before; the volume and grit in his tone were pure venom. While it wasn't directed at me, it was a little frightening to hear. I am sure whatever he does when he is away during the day and night, his fearful tone may be necessary, but here in the comfort of his home, he has never once raised his voice. I can't ever imagine him taking that tone with me, but we have only just started to get to know each other. There is still so much I don't know about him. And him me.

I rub my chest, trying to get my beating heart to slow down, and draw in a breath to fill my lungs with much-needed air. I try to center my thoughts and take the snippets of information I overheard to piece together what is going on and if I should be worried. Our tranquil day is now all out the window.

Dante must see my hesitation at everything that just occurred, and leaving Leo to eat his dessert, he walks around the breakfast bar, straight to where I am standing in the kitchen. I watch him as I wring my hands together, and then without hesitation, he grabs me, pulling my body flush with his, and drops his head to the crook of my neck. My arms automatically run up his torso and wrap around his neck, my fingers caressing his hair at his nape.

"It's okay, Bella," he whispers. "She is not an issue, and will never be an issue for you." His hands remain firm on my hips, pulling me to him, not wanting to let me go.

I blush a little. As Dante breathes me in, calming himself. I look past him over at Leo, who is watching us eagle-eyed, so I reach out my hand to him, to encourage him to come over too. I wait on bated breath to see what his reaction will be. Jumping off the stool and running around into the kitchen, his little body slams into my side, his small arms wrapping around me and his father, and the three of us stand like that for a moment, feeling secure in each other's embrace, before Dante is calm enough to speak.

"It is very good tiramisu, Little Red," he says, as he lifts his head from my neck, a small grin appearing on his face.

I smile at him. "Well, Maria taught me everything I needed to know," I say before looking at Leo. "And little Leo here is a great taste tester..." I add with a big smile, one which he returns. I grip his hand tighter to show him that I am here to support him. Why would anyone want to harm this little boy? There is so much that I don't know, and I am beginning to feel out of my depth a little. But, Leo has one of my hands in a vice grip and Dante has the other now enclosed in his, and I would be lying if I said I didn't think that the three of us made a good team.

Dante lowers his head to my ears. "I can think of something else I would like to eat with my favorite dessert..." My skin prickles as his breath skims across my cheek, where he plants a kiss, and lets go of my hand before moving it to my ass and giving my cheek a squeeze. My breath quickens, but before I can reply, he steps back and scoops Leo up into his arms and flings him into the air.

"C'mon, buddy, Little Red is going to make me another tiramisu—that you can't eat on me—while we go outside and kick the soccer ball around before I need to go out to work," he says, tickling Leo at the same time. Leo squirms in his arms but has a big smile on his face, and I watch the two of them walk down the hall. Turning at the last moment, Dante looks back at me, gives me a wink, then steps out of sight.

The door closes and the house is quiet, and I sit on the kitchen stool that Leo just vacated to take a moment. *Angelina.* From the conversation I overheard just now, she isn't allowed anywhere near Leo, and I wonder why.

Sitting here in my jumbled thoughts is not going to achieve anything, so I release the breath I was holding and look around the kitchen. I need to start baking.

WITH THE TIRAMISU in the refrigerator, Dante out at work, and Leo in bed, I clean up the house because Maria is still not well. Walking up the stairs, I start to relax and think about having a bath before I stop short when I hear Leo whimpering.

Racing down the hall to his room, I fling myself inside and find him crying in bed.

"Leo?" I say as I walk slowly to him. "Are you okay, buddy?" I stop at the side of his bed and kneel down to be closer to him. Reaching out, I wipe a stray tear away, and he pulls the blanket up to his chin.

"It's okay, I'm here. Can I get you anything?" I ask him, before he suddenly flings the blankets back and jumps out of bed and into my arms, gripping onto me for dear life. My heart breaks as he whimpers in my arms, and I cuddle him, rubbing his back to help calm him down. As I sit up onto the mattress, I realize that both his pajamas and the sheets are wet, and it dawns on me that he has wet the bed. Something that is not a usual activity for a boy Leo's age, but after his frightened state today, it's not surprising.

"It's okay. Come on. I will take you to the shower and change your bed while you clean up." He nods into my shoulder.

Standing, I carry him across his room and into the bathroom, where I turn on the shower and get him a fresh towel.

"Okay, you get in and have a quick wash. I will be out changing your bed and then I can stay with you, if you like?" I say to him, trying to be upbeat, and he nods while wiping his eyes.

With a last squeeze of his hand, I close the bathroom door behind me and get busy changing his sheets. I hear the shower turn off just as I am putting the comforter on, and I'm fluffing the pillow as he comes out with damp hair and fresh pajamas.

"Feeling better?" I ask, and he nods before crawling back into bed. I pull up the blankets around his chin. As I am about to walk away, he grabs my hand, then motions for me to lie on top of his blankets beside him.

"Okay buddy. I will stay a while," I say to him, hopefully answering what he is asking of me, and I jump onto his bed to lie beside him, all the while his grip on my hand remains.

I brush his hair with my fingers, lightly, to help him relax, and I hum a little lullaby—one that my mother used to sing to me when I was little. Lost in my own thoughts, I am a little taken aback when he begins to join in. His voice sounds a little shaky at first, and it is quiet, but it is there. Leo is humming. I try to remain calm, not getting too overly excited, not wanting to scare him and wanting to let him have this moment of relaxation. But I am nearly bursting out of my skin and wish that Dante was here to hear it. While he isn't talking, he is using his voice box and that is another step forward.

Together we hum the remainder of the lullaby before I notice his eyes closing, and he begins breathing heavily. I stay close to him, my hand running through his hair, until his grip on mine begins to loosen.

Lying back on the bed next to him, I stare at the ceiling. I don't dare move so as not to wake him. As I lie here in the darkness, his soft sheets like a pillow around my body, I am comforted by his presence and happy that he is now firmly asleep. I want to stay up to talk to Dante, but before long, I succumb to sleep as well.

22

DANTE

Walking into the dark, quiet house, the pounding in my head starts to lessen after spending the past five hours with Carter at Allure. Weeks have gone by without a word from Dominic, and I know he has to be frothing at the mouth, wanting to kill me. He would take great delight in it. I am sure. The fact that he has been underground for so long now is unsettling. The longer he makes us wait, the more likely it is that he will take us by surprise. So, trying to draw him out, Carter and I sat at that stinking shithole all night, hoping that his need for revenge was strong enough to pull him from his hiding spot so we could finish this once and for all.

But it wasn't.

Instead, I have a fucking headache due to my ex-wife screaming at me every time she took a break from the stripper pole, even though she couldn't string two words together and her eyes were bloodshot and half closed. At one point, I thought she fell asleep on the pole, such was her lack of energy and ability. Totally incoherent from whatever drug was in her system.

In the end, Carter and security had to physically remove her from the bar, setting her up out the back with coffee. As the night wore on, my anger at her subsided and now all I feel is pity. It is fucking sad that her life has become what it is.

It has been a long fucking day.

I walk past the kitchen, then stop, intrigued to see if she actually made the dessert that we joked about today. My pace quickens as I make my way over to the refrigerator and open the door. The bright light shines on my silhouette as I lean in to see the large glass bowl full of fresh tiramisu, and I smile. Pulling it out, I grab a spoon and take it upstairs with me.

Thank God for small delights.

It is late as I open the bedroom door and creep in slowly, putting the bowl of dessert next to my armchair before I notice that the bed is empty. Sheets still made, the room untouched from earlier today.

I walk to the bathroom and open the door, but find that empty too.

She isn't downstairs, so I walk out the bedroom door and down the hall to Leo's room, the only other logical place she might be. Stepping quietly inside, I spot her. Curled up on her side, on top of the blankets, lying next to Leo, his hand holding hers. The both of them are sleeping, looking peaceful together.

I haven't seen this before. Angelina never stayed with Leo. Never nursed him or read him stories. She never played with him, ate with him. It was almost like she didn't even want him. Maybe she didn't. Maybe she was just doing her duty as a mob wife. She never spent much time with him at all, which is why her contacting me now to see him is so odd.

I watch them for a moment, looking at how perfect and peaceful they are. Little Red's caring nature is something I have never experienced before. With parents who both left this earth when I was young and an arranged marriage that was a shambles before it even began, this maternal instinct and feminine energy she is bringing to my home, to my boy and to me, is thawing me right down to my bones.

She is all woman, and I fucking love it.

I spot the pile of sheets nearby and put two and two together. Understanding washes over me that Leo may have had an accident. He usually does when his mother starts to crawl back into his life, and I feel the anger beginning to well inside of me at how distressed she makes him.

Looking back at the bed, Little Red moves slightly, obviously feeling my presence.

"Hey," she whispers quietly, sitting up and rubbing her eyes, before looking over at Leo to ensure she doesn't disturb him.

I don't reply, but rather walk over to her side of the bed and reach down, picking her up, her hands immediately circling my neck as I kiss her. Because I've been gone mere hours, but it feels like days.

"Everything alright?" I ask her quietly as my nose caresses her cheek and my lips kiss up her jaw.

"Yeah, he had a little accident and then wanted me to

stay for a while, but I must have fallen asleep," she says, looking back at Leo with love in her eyes.

With Leo still snoring, I carry Little Red back to our room as she curls into my chest. Kicking the bedroom door closed behind us, I walk over to the bed and set her down on her feet. I scan her face, making sure she is okay after today too.

Sensing what I am doing, she laughs a little, rubbing her hands up and down my arms. "I'm okay, Dante."

My hands find her waist, and I pull her close. "Good," I say, holding her tight, my fingers trailing along her hips. "I was serious today when I said I wanted to eat something else with my tiramisu." Her lips part slightly in surprise, and her eyes flick around the room until they land on the bowl of dessert sitting on the table. A small grin comes to her face.

I lean down and kiss her softly, memorizing her lips and her tongue. I have never kissed anyone this way before. My gentle nature surprises us both as I explore her slowly, gripping her skin under my hands. I pour my feelings into the kiss because I want her to know exactly what she is means to me.

She will be my undoing.

I move my hands, lowering them until I hit the edge of her shirt. I pull my lips away from hers just enough, so she raises her arms like a good girl, and I drag her top over her head and off her body. Her body is fucking amazing, even more so now that she has been eating Maria's cooking this past month and her curves have filled out. There is now more for me to own.

My mouth goes back to hers in an instant, as my

hands roam her torso, taking my time to feel her soft skin under my fingers before I begin to massage her breasts. She is addictive, her taste, her touch, her smell, her fucking everything. I reach around her back and unclip her bra, and leaving her lips, I kiss across her jaw, her head falling back, exposing her neck to me. Her breath quickening and the small noises she makes at my touch has me feeling insatiable. I skim my hand up her delicate body, gripping her throat, keeping her head back, leaving her neck open for me. I kiss and nip at her, trying my best not to rip the remaining clothes from her body and fuck her hard and fast on this bed, which is what I am aching to do.

"Dante," she whispers as her chest rises and falls, and her hands start exploring too. Fuck, this woman has me wrapped around her finger. I would do anything for her.

Her breath hitches as I increase the pressure in my grip around her neck. My mouth slides along her shoulder, my tongue tasting her skin as I pull her bra strap down her shoulders.

"Annie, do you know what you do to me?" I grit out to her, nearly in pain due to the need I have for this woman.

"Probably the same that you do to me," she says as her hands glide down my chest to open my shirt buttons. She pushes my shirt off my shoulders, and I let it fall to the floor.

We both stand before each other half naked, as I lean down and grip her by the ass, hauling her up my body, her legs instinctively wrapping around my waist. I pull her hips into mine, so she can feel exactly what she does to me, and she moves her hips to grind into me, wanting the friction as much as I do. Her hands delve into my hair where she begins to massage my head and pull me closer as our tongues lash each other with carnal desire.

"Dante, please, I want you," she all but begs me in her light tone, and I fucking nearly break. Visions of slamming into her, over and over and over again until she is begging for mercy have been in my daydreams. But she is too innocent for that just yet, so I kneel on the bed and slowly lower her down onto her back.

"Tell me what you want, Bella?" I say to her as my eyes canvas her body beneath me.

"I want you inside of me. I want you to own me." As the words leave her, I swallow hard, unable to contain my groan as her hands come up to my chest and trail down my stomach to the top of my jeans. Her eyes remain firmly on mine, and I need to grip onto the bedsheets beneath her before I totally lose control.

"I'm going to go slow, Annie," I say to her as my hands find her jeans, and I begin to unzip them. "I am usually not a slow man when it comes to sex, and you are so fucking goddamn sexy I don't know how I will behave myself, but I will for you." I pull her underwear off with her jeans and throw them across the room.

She is bare underneath me and begins to cross her legs. "Don't. Don't ever hide from me. Open your legs, Bella. Show me how wet you are for me," I growl at her as I undo my jeans and throw them across the room to meet hers.

As I watch her from above, like a blooming flower, she opens her legs wide. Her hands wander across her body, lightly touching her skin, and my dick throbs as I watch her confidence rise while I devour her with my eyes.

"Is this better... Dante?" she asks, knowing that her saying my name like that is the sweetest fucking sound aside from the noises we will be making when I slam inside of her. I grip my cock, stroking it a little, and watch her watching me. It is the hottest thing having her watch me like this, like she is hungry for me. And I want to feed her, every inch, every fucking day.

Leaning down, my fingers find her center warm and wet, and her body shimmies a little under my touch.

"I have wanted you from the moment I first saw you. Are you sure this is what you want? There is no going back, Annie. After this, you will be mine," I grit out to her, barely hanging on and praying that she hasn't changed her mind.

"I'm sure, Dante. I want you. I want you more than anything." Her body squirms underneath mine, begging for me to touch her.

"Are you ready, Bella? Are you ready for me to fuck your tight little pussy?" I haven't talked too dirty to her yet, so I wait for her response to see how she reacts.

"Fuck me, Dante," she whispers out on a whimper, and it is all I need.

I lower myself to her, my fingers continuing to explore her wet core, circling her clit as she continues to writhe and wiggle under my touch, her breaths already panting.

"I want you to come on my fingers, then I want you to come on my tongue," I growl at her as I speed up my fingers on her clit and see her head push back into the mattress, nearly at breaking point.

"Then I am going to fuck this perfect fucking pussy so good..." I don't finish as she comes undone, her orgasm ripping through her, just by my touch and dirty words and that's exactly what I want to do.

Get her dirty. Really fucking dirty.

23

ANNIE

I have no idea if I am quicker than average to orgasm or if it is Dante and his skills, but within an hour of him being home, I am already underneath him, panting. And I want more.

So. Much. More.

As I breathe in, my bare breasts rise, touching his scorching chest, his torso rigid, muscles tense. He looms above me, his dark Mediterranean Italian skin that is full of tattoos, scars and marks is in complete contrast to mine, yet we fit. On paper, we are worlds apart, but here, together, there is nothing that separates us.

I sit up on my elbows and admire Dante's naked body as he gets up and walks away from the bed to the armchair. I am nowhere near as experienced as him, and I am happy to have him take charge, but I still doubt myself a little, wondering how a girl like me can ever satisfy a man like Dante. Before I get too caught up in my self doubt, I see him stop at the armchair and pick up his bowl of tiramisu. My eyes crinkle, wondering what he is doing.

Is he having a mid-sex snack? Is that a thing?

His eyes flick to me as a small smile spreads across his face, and he walks back to the bed. Still holding the bowl, he stands at the edge of the mattress, looking down at me. The power dynamics are clearly evident, his tall statue dominating and demanding as he sucks up all the air in the room.

"Did you learn to make this just for me, Bella?" he asks me with deviant eyes and a smirk on his face. He already knows the answer.

"Yes, Dante," I say, just how I know he likes it.

He scoops out a small spoonful of the dessert and leans over, feeding it to me.

"Do you like my fingers on your body, Annie?"

"Mmmhmmm..." I say in response as I lick the cream from the spoon, which falls slightly onto my bottom lip. Before I can wipe it away, Dante grabs the back of my head and leans in, swiping my lips with his tongue, collecting the cream before kissing me again.

"So fucking good," he growls into my mouth.

He takes another spoonful of the dessert, but this time he doesn't feed it to me, dropping the cream on my left breast instead. The cool mixture immediately causes my skin to prickle and my nipple to peak, and a small gasp leaves me as I am caught off guard by his action.

"You didn't know when you made this, that I'd be enjoying it off your perfect body, though, did you?" Dante asks me again as I watch him closely, my heart racing.

"No, Dante," I reply, totally lost for words and already

wound up so tight I might start moaning before he goes any lower.

"Lay back, Bella, I want to eat this off your body and then I want to eat you," he says in a way that has my sex throbbing. I have no idea who could ever say no to this man, because all I want to do is please him.

"Oh God, yes, Dante." I slowly lie back, my head resting on the mattress as he leans over my body and his mouth finds my breast. He licks, sucks, and nips my nipple, eating the dessert from my skin. His tongue is a tool of magic, his lips and breath warm in contrast to the cool cream. He repeats the action on my other breast, taking his time, sucking my breast into his mouth, and I feel my arousal building.

"This is the best fucking dessert I have ever had," he groans to me as he kneels on the bed, positioning himself between my legs, pushing my legs wide and making me completely open and bare to him.

"You are so beautiful, Annie." He dips the spoon back into the creamy dessert, his eyes on mine. Bringing the spoon down on my hip, he swipes the cream across my skin, before he leans over and licks it off my body. In one long lick across my hip bone, he collects the cream and swallows it before licking and sucking the same spot again, peppering kisses down lower and lower, making my hips twist in delight. This is so intimate and intense, and I can't believe a man like Dante is worshiping my body in this way. I feel my temperature rising, my eyes not able to stay away from watching him.

"Dante... Please..." I'm begging him to touch me again, wanting to feel his hands gripping my body.

His dark hair falls across his forehead, his eyes sparkling in delight at my tone. He likes hearing me beg. My eyes wander down his body, and I take in the patchwork of tattoos, different images paint his body, and I don't miss seeing Leo's name and birthday right on his chest, near his heart. As my gaze travels down, I take in his large, hard cock. I have no idea how it is going to fit. I swallow as I look at him, not quite believing what my life has become.

"One spoonful left," he teases as he takes the last spoonful and puts it on my center before placing the bowl on the bedside table and lowering himself between my legs. The smell of coffee filters through the air and the cool dessert has my skin covered in goosebumps as I lean back into the soft sheets, my body feeling weightless. Again, the power rush I feel whenever I am with Dante fills me, and I watch him with a small smile on my face as he kisses up the inside of my thigh.

He licks me from back to front, and I watch him gather some of the cream on his tongue and swallow it before he does it again. He is taking his time, his eyes penetrating mine as he continues to eat the cream, slowly and deliberately two more times, until there is none left. But that doesn't stop him. He plunges his tongue into me, catching me by surprise. I jolt off the bed a little, but his hands are quick, holding my hips down as he continues to feast. His tongue and lips are everywhere, licking and sucking me, twirling around my clit before he delves his tongue back inside over and over.

"Mmmm. I think I've found a new ingredient for my favorite dessert," he grits out as my head pushes back against the mattress, my hands gripping the sheets underneath me. "What do you think it is, Bella?" I can't answer him, I'm too overwhelmed by how good he feels.

"Ahhh... Oh my God..." I pant out, quivering, my senses overloading, and I arch my back, pushing my head into the pillow. It is like he is everywhere at once, and I can't help the small moans and noises that come from me. I jolt again as he sucks on my clit, his hands sliding up my inner thighs, pushing my legs wider for him, then I feel his finger push inside of me. My heart is racing, and I am panting, wanting more of him, yet wanting him to take his time.

"Maybe it's your sweet pussy, hmm?" He continues to devour me as I moan out at his dirty words. "I'm only ever going to be able to lick it off of you from now on. Next time you make this for me, you better keep that in mind."

I look down, my eyes firmly on him, and he catches my gaze as he continues to explore and lick and tease me until I can barely take it anymore.

"Dante, please,"

"You're tight, Little Red. I need to get you ready for me." He lowers his head again and flicks my clit with his tongue as a second finger glides inside of me and he begins to move them at the same time.

"Oh God, Dante," I moan. Heat begins to build in my body as the feeling of Dante's fingers inside of me have me grabbing his hair, pulling him closer to me, needing the increased friction.

"Ride my face, Bella. Fucking give it to me." I begin to move my hips a little more as he flicks my clit with his tongue again, and I push his face into me, my hips now working with a mind of their own, eager to chase my release. Dante removes his fingers and grabs my ass, as his tongue and mouth work in tandem.

"Dante!" I scream out to the room as I explode, my body convulsing around him, but he doesn't stop. He continues to lick and suck me, growling into my pussy in pure delight.

"Fucking perfect," he murmurs.

Panting, my hand comes up, and I rest it on my forehead, covering my eyes, not quite believing how sexy that whole experience just was. I try to catch my breath and calm my racing heart as Dante crawls up my body, peppering kisses all along my skin, until he reaches my face.

"Like I said, best fucking tiramisu I have ever had," he whispers in my ear.

"Me too," I reply, a big smile spreading across my face, and I move my hand to look at him. His eyes stare deep into mine.

"Now, are you ready for the main course, Bella? Because I am still fucking starving," he growls as he pushes his erection firmly into my stomach.

It is then that I realize that I have never wanted anything or anyone more in my entire life than I want this man right now. And if this is what happens when I make him his favorite dessert, then I am going to be making it every day for the rest of our lives.

24

DANTE

I put my hands under her arms and lift her up the bed. The lamp shines a ray of light across her body, giving her an angelic glow, of which this devil is going to fuck right out of her. Even though I know her body is getting weary, I want to make her come on my cock; something I have been daydreaming about since I first slammed her tiny body into the pavement. If she wanted me to stop, I would, but as I look at her underneath me, she wants me just as badly as I want her. This beautiful young woman is going to end me for all others.

I lean over to my draw and grab a condom. I'd prefer to go bare with her, but I want to be careful. I want her first experience with me to not be something she or I regret later. She watches me as I kneel on the mattress in front of her and sheath myself, my cock growing harder for her by the second and even more so with her eyes watching, taking it all in.

Missionary sex is not something I have done in years, but I want to watch her. I want to watch her face as I push inside of her. I want to see her face when she comes, and I want her to watch me too, to know what she does to me.

It is not something I have had the urge to do before. But taking her from behind like I usually do with any other woman is not even something I contemplate at this moment. It is a surprising thought to me because even with my ex-wife, I couldn't look at her when I fucked her. That alone should have brought up red flags, but it wasn't like either of us had a choice back then.

I lean over her and kiss her neck, my second favorite spot on her because her scent is delectable and I want to drown in it. My hand travels down her perfect body, and my fingers find her clit again, drawing small circles. I want to hear her beg for it.

I fucking love it when she begs for me.

"Tell me what you want, Annie," I grit out, barely hanging on as she withers around underneath me, the slightest touch of my fingers setting her off again. Her need for me is a permanent fucking turn on, and as a man with very little patience, I should win a fucking award for the restraint I am showing tonight.

"I want you Dante," she moans out, her eyes hooded as I look at her, my fingers continuing to circle her as she begins to pant for me already.

"Are you mine, Annie?" I ask her one last time, wanting to make sure she knows who she now belongs to. Because like I said, there is no going back.

"I'm yours. I am all yours, Dante," she whispers back, looking me dead in the eye. My nostrils flare at her words, the beast in me about to unleash if she says my name again. I position myself at her entrance, my knees pushing her legs wider, and I kiss her again to keep me grounded, wanting to remember this moment, wanting it etched into my mind.

I pull back to watch her face as I begin to slide inside of her. I am moving so slowly that I think I will burst a vein, but I watch her eyes as they widen a little, and I push in a little more before I see her bite her lower lip.

"Breathe, Bella, you are so fucking tight, but you feel so fucking good," I grit out to her, barely hanging on.

Her hands glide up and down my back before they rest on my ass and she pulls me in, telling me she is ready for more.

"Keep going. I want this so bad. I want you. Dante," she moans on my name, her words leaving her as I push my way farther, until I am fully inside of her, and pause again.

"You good, Bella? Because you feel fucking amazing to me." I say, about to burst a blood vessel but wanting to make sure she is alright. I am a big man, and she is tiny in comparison.

"Dante," she whispers, and I look at her concerned. "Move, I need you to move. I need you to fuck me. Please fuck me, Dante." Her words unleash me, and I begin to move.

"Your wish is my command, Bella." I slowly pull out before pushing back in, quicker and firmer than before.

Her body relaxes around mine, and I know she is ready, so I don't hesitate for a moment longer. I grip onto her tight and fuck her like I have wanted to.

Her fingers grip around my shoulders, and I lean down and bite her nipple, sucking it and then biting it again, wanting to mark her perfect skin with my teeth, wanting to mark her as mine.

"That feels so good," I hear her moan, her head now thrown back, and her back arched as I continue to thrust into her over and over again.

"Your tits are fucking perfect, Bella," I grit out as I feel my orgasm building. "I could fucking suck your tits and pound you like this for fucking eternity." I am in heaven, and I never want to leave.

Her body molds into mine, and I lift her legs and throw them over my shoulders as I grip onto her hips and push deeper inside of her.

"Fuck. Jesus Christ, you feel too damn good," I growl to her, her hands now above her head, stabilizing herself on the headboard above her as I continue powerful thrusts that have her moaning louder.

"Dante... Dante... Dante..." she pants my name as she begins to squirm, and my grip on her tightens.

"Come for me, Bella. Fucking come on my cock like the good girl you are." And she does.

I thrust into her as she screams my name, her hands scratching the headboard's fabric above her, her face flushed, her mouth open, her back arching, looking like a delectable swan as I thrust into her once more and follow suit.

"Fuuucckk," I groan as I come hard, losing myself in her, burying myself deep inside her, wanting to get as close as I can. We are both panting as I look at her, our bodies still connected, her cheeks still flushed and her breasts scattered with my bite marks. I run my hand across each one, feeling her beating heart underneath my palm, the light sheen of sweat making her skin glow even more in the light.

"Wow..." she says in a whisper, her eyes searching mine.

"You alright, my Bella?" I search her eyes, trying to gauge how she is feeling, because that was fucking amazing for me. I slowly ease away from her, gently rubbing my hands up and down her leg.

"I'm good... that was..." She trails off, lost in the moment.

"Fucking amazing." I bend down and brush my lips against hers, which elicits a small smile and giggle as her hands come up and grip my face either side.

"That was everything I imagined and more," she says to me, and I smile. "I think I need to make more tiramisu if that is what happens when you eat it." I am a fucking simp as I smile wide back at her beaming face. I'm truly happy. For the first time in my life, despite all the shit that is going down outside of this house, I am actually feeling more content than I have in a long time, and I know this woman is the reason for it.

"Come on, let me shower you," I say, and she shrieks a little as I swoop her up, holding her in my arms bridal style. As I walk us into the bathroom, her small body molds to mine. She is exhausted, and while it is not unusual for us to be up late talking half the night, it must be all the activity that has her so worn out.

Turning on the shower, I slowly lower her to her feet and step in after her, keeping her close, her small body curling into my chest as the water flows down our naked bodies. Grabbing my soap, I wash her from the top of her shoulders to her toes and back again, as she leans into me and lets me take care of her. It is a first for me. I have never washed a woman before, during or after sex. I never cared that much. Never had any emotion to want to bathe with them, look after them, or spend a lot of time with them. I am protective by nature, but this level of intimacy is new for me, and I can't imagine doing it with anyone else.

Anyone except Annie.

She looks up at me then, her bright eyes sparkling a little more than usual. She grabs the soap from me and begins to run it over my skin, and I let her. I let her small hands roam my body, discover my scars and my tattoos that all tell a life history of where I have been and what I have done. I watch her look at a few closely, no doubt wondering what they are or how they came to be. I watch her, enamored by her, as her delicate hands continue to roam my skin, her soft touch like electricity through my limbs, my cock already standing to attention again.

"I like your hands on my body, Little Red," I tell her, wanting to make it clear to her. Her eyes flick to mine, her cheeks blushing a little, but she smiles in return.

"I like my hands on your body too," she says in a way that makes me fucking smile. How did this even happen? How did this young woman get involved in my life and totally turn me into a grinning asshole?

I have no idea what we are doing or what the future holds, but I will keep her safe. I will keep her here at the house. I will keep her with me.

25

ANNIE

I wake up wrapped in the sheets, warm, content, and although my body is a little sore, I have zero regrets. If I could do last night with Dante all over again, I would. I would do it every day for the rest of my life. Last night with him was so much more than I was expecting. And I had high hopes, especially after my first sexual encounter at the trailer park was so lackluster. But I knew Dante would be different. The way he makes me feel, the way my body adapts to his, the way he claimed me and made me his. I feel wanted for the first time in my life, and I want to shout it from the rooftops that I am his and he is mine. I feel like we connected, right from the start.

"What's got you smiling like that so early in the morning, Bella?" he says, surprising me. I sit up, clutching the sheets to my bare chest, seeing him sitting in his armchair with a coffee.

"You're still here?" I ask, my heart and body warming at the sound of his voice.

"Well, I have to go soon, but I wanted to see you before I left," he says, looking at me over the top of his coffee cup as he takes a sip of his morning brew. I smile again, because this is the first time he has been here in the morning when I wake up, and so it is a new step for us. One I welcome. He puts the cup down and leans back in his armchair, the same position he has held each and every night since the moment I arrived. He is freshly showered and dressed for work in his black jeans and black shirt, his sleeves rolled up, showcasing his forearms. He looks deadly, yet I am not afraid of him in the slightest. I pull back the blankets, the cool morning air hitting my bare skin, immediately making it prickle. Still naked from last night, I slip out of his bed and slowly pad across the thick carpet floor to where he is sitting.

Watching me walk toward him, his nostrils flare as he looks over my naked body. As I see his jaw clenching, the feeling of power radiates through my bones. I have never felt such power and confidence before in my life. My life before I met Dante was one of survival, weakness, and I was barely existing. Never would I have been confident enough to walk around naked in front of anyone without my clothes on. In fact, I have never done it before. I thought of myself as insignificant, a nobody. But I trust Dante, and he eyes me like he wants to eat me whole. Like he would do anything I ask of him. It is empowering.

As I reach him, I do what I have wanted to do for the past few weeks each time he sits here. I climb onto his lap. I straddle him, fully naked, sitting up on him, and his head falls back. His hands grip onto the arms of the chair, but his eyes wander in appreciation, from my lips down my body and back up again.

"Good morning," I say to him cheekily with a small smile as my hands run up his shoulders and rest around his neck. I lean closer, and he doesn't hesitate to grip onto my neck and pull me toward him, our lips touching briefly before his tongue twirls with mine.

"Fucking great morning," he says back to me, his hands leaving my face and running up and down my thighs before they rest on my naked ass. His fingers sink into my cheeks, pulling and grabbing, massaging my muscles. He runs them up my torso until they reach my breasts, where he again grabs them, molding them in his hands, feeling them fully before he runs his hands back down to my ass.

"Do you want to make it even better?" I ask him, not quite believing that I'm saying that to him, but at this moment, he makes me feel wanted and sexy and I want to please him more than anything. My hands move down his chest, and I feel his tight muscles flex under the material as my hands pass every ripple.

He moves one of his hands across my hips and slides it down to my entrance, where he starts to circle my clit, a move he did last night, and as he spreads my juices around, my heart rate increases.

"You're so fucking wet already, Little Red," he groans, looking at me as he continues moving his finger in circles, and my nipples peak. My breathing quickens, and I lean back a little, my hands behind me resting on his knees as his fingers push inside me. First one, then a second one.

"Dante..." I say as my head falls back, my naked body

completely open to him, as he continues to push his fingers in and out while his other hand grips onto my ass, holding me close.

"What do you want, Annie?" he asks, teasing me, smiling against my skin.

"Everything," I moan, as my hips begin to move against his fingers, needing more.

"You're a greedy girl this morning. By the way you are fucking my fingers, I can tell that you are hungry," he replies, his fingers thrusting in and out in a steady rhythm as his other hand moves, and I hear the clinking of his belt. I lift my head up from my sexual haze and watch him pull out his cock. It is rock hard, standing to full attention, and he pumps it, using the same rhythm as his fingers are.

"I'm starving," I say, needing him to know how much I want him.

"Get on your knees, Bella. Show me how hungry you are." I don't hesitate, sliding from his lap and positioning myself on my knees in front of his chair. My hands slide up his legs before I reach for his cock, which is throbbing in desire. I look up at him, as he leans back in his chair, openly admiring me.

Watching him, I lean down, taking the tip of him in my mouth, before circling it with my tongue, and I hear him hiss a little. I take him in a little farther, taking my time, enjoying the feel of him in my mouth, as his hand comes and rests on the back of my head, his fingers weaving into my hair.

"Fuck, Bella, you are perfect. Such a good girl..." he groans, clearly enjoying what I am doing.

I take him fully into my mouth then, swirling my tongue and sucking him as I find a rhythm, and I feel his hand on my head clench. I moan around him, feeling myself get wetter by the second.

"Fuck, Bella. Fuck, you look so beautiful with my cock down your throat." My eyes flick back to his, and I smile around his length.

"Come up here and sit on my cock, Bella. I want you to ride me," he demands, and I stand up and straddle him on the chair again and let him take control. He pulls me closer, until we both watch as he slides me onto him, his hands now firmly back on my ass as he fills me, the pleasurable pain making me instinctively move.

His hands guide me as I move, a little unsure at first, because having never done this before, I have no idea what I am doing. But he makes me feel so sexy that I begin to rock like I have done this for years, and by the look on his face, I am doing it right.

"Fuck, Bella, you look perfect bouncing on my cock," he grits out, his eyes hooded as he looks at me, before he leans forward, taking a nipple into his mouth. The move puts more pressure on my clit. I can feel my temperature rising, and my hips move faster.

"Dante, this feels soooo good," I say to him, my hands now gripping into his hair as I continue to bounce, and my hips move faster and harder. My hair is out and falls all around me and one of his hands reaches up, grabbing it, pulling it behind me, my head naturally following.

His mouth explores my neck, licking and sucking my skin, as his other hand grips onto my ass, pulling me to meet him in our fast-paced rhythm.

"Fuck, Bella, I need you to come." He leans back in his chair, his jaw clenched as he watches me. Both of his hands are now firmly on my hips, gripping onto my skin, moving me back and forth, and whether it is the new move, the way he watches me, or this innate feeling I have inside of me to do everything he asks of me, I feel myself beginning to lose control.

My hands grab onto his shoulders for support as I rock faster and faster until I can't take it anymore, and I let go. His grip on my hips tightens, and he slams me down onto top of him, harder and harder, until he too lets go. His growl mixes with my scream, the two of us grabbing and pulling at the other, the raw need and want for each other growing animalistic before our movements slow and I fall onto his chest, breathless and totally sated.

His hands run up and down my bare back, his lips peppering kisses to the top of my head, and my hair falls all around me and over his hands.

"Are you feeling alright, Little Red?" he asks me, holding me close.

"Never better," I reply, a little lightheaded. It must be all the activity from the past 24 hours, because I start to feel a little dizzy.

He pulls away from me slightly and zips up his trousers before standing up, taking me with him. My arms and legs wrap around him on instinct.

"You like to carry me around, don't you?" I think he likes that he can just pick me up and take me anywhere.

"I look after what's mine, Little Red." I bury my head into him farther, thinking about his words, never having felt safer before in my life. Walking us slowly back over to the bed, he leans over and places me into the sheets. He kisses my breast, and up my chest to my neck, before pulling back and bringing the blankets over my naked body.

"Sleep a little longer, Little Red. It is still early," he says as he looks into my eyes. "Are you sure you are feeling okay? You look a little pale?" His concern for me is new and welcome, but I begin to worry.

I should tell him.

He looks at me, waiting for me to say something, and I know that this is the time to tell him. To tell him about my lump, about my life being on a timeline, about everything. But as I open my mouth, I can't. I just can't.

"I'm fine. Please don't worry about me. That was the best wakeup call I have ever had," I say with a smile, while on the inside, I am not sure if I am about to faint or throw up. All I can hope is that whichever one is going to happen, it doesn't occur until he is gone. Clearly, I have overdone it again and the bleak reminder starts to haunt me.

"I will see if Maria is feeling better to check on you later," he grumbles before leaning in and kissing my lips, then slowly retreating to the door.

"I'll be seeing you later, Little Red," he whispers.

"Be safe," I reply to him, and he nods before walking out the door.

I lie there in the quiet, taking big breaths, until my heart beats slow. I'm his, I want to be his, but it is all going to be over before it really begins. I already am feeling my body going. I'm always tired, and my appetite is no longer as ravenous as before. I feel the cold more than ever.

I feel terrible not sharing it all with him, but I am in bliss with him. For the first time in my life, I feel what it means to want someone and them want you.

I know Dante told me to relax, but I need a shower and something to eat. Because if this feeling doesn't subside soon, then Dante is going to know something is wrong.

26

DANTE

I walk out of the bedroom door, leaving Little Red in bed wrapped up in my sheets and wishing that I can lie there with her. Her sweet naked body wrapped around mine is all I will think about today.

Her move to straddle me on the armchair this morning surprised me, and I am glad to see her coming out of her shell a little more. She must be feeling more comfortable, and I do like this confidence that she has, especially when I get to start my day with her on top of me or her mouth on me.

But as I walk out my front door and make my way down the quiet hallways to our conference room to meet the boys, I still feel like something is not right. She was pale this morning when I tucked her in. I quickly pull out my phone and send a quick text to Maria to see if she can check up on Annie this morning. Perhaps it was because she is tired and hasn't eaten yet this morning, but I have a niggling doubt in my head that is starting to fester, and I feel like she is keeping something from me. Something she knows I won't like.

I meet Sebastian in the hallway, and watch him as he rubs his eyes, clearly having had a late night.

"I fucking hate getting up early and leaving Goldie in bed," he grumbles to me, and while 6am is not too early, I am beginning to understand what he means.

"Well, she is your weakness, you know that," I say to him as we continue to walk together. I never thought I would see the day that my best friend fell in love, and it has been a privilege to watch. Growing up, we never really saw a happy marriage, all of them arranged and merely business transactions. But when Sebastian spotted Goldie, it was game over for him, and now all he does is grumble when he is away from her. A feeling that I am discovering in myself.

"You will see, brother, you will see," he says to me with a knowing smile as he takes a sip of his morning coffee.

We walk into the conference room and see both Carter and Nico having an animated discussion about one of Carter's upcoming fights, and Sebastian and I take a seat, watching them.

"You really should. You get calls about it all the time!" Nico says, obviously trying to convince Carter to go pro, but we know he will never do that. Nico has a good business mind, and I can see the wheels in his head turning, thinking about managing Carter to become a world-renowned MMA fighter, which he is more than capable of being.

But underground fighting is what he enjoys. Carter loves to walk on the wild side; he doesn't like restrictions, rules, or anyone telling him what to do. He is a tough motherfucker who had a bad upbringing and a rough start at life, and he is now taking out his anger on the poor suckers who think fighting with him in a warehouse, on a cold concrete floor, in the darkness of night is a good aspiration to have.

"Fuck going pro. Do you know how much money you make me, Carter!" Sebastian chimes in, now grinning like the Cheshire Cat, because it's true. Sebastian and I have made a lot of money from Carter's fights. We never bet against him. He wins every time. I feel sorry for the poor guys who step into the ring with him, because I would never want to.

"When is your next fight?" I ask him, knowing he always has one lined up.

"Not sure. We need to find this asshole first, because I want the family safe before I step back into the ring," Carter says, sobering the room.

I nod to him in admiration that he puts the family in front of himself. We all do it, but it was how Sebastian and I were raised. Carter is different, but no less part of our family, and he shows us his commitment each and every day.

"How is Annie, anyway?" Carter asks, and all three of them look at me. Sebastian has a sly smile, clearly reading me like a book.

"She is fine," I reply, not really wanting to elaborate.

"Just *fine*?" Carter presses, trying to goad me into

biting. Clearly, he needs to fight if he is trying to pick one with me.

"Why don't we talk about your woman for a moment, shall we, Carter?" I say to him, willing to entertain him this once. Carter doesn't have a woman and has never had anyone serious, but I like to tease him, regardless.

"Oh, so Annie is your woman now?" Carter asks with an eyebrow raise, quick to pick up my words and slam them back into my face. He is good at it. Due to his history of growing up on the streets, he had to hustle, had to learn to sway things his way in order to survive.

"Let's get to work," I say gruffly, changing the subject, and Carter laughs, shaking his head, knowing he won this battle. He and Nico sit down, and we get busy, strategizing about how to get Dominic and put an end to this shitshow of a situation.

Later that day, I am in my office, going through the list of new soldiers that are coming to New York. Tension is high because we need men, and we are very selective on who we take. But given the trouble we are having at the moment with trying to find Dominic, and needing manpower now more than ever, I have to broaden our scope and take in men who I am not confident are ready for the challenge.

I am tired, stressed, and keep thinking about Little Red on my lap this morning and how much I want a repeat. I haven't seen her today. After the boys and I worked out a new plan, Nico and Carter went out with the team to put the wheels in motion, and Sebastian needed to go and help Goldie at her gallery.

I came back to a quiet house earlier this afternoon, and went to the bedroom to check on her, finding her still in bed, asleep. She sleeps a lot, and while I know our nighttime activities have increased, I am still not sure that is the sole reason for why she is so tired. I sat and watched her for a moment, to see if she woke from her nap, but her sleep was so deep, she didn't even toss or turn, so I left her and have now been in my office for hours.

I need to get things moving because everything feels too slow at the moment. Dominic laying low has really put us out of our ordinary flow. We like to get things done quickly. He is smart, though. He knows how we operate, so by going into hiding and not being available to us, he is slowing us right down, and it is irritating us all. Just when we think we have found him, things change at the last minute. He is sly like that, and I know that wherever he is, he is enjoying toying with us. I look forward to catching him and showing him exactly what I think of him.

I flick through page after page of resumes for soldiers, some from the US, some from Sicily, some have skills, others go straight into the trash. As the pile in the trash gets bigger, I grow more and more frustrated. Standing up, I throw the papers across the room.

"Fuck!" I yell to myself, my temper shorter than normal.

As I pace the office, trying to calm myself, I hear the TV from the movie room. It's soundproof, so whoever is in there must have kept the door open. Now that I hear music and talking, I can no longer concentrate. Already in a terrible mood, I stalk out of my office, ready to yell at someone.

But as I walk through the movie room door, I stop short.

"What the hell is going on in here?"

27

ANNIE

I ventured into the theater room later this afternoon after waking from my nap, and although I know next to zero about tech, I managed to get the system to work. Scrolling through the movies, I finally land on the one I want. I get some throw rugs and cushions and make a cute little picnic area.

While Leo is still quietly playing in his room and Dante is working down the hall in his office, I head to the kitchen and make some popcorn—a request I put onto the grocery list I made for Maria a few days ago. I grab the soda from the refrigerator, along with some glasses, and go back to the movie room to finish setting up my special picnic surprise.

Happy with the set-up, I walk down to Leo's room.

"Leo! I have a surprise for you!" I singsong to him, and he looks at me with a wide smile. "You need to close your eyes and take my hand, okay?" He doesn't hesitate, grabbing my hand in his, and I can see the joy and excitement on his face.

Holding hands, I lead him out of his room and back down the hall, and take him into the movie room.

"Ta-da! Open your eyes!" I announce, his eyes opening wide at the sight before him. He takes in the room, the rugs and cushions, and the popcorn and sodas. He then spots the Lego movie on the screen, and his smile grows to take up his whole face.

"I thought we could have a movie afternoon!" I say joyfully, knowing that although Dante and Maria love him, they would never have done something like this.

"Come on, let's get comfy." We make our way to the cushion floor mound I have made with the blankets, which are a staple for me right now as I am always cold. We submerge ourselves in the billowy softness, and I press play as we begin to watch the movie and eat our snacks.

As the movie begins, Leo stretches and grabs the remote to turn it up, wanting the full movie experience. We devour the popcorn and Leo drinks his soda in record time. I am not looking forward to the sugar rush later.

"What the hell is going on?" I hear Dante ask from behind us, and we sit up quickly. He is not angry but certainly surprised, amused almost, looking around the room like he hasn't seen it before. I follow his gaze; it is like a magical kingdom and not his sleek theatre room it was mere hours ago. Dante struts over to the remote and pauses the film. Obviously, it was too loud and he could hear in in his office

"Daaaad!" Leo says in complaint, and we all stop.

Leo just spoke.

My eyes widen, and I gasp as I gape at Leo. The three

of us are still, not quite believing what just happened. I force myself to breathe and a small smile graces my lips as my eyes begin to water.

Leo is still, his eyes wide, a mirror image of his dad.

"Leo?" Dante says quietly, coming closer to Leo, bending down on one knee on the floor in front of him so they are eye to eye. Dante reaches for Leo's hand, the two of them looking at each other, Dante in awe, Leo a little startled, both in total shock.

"Can you talk again, son?" Dante asks, almost pleading, as he can't quite believe what just happened. He grabs Leo's shoulder, and Dante's eyes begin to water as well.

Leo looks at me, and I smile wide and nod to him, trying not to let the tears fall, not wanting to ruin the moment and giving him the reassurance he is asking for.

"Dad?" he says timidly, his voice a little croaky from lack of use, but otherwise, all normal. It's the sweetest sound I've ever heard.

"Leo. You can... you can talk..." Dante stammers, shock still evident as he grabs Leo and pulls him to his chest. My heart swells. I have studied every textbook I could find. I scoured the internet, read articles, used different techniques from talking constantly, to reading to him, playing with him, and doing generally anything I knew how to, to make him feel safe and secure in my presence. I have spent every day with him since I got here, and I have noticed each time he experiences something new, he opens up more and more. My banter at Lego time, my soft singing at nighttime, my cooking with him and Maria. Whatever it was, I made sure to include

him, speak to him, and care for him. The movie afternoon was another first. I thought we could make this a
weekly tradition, so he could hear different characters,
and to expand his vocabulary.

To hear him speak is overwhelming. Tears burn my
eyes, watching this father and son. Dante doesn't let him
go, as they hug each other tight. I can hear Dante whispering to him while rubbing his back. "I love you, Leo.
Your voice is beautiful, my son." My heart is about to
explode from my chest as I see Leo's head nodding every
few moments, agreeing with Dante. It is a big moment for
them both. Dante is right; Leo's voice is beautiful. It is
wonderful to hear it, and watching the two of them
together makes me feel even more connected, and like I
am right where I need to be.

I turn and start to tidy up our mess a little, trying to
give them some privacy, running our empty glasses back
to the kitchen. When I return, I see them both now apart
and smiling.

"Hey, did you talk your dad into watching the movie
with us, Leo? I could try, but I think you would be more
convincing!" I say with a big smile and look at Dante as
he eyes me walking back to them. Leo is now settling
back in our comfortable rug area, ready to start the movie
again. Dante takes two steps forward to meet me, before
he grabs me by the waist and pulls me to his body, slamming his lips to mine. I gasp in shock at the sudden move,
which Dante takes full advantage of, his tongue slipping
into my mouth and his hand coming up to the back of my
head to keep me in place.

I grip onto his shirt, and my body melts into him,

letting him lead, allowing him to take what he needs. I'm lost in a sea of lust for this man. Leo giggles then, and we pull apart, both of us looking down, forgetting that we had an audience, and I blush.

Dante starts laughing too, and I am caught off guard, having never seen or heard him laugh until now. He looks happy, totally and unashamedly happy, his eyes glistening and his smile wide. He seems lighter, more relaxed. I watch as he and Leo giggle so much it is contagious, and I join in.

"What are you all laughing at?" Maria asks as she steps into the room, and before anyone can answer, Leo speaks.

"Hi, Maria!" he says. Again, he stumbles a little, but the look on Maria's face is priceless.

"Leo!" she says, clutching her chest, her eyes instantly watering. "Oh my God!"

Her disbelief shows on her face as her eyes flick from Leo, Dante, and to me.

"Leo, you're talking!" she says before rushing over and pulling little Leo to her chest.

"Yes. Leo can talk," Dante, says giving me a squeeze. His life has just changed for the better, and there is no wiping the smile from his face now.

Dante looks at me, his hands caressing up and down my arms, before he lifts one and runs it through my hair, bringing me toward him.

"Thank you, Bella. Thank you for getting my son back to me," he whispers to me, kissing me again, before murmuring his thanks in my ear as he peppers kisses down my cheek and neck.

I don't need any thanks, but I feel incredible. The look on Dante's face will forever be embedded into my heart.

Maybe this was my one true calling... Maybe this was what I was put on the earth to do before my soul leaves it forever. I am so glad that I got to experience this, and in some small way help make it happen. I can leave this earth happy now. Happy that I got to make a difference and help my two beautiful boys.

28

DANTE

As Sebastian and I drive through the streets, my mind flicks to thoughts of home. It has been a week since I had my first taste of Little Red, and I am addicted, just like I knew I would be.

I do not wish ill of anyone in my family, but the fact that Maria has been sick in bed with the flu has provided me with the best week of my life. With Maria out of action, Little Red has been taking care of everything, stepping up to the plate in a way that she wasn't asked to, but instinctively knew we needed.

Her cooking is on par with Maria's, which is saying something because Maria's cooking is the best in Sicily. She looks after Leo, the two of them now sharing a bond that is stronger than any other he has made in his short life. I have now heard him giggle and speak on more than one occasion, and it is a sound that lights up my home in a way it hasn't been lit before.

She brings me coffee every morning, pours me a whiskey every night, and I can't keep my hands off her.

We have sex every morning and every night, missionary, her on top, in the bed, in the armchair, in the shower. I even had her naked body spread out on my desk in my den again one night, where I took great delight in fucking her until she screamed. Twice.

I can't get enough of her, and she can't get enough of me. But something still isn't right. She is pale, she is constantly tired, her body is often cold. She could be worn out from our daily activities, but still, there is something that doesn't make sense.

"Dante!" Sebastian growls at me, and I look at him sharply.

"I don't know what kind of magic pussy Annie has, but I need you to focus," he says to me, and he is right. My nostrils flare because I don't like anyone talking about Little Red like that, but I will let it slide for Sebastian.

"Sebastian..." I reply in warning.

"I know, but we need to fucking find him. Leo and Annie are pretty much on total lockdown, and Goldie and her mother too. I know you might be having a fucking fantastic home life in your newly-mated haze, but Goldie is busting my balls every minute, wanting to get to her fucking gallery without me hovering over her head. If we can't make this city safe for our families, then we are failing them. We need to fucking find Dominic and end him."

"Dominic is a fucking dirty rat who is currently living in the deep squalor of New York, waiting to pounce. The minute he does, I am going to kill him. Preferably painfully and slowly," I grit out, making it known that my head is still firmly on my shoulders, and I know what needs to get done.

We sit in silence for a moment, and I decide to let him know about Leo. I have waited all week, wanting to make sure it wasn't just a one off, but he continues to flourish, so there is no point hiding it from my brother anymore.

"Leo is talking," I say calmly, even though I want to fist bump the air every time I think about it.

"What the fuck?" Sebastians says leaning back looking at me like I have grown a second head. "What the fuck are you talking about?"

"Leo has been talking. He is getting better and better every day. He and Annie fucking chat all day every day about God knows what shit. She got him talking. My girl got my son to fucking talk," I tell him, bursting with pride and love for the two of them.

"When, how, what? That is amazing!" Sebastian clears his throat, overcome with emotion, just like I have been. "I need to see my godson. I want to hear his voice."

"She is good for you, you know. I wasn't sure you were ever going to open up to anyone after Angelina, but Annie is your match. I can see it. She is good for you and Leo. She is welcome into the family." I drive in silent shock for a moment. We haven't talked too much about Little Red and I, and although she has been living with me for the better part of a few months now, I thought I was keeping our activities and my feelings about her on the down-low. However, Sebastian's approval and welcoming of her into the fold is a big deal, and I am grateful.

"Thank you, brother," I reply after a moment, looking

at him and nodding my head. He nods to me in return, and we refocus on our task for today.

"Now let's get this slimy bastard so we can both go home and fuck our women. Dominic has made threats against us, against our families, and we need to fucking find him." Sebastian, like the rest of us, is frustrated. The pressure on us continues to build each day that he can't be found, the other families still asking questions.

"We need to work out what he is planning. We killed his best men and his brother. His attack on us is going to be brutal if we don't get to him first," Sebastian looks out the window at the passing shops as I drive us to Queens.

"If today doesn't flush him out, then we need to regroup. Carter is following some intel today back at the compound, so hopefully he finds something too," I offer, even though I'm going to be even more pissed if we have to settle for intel instead of his dead body when we leave today.

The car weaves through the streets until we come to a stop outside Allure. I have been to this shithole more times in the past few months than ever before, and the sooner I can leave it all behind, the better I will feel. It is still a heap of crap, nothing renovated, nothing cleaned. As I survey the streetscape, I can clearly see the spot where I threw Little Red down onto the pavement that first day and that is the only good thing this place has going for it.

Sebastian and I step out of the car, standing tall in the street, showcasing ourselves to anyone who may be watching. In the bright afternoon sun, we are hoping that a visit during the day, when everyone can see us, may be the way to draw Dominic out. Sure, we have our people planted all around the streets and inside, and we are fully armed and ready to kill on sight, but if Dominic is watching, then he'll see it as his chance to kill us both.

Offering ourselves up like lambs to the slaughter is not anything new. We have put our own lives on the line before and we are not afraid. We stop on the sidewalk and look around, taking our time, seeing no one, nothing, the street quiet, eerily so. My skin prickles and I have a feeling that something isn't right. Looking at Sebastian, I can tell he feels it too, but we turn and walk into Allure like we are paying customers.

Stepping inside, things look like they usually would for this time of the day. There are a few patrons sprinkled around the tables, and I spot some of our team undercover around the place. Music is playing through the speakers as women dance on the stage and the smoke haze filling the room is enough to make my eyes sting. My shoes stick to the floor, the peel with every step I take irritating me even more.

As Sebastian and I walk to the bar, all eyes are on us, and I don't miss the sly grins we are receiving from some of the men in the room, like they know something we don't. That uneasy feeling I had outside multiplies.

We brought our best team with us, which means that our compound is now secured by our new young soldiers, and Carter is the only one still there with them. He stayed behind, locking himself in the office, looking at computer files, needing the quiet to piece together the data that might help us find this asshole if we don't on our own.

We reach the bar and lean on it, and I look briefly at the women who are in different states of undress dancing on the stage. Cheap sequin outfits, high heels and tassels abound, and I notice my ex-wife is not here. At least that is one thing I don't need to worry about today. Her calls are now incessant, so much so, I no longer answer her, especially after Leo hearing me yell at her. Something I still feel guilty about.

We stand at the bar, surveying the room, both feeling uneasy. I look at the barman who is currently polishing glasses down at the other end. He is an older guy who has been around for years, never causes trouble, and is always neutral in our activities. He nods to me as he comes closer. I turn to face him, leaning my arms on the sticky bar as he stands in front of me.

"I have a message for you," he states, and I nod for him to continue as Sebastian tenses next to me, his anger permeating from his body. The barman moves his hand, and Sebastian and I immediately do the same, our fingers itching to grab our guns, but instead of pulling a gun, the barman pulls out a note and slides it across the bar. Nodding again, he walks back down to the other end of the bar and continues polishing the glasses.

I grab the folded piece of paper he passed to me, wondering what the fuck is going on. As I look down at the words written, the scrawling handwriting just as messy as this fucking bar, my face drops, my scowl now all but gone and my body rigid as I read it.

"The boy belongs with his momma, and the redhead, I will keep just for fun."

29

ANNIE

I stifle a yawn as I mix the Bolognese on the stovetop. Leo is sitting at the kitchen bench, content with his Lego pieces, trying to skillfully make a small rocket, another one to add to his collection, while keeping me company. I'm tired. More so than usual. I don't know if my health is starting to fail me, or if it is all the extra physical activity I have been doing with Dante. A smile appears on my face at the thought of him as butterflies dance in my tummy.

This past week has been like nothing I could have ever imagined. On the one hand, it has been extremely domesticated, because with Maria unwell, I have been looking after the house and my boys and I love it. The cooking, spending time with Leo, looking after Dante's needs, it has come to me very naturally, my caretaking role one I feel I was made for. On the other hand, the amount of pleasure I have given and received is more than I ever thought I would have in my lifetime. My cheeks heat as I think about lying naked on Dante's office desk just a night or two ago, and how much I love his hands on my body, and how I am enjoying everything he is teaching me. It has been so amazing, I keep forgetting that I am on a timeline, until times like this when I feel more tired than usual and my body aches more than it should.

As the house fills with aromas of basil, there is movement at the door, and I am surprised to hear Dante home already as he only left an hour or so ago. Turning the stove off, I wipe my hands on the towel and walk to the other side of the kitchen to where Leo is, as we both turn and smile, evidence of our combined joy at seeing Dante back earlier than we expected.

But it isn't Dante. It is a woman who staggers into the house looking disheveled. She has two burly men following her, and my heart rate immediately rises.

"Ahhh, can I help you?" I ask her, nerves evident in my tone as my eyes flick between her and the two men, wondering who they are and why they are here. I'm not sure if she is someone who works with Dante's team, or perhaps someone from Sebastian's wing. My head jerks back to little Leo when I hear his Lego spaceship fall onto the floor, smashing into tiny pieces, which skit across in every direction, and I hear him gasp. Looking down at him, I notice his eyes are as big as saucers as he looks at the woman, his breathing speeds up, and his hand grabs onto mine as tight as a vice before he slides off the kitchen stool and stands so close to me that we could be conjoined.

"Leo?" I ask gently, sensing the fear in his body. Now I am even more concerned.

"LEO!" The woman shouts, and both Leo and I jump. My head flicks back in her direction, my eyes wide in surprise. As I stare back at her, trying to work out what is going on, she looks between the both of us, seeming agitated. Leo continues to shuffle closer to me, and I instinctively put my arm around him and tuck him into my side.

"GET YOUR FUCKING HANDS OFF MY SON!" she screams at me, and I jump again at her sudden explosion, taking a small step back until my body hits the kitchen bench. Realization dawns on me that this is Leo's mother, and my eyes widen as my heart rate increases. Looking at her, as she stands mere feet away from us, I notice she is swaying on her feet, her hair is oily and unkept, and her body is covered in bruises and scabs. It is clear she is not lucid. What she is under the influence of, I don't know, but it is more than alcohol, of that much, I am sure.

"It's oka—" I start to say, but she cuts me off as I bring one hand up, my palm facing her.

"It is not fucking okay!" she screams, and again, I jump, pulling Leo even closer to me as he starts to whimper into my side. My eyes flick to the front door, wondering where the hell Dante's team are. They are all usually close by, but not today, it appears.

Looking back at her, I take in her full appearance. Tight black shiny shorts that hide nothing, and a black halter top, which stops short of covering her torso, and I can see her skinny frame underneath. There is nothing of her; I can see her rib bones.

"What do you want?" I ask her tentatively, trying to keep her talking to give me more time to think of a way out of this situation. Leo and I could run, barricade ourselves in one of the rooms, but we won't be fast enough to outrun them all. The two men have already positioned themselves on either side of her, clearly anticipating that option, so I immediately look around for other clues that may help us escape.

"I want my fucking son!" she screams again, and I know that she is not stable at all. Her words are slurred, her eyes are hazy, and there is absolutely no way that Leo is going anywhere near her. Whether she is his birth mother or not. I am not sure of their history, but I can't imagine Dante ever being married to someone like this. I look at Leo again, and he is hiding his face into my t-shirt. I increase my hold on him, silently telling him that he isn't going anywhere.

Feelings of how my own mother treated me begin to filter through my mind, like a rolodex of memories that flash from her slurred words, her stingy hatred, her venom when she didn't get what she wanted. The anxiousness that had left my body the moment I arrived here in New York floods through my system, my palms sweating, and if it wasn't for this little boy gripping onto me so tightly, I would be totally losing it right now.

"I'm sure if you just wait for Dante..." I start to say again, feeling so out of my depth here that I am not sure what to do.

"Who the hell do you think you are?" she sneers at me as she looks around the house. "Are you the nanny, or the housekeeper? Did he finally get rid of that old bag Maria? I know you can't be fucking him because he never brings a woman into his house." She eyes me suspiciously. Looking at her, I still cannot quite believe this is happening. "Do you think he cares? Do you really think a man like Dante Luciano cares about someone like you?" Her voice is cunning now, almost threatening. "He doesn't care about you! NOW GET YOUR FUCKING HANDS OFF MY SON!" she screams again as she begins to pace in front of us.

I look around me to try and find something to defend myself because she is acting unhinged. There is nothing, the house spotless. The benches and floor are so clean and tidy you could eat off them. There isn't a lamp, a broom stick, nothing I can grab that may buy us more time. I am too far away from any of the kitchen utensils and the bench is clear except for some of Leo's Lego pieces.

I hear Leo whimper again and feel something cold. Looking down, I see that his jeans are a darker shade down the leg, and wet against my leg, his little body shaking next to mine. It makes me angry, and as scared as I am, I realize that I am the only person here who can protect him.

"No," I say firmly, and she stops pacing to stare at me, her glassy eyes piercing mine, as her lips scowl.

"No?" she asks me, as if she is toying with me, but I remain firm.

"No. He does not want to go with you," I state, standing as tall as I can, trying to feign the confidence I don't have.

She begins to cackle, laughing at me as her head tilts to one side, looking totally psychotic. I hear a small click then and hold my breath as I notice for the first time since she walked in the door that she has a gun in her hand. The shiny silver metal looks new and unused as she raises it in front of her body, pointing it directly at me.

"Give me my fucking son, or I will shoot you in the fucking head, you fucking bitch." She sways on her feet, and I have no doubt that my time is about to be up. All I can hope for is that the sound of the gun shot will be loud enough to get someone's attention so they come in time to save Leo.

"Well, you better pull the trigger because I am not letting him anywhere near you." My mind is made up. I have no weapon, I have no physical ability to run at her and escape, and no guards are coming to our aid. If my body is the thing that saves Leo, then so be it.

Leo begins to cry, his tears and loud whimpers increasing in volume, and my heart breaks for this little boy.

I look right at her as I pull Leo behind me, my body protecting him like a shield, because I know what is coming. I see her begin to smile as her finger tightens on the gun and she pulls the trigger, just as some men storm through the front door, firing in her direction.

But I see and hear nothing more, the burn through my chest instant, my body pushed back, thumping against the kitchen bench before it slides onto the floor in a pool of vibrant red.

30

DANTE

I meet Carter and the crew in the hallway—where the fuck they have been I have no idea. But I have little time to worry about it now until I know Leo and Annie are safe. I push through my front door and my heart immediately stops beating. There, in my living room, is my ex-wife, along with two men. Angelina's gun is raised, and as I walk farther into the house, I see that she is aiming it right at Annie, who is shielding Leo with her body. The two men both pull their guns as they see us come through the door, but my team and I don't hesitate, and I pull my gun, walking straight toward Angelina.

"Put it down, Angelina!" I yell out to her. The two men have turned, training their guns on me and my team, who now surround the space behind me.

She looks my way and smiles an evil smile, and in that split second, she pulls the trigger. Disbelief washes over me as Carter is beside me in a flash and doesn't hesitate. He pulls his gun and shoots her just as she is about to turn the gun on us.

"Annie!!" I scream as I watch her small body take the bullet into the top of her chest and slam backwards into the kitchen bench, falling to the floor on top of Leo. This can't fucking be happening. I run straight to them, not caring about the bullets that are still flying in all directions as Carter and Sebastian take care of the other two men.

My heart thumps as I drop to my knees, pulling Leo out from under Annie's body where he is a shaking mess, but alive and physically unharmed. His small hand is still clutching onto Annie's as I look down at her limp body. I rip my shirt off and push it tightly into the gunshot wound in her chest, praying that it missed her heart. There is blood all around her, and I feel it seeping into my jeans.

"C'mon, Annie. Fuck!" I yell as anger, stress, and fear sweeps through my body, and my fingers press on her neck. I feel her pulse which is still strong and see the rise and fall of her chest so I know she is still alive.

"Stay with me, Little Red. Fucking stay with me," I demand of her as I put pressure on her wound, the blood loss is so severe I feel the dampness seeping through the ripped fabric of my shirt and onto my hands.

"Annie?" Leo says in his small quivering voice, breaking my heart in two as he starts to sob next to me. I have waited years to hear his voice and to hear it now pained cuts me to my core.

"Fuck," Sebastian says as he comes and kneels next to me. Grabbing Leo, he tucks him into his side, a move not dissimilar to the hold I saw Little Red have on him moments ago when I stormed through the door.

"Doctors are on their way up. I will call an ambulance!" Carter yells from behind me, and I can barely hear him from the thumping in my chest that is vibrating around my body.

She protected my boy... she protected my little boy with her own body. I look at my son, who's now standing next to me. "It will be okay, Leo, it will be okay." Tears streak his cheeks as his little hands cling onto Sebastian white-knuckled, trying to remain strong. The words I say I drill into my own mind as well as I look back at Annie whose skin is even more pale than usual.

"She is losing too much blood," I grit out to Sebastian, before I realize that the gunfire has stopped, and the room is full of activity as our doctors rush in.

"She needs a hospital," our doctors order, already scurrying about, getting bandages out of their kits and applying pressure onto the wound.

"It's a gunshot. Can't you treat her here?" Sebastian asks quickly.

"She is losing too much blood. She needs to go now," they reply as they work around me, checking her vitals and trying to stem the flow of blood, even though my hands are still firmly on her chest.

"Ambulance is on its way," Carter announces as he comes up to us, phone still in his hand. Sebastian nods, not happy that our mess will be now made public but understanding that we need to do what is right.

I haven't moved from my position. My hands, now tainted red, remain on Little Red's body as the doctors continue to administer medication and take her vitals. He face is growing paler, with little splatters of red like freckles across her cheeks, and I wipe them away with my thumb.

"Fuck, Annie, hang on. Please just fucking hang on," I beg her, and I hear Leo whimpering beside me. He has seen so much, this little boy of mine, and the guilt I carry for his life being exposed to this shit builds inside of me daily. He has seen more in his young lifetime than many see in decades. How he will get over this, I have no idea.

For his own mother to walk in and fire her gun at a woman who was protecting her own son... my brain is incapable of understanding any of it right now as I continue to beg Annie to stay with us.

Annie's body starts to convulse as she coughs a little before her eyes open into small slits.

"Dante?" she whispers out.

"I'm here, Little Red. Don't worry, you're going to be okay. Everything will be okay," I say as I kiss her forehead, my voice falling onto her skin as I try to believe it myself.

"Leo?" she asks about my son, even now as her body lays broken, and he rushes to her, burying his head into her shoulder.

"Annie?" Leo says again, sobbing into her shoulder, asking her in his own way if she is okay.

"It's okay, Leo," she whispers to him. "It is all okay." She's giving him the support he needs, her continued thoughts of others during this time astounding me.

"Ambulance is here, Dante. You need to move to the side," the doctor says to me as paramedics fill the room with their stretcher. But I don't want to move. I am too scared to move my hands for fear she will leave me.

"Dante! Move!" Sebastian yells at me, trying to shock

me from my haze, and it works. I lean back and remove my hands, looking at Little Red as her eyes close again the minute my hands leave her body. A small smile stays on her lips as she falls unconscious from the blood loss.

"Red?" I say to her, already knowing that she is out but hoping that she comes back to me. I stand back as the medics take care of her, feeling useless and extreme shame and responsibility that this happened to her, in my house, by the hand of my ex-wife.

I notice Sebastian on his phone, no doubt already talking with the police chief to keep this off the record. Carter and our men form a barricade around the three other bodies on my living room floor, ensuring that no one sees them there. The less they know, the better for everyone.

Little Red is picked up and wheeled out of the room. I follow along with her as they wheel her out of the house and down the hallways to the outside. Carter and Sebastian grab Leo and follow me, leading him out of the house, ensuring he doesn't see the mess that we made, shielding his eyes from his mother as she lies dead.

Outside, in the bright light of the day, I grip onto her hand before I need to let go, so they can put her in the back.

As they do, I lean down to Leo. "It will be okay, Leo. Stay here with Sebastian. I am going with Annie to help her at the hospital. She will be okay," I say, before kissing his head and rushing to jump in the back of the ambulance with Annie. Sitting next to her and gripping her hand in mine once more.

31

ANNIE

The constant beeping in my ear rouses me as I stretch out my legs and roll my head away from the bright light. Slowly opening my eyes, I groan as I wake and feel slight pain in my shoulder. I am in a room that is not familiar, and as my eyes begin to focus, the beeping noise gets a little faster.

My eyes search the room as I try to get my bearings. I have no idea where I am, and I look for clues as I observe the white walls, bright lights, and scratchy linen underneath me. Taking a breath in, I get the whiff of strong disinfectant that travels up my nostrils, burning the hairs slightly, and I swallow hard, trying to encourage moisture to my dry throat.

"Red?" his voice echoes around the empty room, and I immediately feel safe.

"Dante?" I say, as I try to turn my head to meet his voice, but it comes out scratchy and hoarse from lack of use.

"Here," he says gruffly, his tone not warm and inviting

as it usually is, and I spot him leaning farther away against a wall. I watch him walk across the room and pour me a glass of water from a jug that is sitting on a small table nearby, before walking it over to me. His eyes are steely as they look at me, his face set.

"What happened?" I ask him, my brain slowly waking as I try to sit up and take the water from him.

"My ex-wife Angelina shot you in the chest when she came to the house yesterday. You came to the hospital, had an operation to remove the bullet, and now you are in the ward recovering." He's so matter-of-fact, and I can't get past how his voice no longer feels like the familiar warm hug I remember, but distant and cold. So much so, my body shivers under the featherlight white hospital gown I am wearing.

"What's wrong?" I ask him, but his lips press together. He is clearly unhappy.

"Oh good, she is awake," a doctor says as she walks in the door, interrupting our moment. She is stunning, dressed in a crisp white medical coat, her hair long and glossy, her face immaculate in perfect makeup, as she walks up to my bed and begins to look over my chart.

"You are a very lucky woman, Miss Peterson. I'm Dr. Wakeford. I have been looking after you since you came in the ambulance yesterday. Tell me, what do you remember?" she asks me, looking at me with caring eyes, the type I expected from Dante who is now back across the room, leaning against the wall, his arms crossed over his chest, jaw clenching. He couldn't get farther away from me if he tried.

My eyes dart between him and the doctor.

"She is trusted, Red. You can tell her," Dante grits out to me, and my eyes widen, still shocked at his tone.

"Ahh... well, I remember being at home..." I start, but don't miss the cracking noise that comes from Dante as he moves his head from side to side. Why is he so angry?

"Umm, and then Leo's mother came in..." My eyes widen, and I sit up. "Leo?" I say in a panicked tone.

"He is fine, Red," Dante says, softening a little, and I take a breath and relax back down against my pillow.

"Go on," the doctor says as she records my pulse and listens to my recollection.

"Then she shot me, and that is all I remember," I say as my mind flicks through the mental images that float in my brain of the memory.

"Okay. Well, all your vital signs are good. We had you in surgery yesterday. The bullet went into your right upper chest, between your breast and shoulder. We managed to remove the bullet. You were very lucky, as it missed your main artery and was easy to remove," Doctor Wakeford says, and I nod as I take in her prognoses.

"While we had you in surgery to remove the bullet, we ran some scans and they showed a mass in your right breast. Were you aware of the lump, Miss Peterson?" she asks me, and my breath gets caught in my throat. I look at Dante, whose eyes are laser-focused on me, and the penny drops. He knows. The beeping on the monitor quickens, and Dante clenches his jaw.

"Yes," I whisper to the doctor, all the while looking at Dante, and I see his face visibly contort with rage at my confession.

"Does breast cancer run in your family, Annie?" the

doctor asks, grabbing my hand. Tears fall from my eyes as I watch Dante, who is now standing tall and seems even more distant. He knows I lied to him... he knows I kept this from him.

"Yes, my mother passed away a few months ago from it," I barely whisper, my heart thumping in my chest. His body isn't moving, but I know he is retreating. He is removing me from his heart. I can see it, I can feel it, and my heart is beginning to break because of it.

"Okay, well, we have removed the mass and sent that off for testing, and we should have the results later today. I had a look around at your lymph nodes and other areas, and I couldn't see any other masses or any other issues. I will talk to you later once we have the results and we'll work out a plan of action after that. I will organize the nurses to come in now and help you with a shower and something to eat. Rest up, and I will be back later today," she says to me with a small smile, but I can't look at her, my eyes filling with more tears as I stare at Dante. I can feel his anger permeating from his body. The doctor looks from me to Dante and back again before patting my hand and walking out of the room.

"Dante..." I begin to speak, but he cuts me off.

"You fucking lied to me, Red. I asked you, time and time again. We spoke about your mom, your past, and not once did you mention having a fucking lump in your body. All I ask from people is honesty. All I wanted was for you to tell me the goddamn truth!" His voice rises as he begins to pace the room at the foot of my bed.

"I'm sorry. I'm so sorry," I cry out, tears now falling freely, my weakened voice now betraying me because I can't get his attention like I need to. "Dante, please, let me explain." I try and gather my racing thoughts, the drugs in my system doing nothing to help clear my foggy mind.

"I told you I hate liars. I told you that small white lies fester and things get out of control. This is exactly what Angelina did, she lied. Her small lies grew into bigger ones, and because of her, Leo suffered. I told you, Annie, I fucking told you!" I can see the pain and torment in his eyes, and I hate myself for putting it there.

"Dante, please, please, just listen to me. Let me explain," I plead, but I can't even hear myself through my sobs.

"It's too late, Red. I fucking loved you, and you lied. If you can lie about something this big, what else could you keep from me? I don't even know you. You are no better than her," he spits out at me, before throwing my medical file across the room and stalking toward the door.

But all I heard was... *he loved me?* And that's enough to give me the strength to push through my nerves and exhaustion to tell him what I need to. The truth.

"Dante! Please! I was scared to tell you. I was scared that you would treat me differently, that you wouldn't want me once you knew!" I plead out to him, my hands trembling as I try and sit up. I reach for him, but he is too far away. He stops right near the door, but doesn't look at me.

"Nico is here. He will stand guard for you while you are here, and then you will be taken to our safehouse until those assholes are caught and it is safe for you to leave," he says, his voice low. "After that, you will be on your own. I don't want liars in my life. Leo doesn't deserve any more of them either. Forget you know us, forget what you saw and heard, and forget what we had, because it all meant nothing."

"Dante! No!" I shout to him, tears running down my cheeks, my heart feeling like the bullet went through it yesterday instead of my shoulder. I try to move, to go to him, but I am trapped onto the bed by a mess of cords and tubes. I feel like my life is ending; right here, right now. Like the minute he walks out the door, it is all over.

"Dante! Please! I love you!" I cry out for him, needing him now more than ever. Admitting my love for him, only to have him look away.

"Goodbye, Red." He flings open the door so hard that it bangs against the wall, leaving a dent in the plaster, and I watch helplessly as his tall frame stalks out of the room. And out of my life.

32

ANNIE

It has been a week since Dante walked out of the hospital room, and I haven't seen him since. I have been here alone, lost in my grief and memories of the past few months, wondering how it all went so wrong.

I have had no visitors aside from the lovely Doctor Wakeford who has become a close confidant. Checking on me twice a day, she's taken great joy in telling me that I didn't actually have breast cancer. It was merely a benign fatty lump, most likely due to a bad diet and a lot of stress from looking after my mother for all those months. Although I am pleased I do not have a body riddled with cancer, I also feel sick to my stomach that hiding the truth from Dante was all for nothing. Had I come clean with him from the start, I could have been checked out and cleared before this even became anything. It is a deep regret that sits heavy in my stomach, making me want to vomit every time I think about it. I was stupid. Stupid to think that a girl like me could have the dream man, dream child, dream house. I was naïve. How quickly it all disappeared, just because I didn't want to face the truth, and took that option away from Dante as well.

Stupid. So stupid.

"Good morning, Annie," Doctor Wakeford says as she walks into the room for her routine morning check-in. "How are you feeling today?" She grabs my files from the end of the bed and looks over the results of the test that the nurses took over night.

"I'm good, Doctor Wakeford," I reply, trying to be cheerful but not feeling it at all. Over the course of the past week, Doctor Wakeford has run additional tests for me to ensure I didn't carry the breast cancer gene or have any other ailments. I have had iron infusions, a steady dose of antibiotics, my stitches removed, and a daily physio to help my shoulder heal, although it is still bandaged, and I need to protect it. But that is not what weighs heavy. My heart is broken, my spirit too. I hate myself, more than ever, and I wish I could crawl up somewhere and hide.

"I think we may be able to discharge you today, Annie!" I should be excited, but I am not. I have no idea where the safehouse is or what to expect.

"Okay," I say quietly, and my eyes travel to the duffle bag containing my life that sits over in the small wardrobe to the side of my hospital bed. Reminding me that I have nothing, I have no one, and I am unwanted.

"The nurses will get you up and dressed, and I will just need you to come back in within the next week or so, so I can check over your shoulder and ensure it is progressing well." I nod to her, as the fear of being alone and eventually out on the streets starts to well into my bones.

Doctor Wakeford looks at me then and pauses. Her eyes flick to the door and she walks a few steps around the bed to talk quietly to me.

"Nico will be taking you to a safe house, Annie. Dante still needs to keep you hidden because there is still a threat, I believe. You will be okay, don't worry." She gives me a small smile and squeezes my hand.

"Okay, thank you," I say on a sigh.

Doctor Wakeford puts the medical files back, and with one last small smile, she walks back out the door, leaving me with my thoughts.

I am devastated that I won't see Leo again, or Maria, and I am heartbroken from the loss of the home I had, albeit for such a small time. I knew he would be angry at me for not being totally honest with him. He said multiple times that he hated liars, yet that is exactly what I did. I lied. Every time he asked me if I was alright, I lied. Every time he asked me if anything was wrong, I lied. During our nighttime chats, there were multiple opportunities for me to talk to him about my health. I could have been honest with him, but I didn't want my perfect bubble to burst. But keeping it all from him has shattered anything we had and any hope of a future with him. Who am I kidding, I am not Little Red, or Annie, I am no one. And I have no one. I have nothing, I am nothing.

The door opens, and I look up quickly, expecting to see the nurses, but it is Nico. We have met briefly, but he stays outside my room each and every day, like a bodyguard. I watch him with interest as he walks in, closing the door behind him.

"Hi, Annie. Today is the day we move you to the safe house," he says quietly, approaching me like I am a dangerous animal and he needs to proceed with caution.

"Okay. I will cause no trouble, Nico. I am sorry you got stuck with me," I say with a soft smile.

"No need to apologize. We will get to hang out together for a little while because I will also be at the house with you. We won't leave you on your own, Annie. Dante has told us you must be 100% protected at all times," he says, smiling as he stands at the end of my bed.

Dante. Just the mention of his name breaks my heart all over again.

"Everyone is on lockdown. Things are getting a little crazy out on the streets because we can't locate the man who is a threat, but Dante, Sebastian, and Carter are all hunting for him, so it is only a matter of time. Then you will be safe."

Nico is nice. A bit younger than the others. His accent is thicker but similar to Dante's.

"What part of Italy are you from?" I ask him. If we are going to be hanging out with each other for a while, I might as well make a friend of him and get to know him a little.

"Ahhh, Sicily, where all good Italian men are from!" he says with a big grin, and I laugh at him. It feels good.

"Tell me about where you grew up? I would love to learn more about Italy." He begins to tell me all about his homeland, and it becomes evident that Sicily is a place loved by many, not just Dante.

The morning flies by quickly and after eating, showering, and having one more check-up by the nurses, I sign a few papers. Then there is nothing left to do except leave. I feel hollow, like a shell of myself. It is the same feeling I had on the plane ride here, when I didn't know what to expect or what I was doing. Nico bends down and grabs my duffle bag. "Come on, Annie, let's go." When I don't move, he nods at me, silently telling me that it will be okay, and slowly, I move, one foot in front of the other, down the hospital halls and out the front entrance. The sunlight burns through the sky, the brightness something I haven't seen in forever. The warm feeling on my body is humming through my skin, and I take a big breath of fresh air.

"This way. We can't stand around outside, we need to move," Nico says, putting a hand at my back and pushing me along at a quicker pace. The stark reality of my situation slams back into my face as my heart rate picks up, and I follow Nico to a black car parked at the curb right out the front of the hospital.

Nico opens the door, and I slip inside, my body sliding on the soft black leather as he gets in beside me. Before the car begins to move, I sit in silence, looking out the window and wondering where the hell my adventure is going to take me next.

33

DANTE

Watching her step out of the hospital, Nico next to her, holding her small duffle bag, my heart feels heavy. Every day, I have had to restrain myself from visiting her, forcing myself into my work and trying my best to ignore the situation. She takes small, unsure steps as the bright light of the day hits her face, and all I want to do is run to her and tuck her into me and never let her go. Nico says something to her, and her eyebrows rise and she walks quickly to the car, but not before I notice his hand touching the small of her back. My grip on the steering wheel tightens, and I push my body back into the car seat, willing myself not to move.

She lied. I can't have liars in my life. I have to protect Leo. Nothing else can happen to him. I continue to tell myself the same things over and over, trying to drill into my brain that she is not the person I thought she was, when really, all I want to do is grab her and hold her tight.

"You like torturing yourself, don't you?" Sebastian

says next to me as he types into his phone, messages to Goldie, no doubt, who like Maria and Leo are ignoring me because I have let Little Red go. The silence that is directed at me in our compound is near stifling and has been going on ever since I left her at the hospital. With no signs of it letting up, I question myself every day, something I have never done before in my life. Especially over a fucking woman.

"I need to make sure she is okay," I grit out, angry at her, angry at myself, angry at the whole fucking world.

"Well, let's fucking find and kill Dominic so you can ship her back to Oklahoma and get on with your life, then," Sebastian says, and I look at him and snarl.

"Yep, thought as much." He rolls his eyes at me, an annoying trait that he picked up from his wife. "Okay, they are moving. Let's go." I look back at the car she just got in, and I start the engine to follow them.

"Why did you move her to the fucking safe house? Of all the places..." Carter chimes in from the backseat, and my eyes flick to him in the mirror.

"Where else should she go?" I grumble back to him, not in the mood for his questions.

"Well, she could have stayed at my place?" Carter says seriously, and I pull on the steering wheel and slam on the brakes before turning in my seat to see him grinning like the cat that got the canary.

"Fucking asshole," I snarl at him, before facing forward and driving again. He goads me on purpose, and if he is not careful, I will punch him in the fucking throat.

"Calm the fuck down, you two," Sebastian growls from the front seat like a parent disciplining his two children. "But I agree with Carter on this one. The fucking safe house is shit. Couldn't you just put her in a spare room at your place and ignore her?"

I huff out at his question. There is no way I could have Little Red in my house and ignore her. That was my original plan and look how it ended up. "It is the safest place for her. No one knows about it, and it is off the books."

Moving her to the safe house is something I should have done the moment I met her. It would have saved me all this fucking heartache and complication that has seeped into my life. The guilt and remorse I feel for having her and Leo attacked in my own fucking home runs deep, as I know it does for both Sebastian and Carter too. The compound is our home. It is the one place our families have always been safe. The fact that it came under attack has made us all feel uneasy and each of us blames ourselves for it happening.

Carter was the contact on site, but due to him being down in the computer room, locked away, reviewing footage and data, he was hard to reach and farther away than usual. Sebastian and I took the whole main team with us to Allure, leaving just the new soldiers behind. A rookie error on our behalf, because they were no match for Angelina who walked right in, claiming to be my wife there to pick up Leo. They just let her walk straight in; no one questioned her, no one wanted to upset the wife of their boss, so assumed she was not dangerous as her and her two men walked into the compound and straight to my place like they had every right to be there. The confidence that rolled off them was astounding, and every night when I watch the security footage over and over again, I still cannot believe that Angelina did it. What is not surprising is that Dominic didn't show his face. Of course, he wouldn't, preferring to leave all the dirty work to others, laying low to extend his life, because he knows I am gunning for him now. There is no coming back from this.

Angelina died of multiple gunshot wounds, something that the team and I are extremely remorseful for. Harming women and children is not what we do, and even in self-defense for one of our own, it is still something that doesn't sit well with us. Her body, along with those of her men, were cremated, and we put her ashes into a lot at the cemetery for Leo. Because I know one day, he will grow up and need a place to reflect and remember.

Our whole team was replaced, shipped back to Sicily for further training, and new soldiers arrived for us to use in the meantime, with strict new protocols in place so nothing like this can ever happen again.

My house is no longer our home. The whole place has been gutted and it is currently nothing but a shell, ready to be remodeled. Leo, Maria, and I are living in another part of the compound, on the other side of Sebastian, with Goldie now taking care of them both while Sebastian and I continue to scour the streets all day and all night, looking for Dominic.

I haven't slept. I can't sleep without Little Red in the house, without Little Red in my bed. Every night, I continue to sit in my armchair, looking at the empty bed, hating myself more and more with each passing moment.

"Where the fuck can he be?"

"We have looked everywhere, my friend. Now we just have to wait," Sebastian says calmly, eerily so, his anger buried deep. Like me, he doesn't take kindly to anyone threatening our family, and we know Dominic has not finished yet. There is no doubt that he put Angelina up to the task of killing Little Red and taking Leo.

The target on Dominic's head grows, because although Sebastian is still being asked questions, the entire fold knows what happened in my home. They now know who was responsible, and tides have turned. Everyone is searching for Dominic, because to have such little respect for the head family means that everyone is in danger of his crazy ways.

I stop the car outside on the street as we watch Nico and Little Red pull into the driveway of our safe house. Positioned on the other side of town, it is small, but secure, and I grind my teeth as I see Nico grab her hand and help her out of the car, her frail body needing his support. I am white-knuckling because I want to run over and pick her up and bring her home with me. My eyes zone in on them both as she takes his arm to steady herself, and they walk down the path and inside the house. Nico turns and gives us a small nod before he closes the door, knowing full well that we were watching.

"We need to get rid of this fucking house," I spit out to Sebastian, and he nods.

"When this is over, we will demolish it and find some-where new," he says, in agreement with me.

I don't like this house, not one bit. It is where I locked Angelina up to get her to dry out a few years ago. Her screams and her tears are still etched into my brain. The nondescript brown brick home is something that fills my nightmares. It is not good enough for Little Red, but at least she will be safe.

"Let's go. You can't sit here like a fucking stalker all day. You either want her or you don't. You can't have it both ways," Sebastian says to me, startling me from my thoughts, and I don't answer him. Instead, I start the car, and without looking back, I drive down the street, making our way to Allure.

Now that everyone in the fold knows exactly what a piece of shit Dominic is, we have more flexibility in what we can do to flush him out and we are starting with Allure. Our team is already there, positioned inside and out, because we are going to annihilate the place. It is a shithole anyway, but we will take everything from their office, smash every glass and mirrored surface, destroy it before we turn it to ash. And I can't wait.

I have so much anger inside my body that I am at breaking point. Leo is so upset at me for letting Little Red go that he doesn't come out of his room. Maria tries to get him to eat, but he picks at his food like a bird. He has regressed to the point that Legos don't seem to entertain him anymore, and he hasn't spoken again. His sweet voice is only reserved for her.

Likewise, Maria is huffing around the house like a scorned woman. The entire family hates me; even Sebastian thinks I am an asshole.

And maybe I am. But one thing I know for certain is that Dominic needs to pay for everything he has done, and I am going to collect, even if it is the last thing I do.

34

ANNIE

T he safe house is cold, quiet, and lonely. Although full of furnishings and heavy drapes, it is dark, desolate, and defeated. Just like me. It has been two weeks since I arrived, and no amount of sleep and Italian cooking can remove the empty feeling I have in my chest.

With the stitches all removed and my physical healing near complete, I am back to my old self, apart from the small ache that sometimes occurs in my shoulder, right where a bright red scar now resides.

Dante always used to compliment me on my unmarked skin, and now it is tainted. The way he looked at me in the hospital, with pity and disgust, is burnt into my brain, the image not something I will forget in a hurry. The fact that I put it there by lying to him sits heavy in my gut, twisting and turning, keeping me up at night until the wee hours of the morning until exhaustion finally pulls me under. Dark circles are now a constant under my eyes. I stifle a yawn, my fifth already this morning.

"Tsk, tsk, you need to sleep better, Annie," Nico scolds me as he walks into the kitchen, taking a seat at the table and pulling apart his handgun to clean it. This is an activity he does every morning, before leaving it at the back of the kitchen behind a large vase.

"Easier said than done," I sigh out as I contemplate whether to cook, grab a coffee, or just relax.

Aside from Nico, I haven't seen another soul. No one else has been in or out. The kitchen is replenished with supplies during the dead of night when I am asleep, and each morning it is like a surprise for me as I see what is new to eat or to cook with.

We haven't left either. We don't go outside, and I can't stand near the windows or even open one for fresh air. Nico and I spend our time in the kitchen or the living room, and although we only have each other for company, we are not yet sick of each other. In fact, it is the opposite; I feel like I have found a brother. I now know more about Nico than I ever thought possible. He has been in New York for only a year or so, coming from Sicily, where Sebastian and Dante picked him up and helped his sister, who was battling cancer herself. Given this common history, Nico and I formed a bond quickly, and I know he has a soft spot for me, helping me more than necessary.

Together we have eaten our weight in food and devoured every last decent movie. My cooking repertoire has expanded as well, since Nico is a fantastic taste tester. Now I have to say my love of Italian cooking has grown.

"Why don't you do your exercises, keep building your strength?" Nico suggests, his eyes flicking to me, clearly seeing my indecision on what to do this morning as he pulls out the cleaning cloth and begins polishing.

"Fine," I sigh like a sulking toddler, and I grab the small stress ball nearby, squeezing it in my palm before releasing it again, repeating the task. The exercises are helping, doing them multiple times a day, every day out of boredom working wonders.

"Have you heard from Dante?" I ask, as my heart begins to pound at the mere mention of his name. I ask every day, and I always get the same response. Today is no different as Nico just shakes his head silently, not offering me anything.

I still make tiramisu a few times a week, and Nico loves it too. It appears that every Italian man has a soft spot for that dessert; however, every time I make it, I think of Dante. I take my time, soaking the biscuits and placing the ingredients in the large bowl with precision, in the hopes that he will walk in the door and want a serving, and that maybe it will be enough for him to remember what we had.

For days, I moped around the house, wishing I was back with Leo and Maria, wishing that I was back in Dante's bed, having one of our nightly chats. But I am not. And it is all my fault. I have no one to blame for my situation other than myself. But even though we are no longer together, I am thankful for the time we had, even though I still feel empty.

I spend a lot of time alone in my room, trying to organize my thoughts, and come up with a plan. There will come a time that I leave this place and Nico or one of the other team members will probably drop me off at a bus station to send me on my way. So I have been looking for jobs on my cell phone, the only time I ever look at it, trying to understand what work is available for a woman like me.

A woman with nothing.

No education, no skill-set, no family, no friends. I could wash dishes, but the urge to make something of myself now that I know I can, now that I have no time limit, rumbles in my chest. Dante taught me many things, but the time he devoted to me, the trust he had in me, a stranger in his home, it built my confidence. I want to be more, do more, and not just survive, but flourish.

"What are you dreaming about over there, Annie?" Nico asks me as he looks at me from the kitchen table, his gun now nearly sparkling. Weapons no longer scare me, and Nico has even spent some time showing me his gun and how to operate it. Not that I have ever fired it, nor do I plan to, but it is yet another thing I have learnt in this weird situation I am in.

"What I want to be when I grow up," I say shyly, grateful that he takes an interest.

"Well, you know you can be anything, right?" He smiles, the polishing cloth in his hand still moving up and down the barrel of his handgun as he wipes the already pristine metal.

"But that is just it," I say in slight frustration, and put the stress ball back onto the bench. "I don't know if I can. I have no education, no skills, no people around me to help me. I will be starting from the very bottom."

"Well, you are a great cook, quick to learn. Everyone saw how great you were with Leo, so you could work with kids..." Nico offers, and I nod quietly, my heart splintering at the thought of Little Leo, the precious boy who dug a place into my chest alongside his father.

I do love working with children, and it is something that I do have experience with. But with no education and no references, it will be hard to get started.

I walk to the fridge and grab the large bowl of tiramisu, then serve two heaps and walk them over to where Nico is sitting, plonking down beside him. He scoops up the dessert, and I hear his appreciation.

"MmmmMmmm! Damn, Annie, this is good. Maybe you could open an Italian dessert bar?" he says with a big grin.

I smile as I take a spoonful myself, the coffee hitting my taste buds and awakening my senses. A small flame builds inside of me. For the first time in a long time, I feel the excitement of possibility instead of the dread of a dead end. And while my mind is still firmly on Dante and Leo, and my chest hurts not from the injury, but from my broken heart at losing them both, I know that if this is all I get, if I never see either of them again, then they have given me more than I ever thought possible.

Because now I understand that the possibilities are, in fact, endless.

35

DANTE

I watch her as her pink lips puff out with each exhale. They are soft, pouty, and one of my favorite things about her. I squeeze the back of my neck, the small wooden seat I am sitting on making my back ache, but I never leave.

Like a fucking fool, every fucking night, I come here and watch her sleep. During the dark hours of the morning, I sneak in with groceries, the ones I know she likes to cook with, and then I sneak out before she wakes.

She has Nico wrapped around her little finger. Every night when I come, I smell the amazing food she cooks for him, and my heart pounds in time with my stomach rumbles. My food doesn't taste the same anymore, and I grit my teeth when the burn of my whiskey runs down my throat as I try to dull the ache I have in my chest. It has been there for weeks, and it is showing no signs of leaving.

Nico loves to taunt me with tales of their friendship, the way she smiles when cooking, or the way she laughs at a TV show they're watching. If he wasn't my best soldier, I would stab his eyes out for even looking at her. The fact that she is here laughing with him makes my blood boil. Did Leo and I even mean anything to her? I shake my head at myself and my thoughts. I was stupid for even thinking she was any different.

Even after death, Angelina's actions haunt me. Leo hasn't had a dry night since the incident, and I no longer have a fucking home. Her drugged-up antics ruined everything. But she was merely a puppet. Dominic the puppeteer. Pulling the strings, using her to get to me, and he fucking succeeded. That alone makes me livid.

My teeth grind as I crack my knuckles, the desire I have to drain his body of any life now thicker than ever. My team and I have shown no mercy. As soon as the incident happened, and I knew Little Red was okay, I scoured the city removing every lifeline he had. All his associates now know we mean business, and while we have ended a few, many have been forthcoming with information, and we have used that to our advantage.

We have drained his bank accounts, we have stolen and sold all his assets. Allure and all his other clubs are now mere shells, everything removed, and the city closing them down for demolition. Sebastian and I are buying the property for mere dimes, since Dominic hasn't resurfaced to claim them.

But no matter what we have done, it isn't enough, because wherever he is, he is still breathing. I dream of how I am going to end him. Whether it be by gun, knife, or my bare hands. The craving I have to get my hands on him is only surpassed by the craving I have for Little Red.

I want her. I want her back in my home and in my life, but I can't. It is too dangerous for me and too dangerous for Leo to have a liar around after what we've experienced with one. Running my hand through my hair, frustrated at my constant push and pull for her, I see the sun starting to poke through the closed curtains. I know I need to go, but I am not ready to leave her yet.

Again, I look through her medical files. Something I do every night when I am here. Nico tells me her daily physio is going well and she nearly has all her strength back in her arm. He ensures she eats and keeps a positive mindset. Given that she didn't have a lot of body strength to start with, I am not surprised she is doing well. I continue flicking through the pages until I get to the one I am looking for. Her psych evaluation. I wanted everything checked out. I wanted no more surprises. My eyes continue to flick through the typed words until I get to where the notes are about her lump in her breast. Her thoughts on why she was scared to get the lump checked and why. *"I didn't want the drugs. They would kill me before I die. I wanted to live first."*

The memory of the time we talked most of the night and her telling me about how drugs affected her mother is also vivid in my mind. I know it was tough, so I am not surprised she didn't want to be the same.

A small tap at the door interrupts my reading. Nico is standing there, peering in and flicking his head back to motion for me to leave before she wakes. I snarl at him. The fact that he even knows what time she wakes up makes me wonder; if I wasn't sitting here, would he be?

He puts his hands up in mock surrender and backs

away. I am a bastard; I know that, and I have been a total asshole to all my men since she has been here.

Turning back to look over at her, I see her body move, and I freeze, watching her, before I silently stand, placing her files down on the chair and quietly walking out of the room.

I strut down the hallway and into the kitchen, where I find Nico preparing a morning coffee.

"Want one boss?" he asks, already knowing the answer.

"No," I reply. "How has she been?" I ask him. It is the same question I ask him every morning.

"Doing well. Although she is starting to talk about what she will do when she leaves here," he says, raising an eyebrow at me.

Leaves here? The thought of her leaving hadn't entered my mind. I take a big breath to steady myself. *She is going to leave me?*

I watch as Nico shoves off the kitchen bench and walks to the refrigerator to grab some milk. Looking inside, I immediately wish I hadn't. I see the large tiramisu staring at me from the bright white shelf. I scrub my hands down my face to erase the image, as it makes me miss her even more.

"I told her she should open an Italian dessert bar or perhaps work with kids. I know her and Leo got along really well, so I thought she would be good at it." He wanders back to his coffee.

"Of course she should. She should do both!" I say like it all makes perfect sense, although I need to rub my chest due to the twist in my heart at the thought of her with other kids and not Leo. "Why is she talking to you about this?" I ask, eyeing him. I feel like the two of them are getting too comfortable with each other. Nico jerks back at my comment.

"Why do you think?"

"Explain," I grit out to him, not liking his tone and not sure I want to hear what he is about to say.

"She cries herself to sleep every night. Does that make you feel better? Yes, she laughs at the TV shows and cooks YOUR favorite meals, but she's not okay. What did you think would happen when you left her in the hospital after ripping her heart out when she just woke up from major surgery? What the hell do want from her?" Nico says, exasperated, and I clench my hands by my sides, the urge to punch him running rampant through me.

Nico looks at me like I am stupid and crazy, and I am both, I know I am, but she lied to me. Although the more I think about it, the less upset I become because worry for her, my love for her, tries to take over.

"She will be awake soon," Nico says, taking a sip of his coffee, reminding me I need to leave.

I nod. "Call me with anything," I tell him with a nod.

"Sure thing, boss." I begin to walk away and out the door.

I need to get my shit together. I need to find and kill Dominic and then I can sort out what to do with Little Red.

Because even though I miss her, I am still not sure if I can trust her.

36

ANNIE

R aising my arms above my head, I stretch my body slowly as the soft light of the morning peeks through my curtains. I lay quietly for a moment, having a small amount of peace, and then open my eyes and begin to yawn. But then I immediately gasp.

Sitting up quickly, I rub my eyes to ensure I am not seeing things. The wooden chair sits in my room just like it does every night, but resting on the small table next to it is a glass. A whiskey glass.

He was here.

My eyes water as I am overcome with emotion at knowing that Dante was here, watching me as I slept. Something he has done since the moment we met. If he comes, it means he still cares, and if he still cares, there is a chance. For the first time in weeks, I allow myself to believe that what we had meant something to him, and my heart begins to fill with hope that maybe we could still be together. Maybe he could forgive me.

Sitting up, I pull away the blankets from my body and

sit on the edge of my bed, staring at the glass. Too scared to move in case it disappears. I rub my eyes again and the glass remains, so I stand up and move slowly toward the chair, still scared that it may disappear in a moment, afraid that I am dreaming.

Leaning over, I grab it slowly and lift it to my nose, breathing in. The familiar scent of his favorite honey whiskey hits my nostrils, and I close my eyes, letting my mind and body feel at ease. The glass is still warm where his hands had gripped it, like he only just left. I gently place the glass back down like it is an artifact in a museum and look around the room to see if anything else is out of place. My medical file sits on the chair, and I pick it up to read what is on the open page. *He must have read it.*

I read through quickly, noticing it is my psych evaluation, the one that says I am perfectly normal, albeit a frightened woman who just needs stability in her life. It also refers to the lump in my breast and why I didn't seek medical attention, the various reasons listed but with emphasis on not wanting to die the same way my mother did. I sigh and place the file back down before I look around the room to see if anything else is amiss.

Seeing everything else where it is supposed to be, I grab some clothes from the wardrobe and get changed. The small timber robe is empty except for my few t-shirts and jeans, once again reminding me that I am lacking. Closing the door, I go out to the kitchen to start my day with Nico, this time with a small spring in my step because of Dante.

"Good morning!" I say cheerfully to Nico as I walk

into the kitchen. He looks up at me from the kitchen bench where he is again polishing his gun, just like he did yesterday.

"Well, you sound happy this morning?" He looks at me curiously.

"I am." I grab a coffee and lean against the bench, watching him.

"Good night sleep, then?" he asks, before flicking his head toward the stress ball, reminding me to do my physio routine.

"You could say that," I reply, as I grab the ball and start squeezing with renewed enthusiasm.

"Are you going to tell me, or are you going to make me guess?" He's clearly intrigued, and I can't blame him. I have been moping around this house since I arrived, and today, I am acting like it is Christmas morning.

He clicks his gun back together and loads it. Standing, he walks it to the back of the kitchen, leaving it on the bench near the back hallway, behind a vase, out of sight. He has another one at the front of the house, close to the front door, and I am sure many others are hidden where he can access them a moment's notice, if needed.

"Well, I am sure you know that Dante was here," I singsong, and he stops suddenly, looking at me in slight panic.

"Don't worry, I didn't realize until he was gone, so he doesn't know that I know, but if he was here, then that means he still cares for me, right?" I ask, hopeful that he gives me the response I need to hear.

He simply nods. "He does. But he has a lot on his

mind, Annie. Give him time," Nico says honestly, and I calm my excitement just a little. Of course he has a lot on his mind. His ex-wife tried to kill his son, and he is still trying to find the man behind it all. Thinking about me must be his furthest concern.

"I know," I say quietly, taking another sip of my coffee as the flame inside me dims again.

Nico goes to say something, but before he can, a loud bang interrupts us, followed in quick succession by another, then another.

Startled, my cup falls to the floor, the porcelain breaking into pieces at my feet, the hot coffee making me hiss.

"Fuck. Get down!" Nico yells, and I drop to the floor, scratching my hands and knees on the broken pieces, before Nico launches himself at me.

"Quick, come with me." He pulls me hard by the arm. It nearly comes out of the socket as we run down the back hallway.

His cell phone is in his other hand. "Fucking get here! Now!" he yells to whomever is on the line, and I begin to panic.

"What's happening?!"

"Somebody is shooting at the front windows. We have bulletproof glass, but it will only hold them for so long," he says, his demeanor now changed from the friendly laughable Italian to the fearful mob soldier that he is hired to be.

He yells into his cell phone again, just as gunfire starts, and I can hear the glass cracking. I scream, dropping to the hallway floor, covering my head with my hands.

"Come on!" he yells to me, the bullets not making it all the way through the glass, so I jump up and I run with him, into the safety of the bedroom.

"Get in the cupboard" He opens the small cupboard doors where my clothes are folded. It is tiny, but there is a small space where I will fit. I don't question him and get in before he closes the doors, and I hear his footsteps retreat back out the door.

"Be safe," I whisper to myself in the darkness of the cupboard as the house is now quiet, and I try to slow my breathing to calm myself. We didn't really talk about what to do if anyone comes here. It is a safe house. Nico told me no one knows we are here. But if the gunfire I heard earlier is anything to go by, I know we are in trouble. With only Nico here to protect me, I am not sure how we are going to get out alive.

Tears begin to fall, my body shaking uncontrollably as I fold myself into my knees, curling up as tightly as I can, wishing upon everything that I don't die today. It is funny how only weeks ago, I was willing to die, thinking that my end was near anyway, happy to go out while protecting my little boy.

My body jolts as I hear more gunshots, and they appear louder this time. With each pop, I squeeze my eyes shut tighter to try and block out the fear that is building inside of me. As I wriggle my feet a little to get more comfortable, my toes hit my duffle bag. The small bag that contains my life. It is ironic that me and my life fit inside the small wooden robe, and that this may actually be my last resting place.

I begin to pray as that crosses my mind. I don't want to die. I want to be with Dante. I want to have a life with him, a life I am only now ready to fully live. My life is just beginning, and this time, I don't want it ripped away.

For the first time in many years, I want to live.

37

DANTE

After making my unwilling body leave Little Red's room this morning, I picked up Sebastian and Carter from the compound. We are now in the car on the way to see one of the families on the Upper East Side, one who we think may know where Dominic is hiding.

"If they know where he is and have kept it from us all this time..." I start to grit out to Sebastian as he looks out of the car window, rubbing his chin.

"We will find him, Dante. I feel that we are close," Sebastian says, trying to calm me, knowing that I am on the edge and have been for weeks.

"I can't find anything in their files that says they know. Maybe they are completely innocent in all this. Who gave us the tip off, again?" Carter asks from the backseat, his tone not filling me with confidence.

"A note was passed to one of our men. We need to check it out," I reply, my hands gripping the steering wheel. My body tenses under the stress and anger that are now permanently vibrating through my body. I don't trust the note, not one bit, but with no other leads, I can't ignore it.

"Look, man, we will find them. Little Red will be back with you in no time," Carter says, obviously feeling my frustration. "She is a little pocket rocket that can survive anything... including your wrath." As he continues, I shoot him daggers in the rearview mirror.

"You know, Dante, when all this is over, it will be time for you to move forward, with or without her," Sebastian adds, not looking me in the eye, and I grind my teeth in reply. "I'm serious, you need to make a decision; either be with her, or let her go." He turns to look at me. "I think we all know what you want to do, so just fucking claim her already and bring her fucking home. She is not Angelina, so get rid of this fucking chip on your shoulder that has been there for the past few years and fucking get your girl."

I know he is right. Little Red was made for me. I knew it the moment I saw her, and I have been a stupid, stubborn asshole these past few weeks. Before I can reply to Sebastian, my cell phone rings, and Nico's name flashes on the screen. Since I only left him less than an hour ago, I am surprised he is calling, so I pick up the call quickly.

"Nico," I say, but that is all I get out.

"Fucking get here! Now!" Nico screams down the phone line, and I hear loud pops in the background. Then I hear her. Little Red screams, and I slam on the brakes, turning the car around so fast, I am surprised that we are not rear-ended.

My foot is planted to the floor as Sebastian, Carter,

and I speed through the streets, listening to Nico on the other end of the phone. I hear him yell at her to get in the cupboard, and I know she is being placed in her wardrobe. Thank God, she is so small and able to fit.

My eyes look straight ahead, deep in concentration, as I weave the car in and out of traffic, running red lights and trying to miss the pedestrians that have begun to move around the streets in search of their morning coffees.

I have never moved this fast in my life.

"Fuck! Fuck! Fuck!" I yell as I continue to speed. "How the fuck did he find her!" I cannot believe the safe house has been discovered. But as soon as I think that, it clicks. Of course Angelina would have told Dominic about it. I am surprised she remembered it since she was withdrawing and completely out of sorts when she was there, but it all makes sense now. I was too clouded by my anger at Little Red lying to me to think properly, and now because I didn't keep her with me, I put her right into his arms. I delivered her to him on a fucking silver platter.

"Why didn't I keep her with me? If anything fucking happens to her..." I grit out, my heart pounding, my temper rising, so enraged by my own actions that my body is vibrating.

"We will get there, Dante. Concentrate on the road," Sebastian says, attempting to bring me back down, but even I see him clenching his jaw. This fucker has given us the run-around for so long, made us look like fools, stolen our money, and now he is planning on taking Little Red right out from under me. One of our own. My woman. My everything.

"I have prepared your guns, Dante. You are good to go," Carter says, stoic from the backseat, where he is now going through his guns, ensuring they are fully loaded as well.

"Nico, what the fuck is happening?" Sebastian barks out, so we can try to get a feel of what we're walking into.

"Rapid gunfire at the front windows," he pants out, and I can hear him gathering his guns too. "I can't see how many, four, maybe five of them," He must stand then to get a better view, because I hear more popping and a loud crash. Understanding washes over me that they are now through the front door. My heart drops as I will this car to go faster. We are now only a few blocks away, but it feels like it's taking a lifetime.

She better be alive, because if not, I am going to kill every last motherfucker within a 20-mile radius.

I speed down the street and see the house, our car tires screeching as I pull up out the front. And, immediately, gunfire is aimed at us. Good. Because if guns are trained on us, they are not on Little Red. The three of us jump out of the car and spread out, beginning to shoot back, each of our aims direct as we see three men fall and another run back inside the house. Still no sign of Nico or Dominic, though.

I stand then and head straight in. I am going in to get Little Red, and no one is going to stop me.

Walking in the door, my gun raised, I get my first glimpse of what I am dealing with. Sebastian and Carter are both right on my tail, watching my back and sides. We make our way into the house in perfect synchronization, the three of us knowing each other's moves before we even take them. Our defense is strong, strong enough to handle the two or three men that must be left.

"So glad you could join us!" Dominic blurts out from the open plan kitchen, where he is standing toward the back, not far from the hallway. His smug smile makes me want to smash his face into a million pieces, and I would if Nico wasn't on his knees on the floor in front of him. Dominic has his gun pointed to the back of his head, execution style, and my heart drops for a beat.

This is less than ideal.

As my eyes sweep the room, I see one other man standing to the left of Dominic, his arms both raised, a weapon in each, trained on us. Fool, there is no way he can get a clear shot at all three of us; his life is most certainly on a short timeline. Aside from Dominic and his man, I can't see anyone else. Little Red is nowhere in sight, and I pray that she has stayed in the cupboard where Nico put her.

My eyes drill Nico, and he gives me a small nod, confirming my thoughts. He then blinks twice, indicating that there are only the two men, no one else in the house, and I am not surprised. We killed every one of Dominic's associates weeks ago. Who the dead bodies are outside, I have no fucking idea. He must have picked them up from the streets, promising them the mob lifestyle, only to have them killed before their dream began.

"Drop your gun, Dominic," Sebastian yells to him, as the three of us take slow steps forward toward him, spreading out.

"Don't move!" Dominic yells back, pushing the gun further into the back of Nico's head, threatening us, but we don't listen. Sebastian moves to the right toward Nico, with Carter to the left, his eyes trained on the man holding up the two guns at us. I move forward, not flinching for a moment as I look Dominic directly in the eye.

"You're a fucking dead man, Dominic," I grit out, barely hanging on by a thread, my hand clenching and unclenching my gun with each step I take. I want to take his life. I want to make him pay. For all of it. Angelina, Leo, Little Red.

I hear the click of his gun then, and the three of us pause as he begins to smile.

"I will kill your little soldier here if you take one more step. Don't test me!" I look at Nico. He is our best man, and I don't want to lose him. I have no plans for Dominic to take yet another person away from me.

But I need to get to Little Red. I need to make sure she is safe, because if she isn't, I already know it will break me.

"You lay one hand on him, and I will slice your fucking throat and hang you upside down to bleed out in front of the whole mafia family," I growl, my voice dripping with venom.

A small flash of panic runs across Dominic's face, so I know I unnerved him, and he must know that no matter whether he fires the gun at Nico or lets him go, he will be dead either way. There is no way out of this for him. It is the end of the line. As long as Little Red stays hidden, everything will be okay. She will be safe and be in my arms very soon. Where she belongs.

"You think you know it all, don't you, Dante?" he spits

out, his face flushed, sweat beading down his cheeks. He is under pressure and at the end of the road.

"You all think you are just so high and fucking mighty, so impenetrable. I have waited YEARS for you to accept me. YEARS, I have worked for you, doing every shit piece of work you gave me, and you still didn't accept me as part of the fold!" he yells, sounding completely unstable.

"Was that before or after you fucked my wife and got her hooked on drugs?" I yell to him. I am livid. I have never hated someone as much as I hate Dominic fucking Russo, and my insides swell with the intense need to end him right this second.

He laughs then, a cackle. "She was so fucking good at sucking my cock, Dante. All I had to promise her was an ounce, and she would be on her knees in a flash." He's trying to goad me, but it isn't working. All that matters to me now is Little Red. My heart is pounding wanting to get her out of here, wanting to end him, so I can get to her.

He must see that I am not stirred up by his words, and a sly grin comes to his face.

"I wonder if your little redhead will also be as accommodating." His voice edges out to me, and I take another step toward him, about to explode. It takes all my energy to try not to respond, to try and remain calm, because one false move here and Nico won't make it.

"I am going to end you." I have never meant anything more in my life. He is not going anywhere near Little Red, and every last man in this room will die before I let that happen.

Little Red is mine, and Dominic is going to pay.

38

ANNIE

My head rests on my knees, my teeth drumming in my ears as they chatter in fear. I am still curled up in the dark cupboard where Nico left me. I have no idea what is happening, but the loud gunshots have stopped. I strain to hear any signs of life, and I hear people yelling, men, how many I don't know. I try to concentrate to see if I can hear Nico, praying that he is alright, not wanting anyone to die on behalf of protecting me.

Still not able to distinguish who is talking or what they are saying, I peer out the small crack in the wardrobe door, pushing it open a little wider, and then I hear his voice.

Dante is here.

Relief floods me immediately as his voice soothes my shaking body, and I slowly open the wardrobe door wider. I am as quiet as a mouse as I step out from my hiding place, stretching a little before I walk toward the bedroom door to see if I can hear them any better.

Leaning my ear against the bedroom door, the voices are still muffled, so I reach out and slowly turn the brass knob, praying that it remains silent as I quietly open the door and peek down the hallway. I am eager to see him. It has been weeks since I last saw him, and if he is here, I just want to look him in the eye. Then I will know for sure. I will know if he still feels something for me.

The hallway is empty, so I open the door wider and slip out of the bedroom, making my way quietly down the hall, featherlight on my feet, tiptoeing toward the kitchen. I know I shouldn't. I know I should stay where I am, but it is like he is a magnet. My body is being pulled toward him, needing to feel his safe, protective arms around me, telling me everything will be alright. Just like he did the first time we met.

There is more yelling then, and I stop suddenly as fear sweeps over me. For a brief moment, I wonder what the hell I am doing. Panic seeps into my bones, and I start to shake again as I come to my senses. But as I turn around to walk back to the bedroom, I hear him again.

"You lay one hand on him, and I will slice your fucking throat and hang you upside down to bleed out in front of the whole mafia family," Dante says in an evil voice I have never heard before, and a cold shiver runs down my spine.

I decide to take a step closer, to see what I can see from the back of the kitchen. As I take a few steps farther, I stop short at the side. I see a man, with Nico on his knees in front of him. He is pushing a gun into the back of Nico's head, and I cover my mouth with my hand to prevent my gasp from hitting their ears. He is a skinny man, the dark suit he is wearing ill-fitted, almost comically enveloping his frame. His dark hair hangs a little in front of his face, and although I am hidden behind him, I can still see his head when he turns. His lips protrude from his brown buck-teeth, and oddly, he looks a little like a rat, as his nose is long and pointy. My eyes then drop to Nico. Kneeling solidly on the floor, not shaking like I was. I see him breathing slowly, his eyes flicking everywhere around the room, no doubt trying to see a way out. I can't let him die. I can't let him die protecting me.

I raise my eyes and take in Sebastian standing by himself, his gun raised at the man. Sebastian is casual, but I can tell by the throbbing in his jaw that he is anything but. His eyes flick to me and widen slightly, before he masks his surprise at seeing me there. But he doesn't move, doesn't say anything. He remains focused on the man who is still holding a gun to the back of Nico's head.

The tension is stifling. My bones feel like they are seized, my body no longer willing to move as understanding washes over me at exactly what I have walked into.

I can't see Dante, but I know he is here, and I would rather die than have him be shot because of me. I remain still as my eyes continue to roam the room before they land on the shiny silver of one of Nico's guns that he was cleaning earlier. I saw him arm it and place it here on the bench this morning, hiding it behind the decorative vase, so I know it is good to go. I have never shot a gun before. I have only ever held one in my hand when Nico was showing me his collection and how to operate them, so it will become another first for me. I slowly and quietly lean across and grab it while the men continue to yell at each other and negotiate between them.

It is heavier than I thought it would be. It looks so small in Nico's hand, but as I hold it in mine, I barely have the wrist strength. I bring my other hand up automatically to support my grip.

"You have taken everything from me!" the man yells, pushing Nico's head with the gun. "Now I plan to take something of yours. That little redhead will be mine, she will fill my bed, look after my needs, just like Angelina did. I may not be part of the head family, but I can steal your women with ease, Dante," he spits out, talking about me like I am a possession, like I don't even matter. He disgusts me, and I hope like hell he never has a chance to touch me.

"You fucking touch a hair on her perfect head, and I will rip you apart, limb from limb. I will slice you up with small, but deep cuts, spilling your blood so slowly, so painfully, that you will wish you never mentioned her name," Dante replies, and if I didn't know him, I would be so scared of him right now. My breathing slows when I hear him talk about me so protectively. I want to rush into his arms, knowing that is the only place where I feel truly safe.

I look down at the gun in my hand, then flick my eyes back at the man. His anger is evident, but he is so focused on Dante, his hatred for him palpable, that his gun hand has slackened a little and no longer points directly at Nico.

The man's gun now is aimed slightly away from Nico's head, and is moving around a little as he yells back at Dante, the two of them throwing heated words at each other, about me, about Angelina, their rivalry running deep. But as I look back at Sebastian, I realize that no one else can see that they can shoot him. Nico is moving away ever so slightly, trying not to cause the man to notice, but trying to edge away, and I see a gun on the floor in front of him, but it is too far away for him to reach without being noticed.

I love Dante. I would do anything for him. So, gripping the gun in both hands, I raise it up. My mind now no longer connected to my body as it operates on autopilot, and in a blink of an eye, I no longer think. I just do.

39

DANTE

Dominic continues to stare at me, the rage he has for me evident on his face. We have thrown words back and forth, and I know that soon he will get lazy and point the gun at me instead of Nico, and in that split second is when I will shoot. I aim my gun right for his head in wait, as I see Sebastian stiffen a little from the corner of my eye.

We are both out for blood. For stealing our money, for what he did to Angelina, and for now thinking he can just storm our safe house and take the woman who I love from me. I haven't fucking loved anyone before, and I love Little Red with everything I am. I am not going to stand by now and let him take her.

Because she is mine.

I notice his gun hand has lowered, no longer aimed directly at Nico's head, but slightly lower near his shoulder. Gripping my gun, feeling the cold metal under my grip, I pierce my eyes, looking right at him. This is it; I am finally going to end this piece of shit. But just as I focus on his head to aim, a gunshot rings out, and we all duck, falling to the floor in unison. I watch Dominic as his body drops, bright red exploding from his head, but his arm swings wide and his gun fires, shooting his own man, who goes down hard, the bullet hitting him right in the chest. Nico scrambles to the side, retrieving his gun and Carter makes quick work of Dominic's accomplice, ensuring he doesn't get up again.

As I slowly stand, I notice Dominic's body. It was a clear shot, straight through his temple. I glance at Sebastian and then Carter and Nico, and they all look shocked. We must have had another gunman here at the side, but I can't see who it is.

"Fuck," Sebastian says as he lowers his gun. With a clear visual of the shooter, he rubs his eyes in shock and disbelief as I lower my weapon and take a step forward before I stop dead in my tracks and my heart stutters.

It's Little Red. Her tiny frame stands stock still, holding a shaking gun, staring at Dominic's body on the floor, blood seeping from around his head. She is wide-eyed, barely breathing as her eyes flick to me. She lets go of the gun, and it falls from her grip, the thud startling me from my shock. Her beautiful body is splattered in bright red, the strong metallic smell now filtering through the air. She covers her mouth with her hands as she takes in what just happened.

I run to her then and grab her around the waist.

"Annie." I take her in my arms, the color has draining from her face as her body starts to tremble. Her expression still unmoving.

"ANNIE!" I bark at her, trying to startle her out of her

shock, but it doesn't help. I see Nico and Carter running around, cleaning up evidence, as Sebastian is screaming into his phone. Little Red slumps into my embrace, and I look back at her in time to see her eyes roll back into her head. She is out cold.

"Little Red," I say to her, slapping her on the cheek lightly, trying to rouse her. She doesn't move, so I lift her up bridal style and walk swiftly down the hallway, leaving the boys to clean up the mess. Kicking the bedroom door shut, I race her to the bed and slowly lower her onto the soft mattress.

"Little Red," I say again, louder, as I shake her shoulders, trying to wake her up.

"Fuck. Annie!" I yell at her, panic now filling me.

"Dante?" she groans softly, shaking her head as she comes to.

"Fuck, Little Red. Bella, are you alright?" My hands run over her body to check for any injuries. I see blood, but I don't think it is hers.

"What did I do? Dante, what did I just do!" she screams, and tears break through, spilling out over her cheeks as the realization washes over her that she just killed a man in cold blood.

"Fucking nothing, Annie. You protected your family is what you did." I pull her into my arms, securing her small, shaking body to my chest, and hold her as she weeps, with no plans to ever let her go.

My arms wrap around her like a vice. "I fucking should have kept you with me. I'm so sorry, Annie, I am so sorry I let you down," I grit out to her, keeping her with me with no space between us, where she should have been for these past few weeks. I run my hands up and down her back as she cries. I kiss the top of her head, breathing in her scent. My shirt is wet from her tears, and I hear her slowly quiet her crying and take a few deep breaths.

I grab her head with my hands and look at her, my beautiful broken woman, and I lean down, kissing her tears away. "I want you with me, always. I was such a fool to walk out on you like I did," I say to her softly, peppering kisses all over her face, willing her to stop crying.

Pulling away from her again, I look down at her beautiful, big wet eyes. "I fucking love you, Annie. I have from the moment I first saw you, and I haven't stopped. I am sorry for being an asshole, but I want you to come home. I want you to come home with me." Desperation seeps into my voice, hoping that she still wants to be with me after everything that I have put her through.

She takes a big breath in, and I let her have a moment for my words to sink in. She reaches up to me, her soft hands running down the side of my face, her eyes glistening as she looks at me, taking me in. "I love you too, Dante. I couldn't bear the thought of that man shooting you. I had to do it, I just had to," she whispers quietly to me before she leans in and puts her lips to mine. Relief sweeps over me that she still loves me, and I wrap her in my arms again. We stay together, on the bed, not wanting to let each other go.

I hear sirens in the distance, so I pick her up and walk farther down the hall and out the back door, through the back patio, and down a laneway. We have our back-up team here now, so I step into the back of the waiting Escalade, keeping her on my lap, and Tony the driver takes off back to our compound. She sits on me, not unlike the day I met her, the car speeding through the streets, and deja vu washes over me. Our safe house is now crawling with police, and I want Annie as far away from it as possible. Sebastian will be handling them all, with Nico and Carter no doubt by his side, because Annie saved us all. While I may have had a clear shot, she had the better one, and she took it. That is twice now she has put herself on the line for me and my family.

As I keep her close to me, rubbing her back, I think back to the past weeks and months. How I found her at the shootout at Allure and then kept her at my place. How well she fits into my life and how much light and love she brings to it. The way she protected Leo from his mother and how she protected Nico and me just now. She is like a fierce mother lioness, protective of everyone, yet the sweetest and most loving person I have ever met.

The house hasn't been the same without her in it. It is like all the color drained away and Leo, Maria, and I have been living in greyscale. No light, no color, no laughter. I want color again. I want her in my house, in my family, in my bed, all day, every day.

I trust her with my life. I trust her with my heart. She is my equal. My person. She was made for me, I am sure of it. She is my destiny.

40

ANNIE

I lie back on the bed, looking out the window, enjoying the warm sun as it creeps inside. I sigh as my body relaxes in Dante's bed, the familiar soft sheets wrapping around me, his smell infiltrating my senses. It is the same bed I spent all my nights in, albeit, in a totally different room.

I haven't been to the old house. From what Maria tells me, it is nothing but a cement shell now, Dante gutting it all immediately after the incident with Angelina. Not wanting any reminder to be present for Leo.

"Can you hold this?" Leo asks quietly, and I turn and smile at him, taking the small building block from his hand so he can put together a few other elements of what looks like a boat that he is building.

He hasn't left my side since Dante brought me back here a few days ago. Everywhere I go, he is with me. It is sweet, but I also know we will need to work on his attachment in time. Maria is equally protective of me, now ensuring that I am fed regularly, resting, and not lifting a finger until I am fully recovered. Dante is the most protective of all, though. He won't let me leave the bedroom, believing that my body has been through so much this past month, both physically and mentally that I need to just rest. I feel fine, but I have nightmares, and I don't hide them from Dante. I don't hide anything from him anymore.

"It looks like a lovely boat, Leo," I comment, taking in the bright white blocks and the clever way he has curved the square ones into the shape he required. He is such an intelligent boy.

"It is our boat," he says, as his tongue juts out of his mouth. He is in deep concentration.

"What do you mean, our boat?" I ask, intrigued now.

"This is our boat in Sicily. Dad said we are taking you there," he says, not looking at me, still struggling with some pronunciation, but making good progress the more and more he uses his voice.

"Sicily?" I question as I sit up a little more. "What do you mean?"

"What he means is we are going on a family break together," Dante says, walking into the bedroom, his footsteps still stealthy because I didn't hear him enter at all.

I look up at him as he stands next to the bed, peering down at me.

"What?" I gape, in complete shock.

"I'm taking you to Sicily, Little Red. We are going at the end of the week." He's telling me the most exciting news like it is nothing more than a trip to the grocery store.

My eyes widen in surprise, and a smile takes over my face as pure joy radiates through me.

"Sicily? You are taking me to Sicily?" I ask again to be sure, as I sit up onto my knees in front of him.

"Yes. We are all going on a holiday," he replies, my smile now a mile-wide and contagious, as one appears on his face as well.

"Dante!" I scream and jump into his arms, full of excitement.

"Ahh, stop it already. I'm outta here," Leo says, grabbing his blocks and moving off the bed. Dante and I look at him in shock because that is the most words he has strung together in front of anyone. His cheeks flush, clearly embarrassed at our affection for each other, and we laugh at the situation. We now have a very talkative little boy on our hands.

"Maria has done some baking Leo. You might want to go grab something while it is still warm," Dante offers to him as we both watch him speed-walk out of the room, and we again chuckle as he closes the door behind him.

Dante looks back at me, as I wrap my legs around his waist.

"Sicily? Really? You are really taking me to Sicily?" I ask again, my gaze on him softening as I take him in.

"Yes. Does that make you happy?" he asks me, already knowing the answer.

"You make me happy, Dante," I reply, leaning forward in his arms and kissing him softly. His hands grab my ass, kneading the muscles, as our kiss deepens.

"Do I make you feel anything else, Little Red?" he teases me as his mouth wanders down my neck.

"You tell me," I say, as my breathing speeds up and my breasts push against his chest, the thin nightwear I am wearing doing nothing to hide my arousal. Holding me with one hand, he moves the other up and down my thigh, before he slides it up the inside of my leg to my center.

"Do I make you wet, Bella?" he groans as his fingers explore my clit before he pushes one inside of me.

"Yes... Dante..." I say, moaning his name. Since I got back here from the safe house, we have kept our activity to a minimum. The doctor said no sex or much physical activity, but Dante sleeps with me every night, holding me tight, never letting me go, just like he promised me. We often talk until we both fall into an exhausted sleep, and I love waking up to him every morning. I can't believe that he now sleeps with me all night, something he never did before. Often, he is the one that wakes me from my nightmares. Always talking me through them, until I feel good enough to fall back asleep.

He growls into my neck. "Do you like my fingers on your body, Annie?" he asks, his voice growing husky. I know he is trying to be gentle, scared that I am still too broken from the safe house incident.

"Yes, Dante," I say again, knowing that me saying his name is going to push him over the edge, and it does.

"You know I missed your little moans." His fingers continue to circle me, bringing me closer.

"I missed your growls."

"I missed your cooking." I smile then; he really wants me to make tiramisu.

"I missed our talks."

He pushed his fingers inside of me, and my breath hitches. I lean back, my back arching slightly as I let out a moan.

"Fuck it," he says as he leans over and lays me back onto the bed, getting on his knees on the floor beside me. His hands trace down my body until they reach my underwear, and he pulls them down my legs.

"It's been too fucking long since I have had my mouth on you. You need to be quiet because I wasn't planning on doing this right now, especially with Maria and Leo awake and moving about downstairs, but I can't wait a fucking second longer." Pure carnal desire etches onto his face as he grabs my legs and pulls me toward him, pushing his mouth onto me.

"Ohhh God..." I moan at the sudden contact, my hands immediately going to the back of his head. He grabs my legs and throws them over each shoulder, his hands resting on my hips and his fingers opening me up for him.

"Dante... Oh God.. Dante..." I pant out at his veracity and appetite for me. Like I am his last meal.

I look down at him and see him watching me. "I have been fucking dreaming of tasting you for days. Fucking perfect, Bella," he groans out before getting back to his task. Clearly, only hugging and kissing as advised by the doctor has reached its limit.

My hands thread into his hair as my hips begin to move. It has been weeks since I was with him last, and I have missed him just as much as he appears to have missed me.

"I'm... I'm..." I can't even talk as my back arches, and I

grip his hair tight as my orgasm washes over me. My hips rocking against his face, he doesn't release me, but slows his tongue as I catch my breath.

"I could fucking die happy right here in your sweet pussy, Bella." I blush a little, still not quite used to the way he talks about me. He grins before sitting back and rubbing my legs, ensuring that I am warm. "I promise that is just the appetizer, Bella. I will keep main course and dessert for later." He winks, then pulls my legs back into the bed, fluffing my pillow and covering me with the blankets.

Just as he stands, I think he is about to leave, but he actually jumps in beside me, fully clothed, and pulls me toward him, his nose once again in my neck.

"What are you doing?" I ask him, smiling in surprise that he is hanging around, but enjoying this new side of him.

"I nearly fucking lost you, Little Red..." His voice breaks as his face buries into my neck. "I nearly fucking lost you to that asshole, and I am never, ever going to let you go again." He peels his face back to look at me, cupping my cheeks.

"I'm so sorry, Dante, that I didn't tell you everything. I thought the life that I could've had with you wasn't possible. I thought my life was nearly over. Even though I dreamed and wished every day for it to be my future, I really didn't think that it was going to be. Now that it is, I want you more than anything. I want to be with you always. I love you and I love little Leo, and there is nowhere else I want to be."

His face is serious as I stare into his eyes, waiting for

his next words. "My life is not for the fainthearted. You have already seen what devastation and violence come with being with a man like me. It isn't pretty, it isn't always safe." He leans in and kisses my shoulder, his lips caressing my scar. "You saved my son, and in a way, you saved me too. I never truly loved anyone until I met you. I want you with me forever. Is that alright with you?" he asks, a small smile dancing on his lips.

I nod. "I want to be with you forever too," I whisper, and I see his eyes gleam before he tucks me back into his side and we lie there in peace, together.

ANNIE - 12 MONTHS LATER

My fingers ache as I continue to type on the nice new laptop Dante bought for me. I have about 200 words to go until my final assignment is finished. Then all I have to do is pass my final exams next week, and I would have successfully passed my first year at college.

Enrolling in a degree of education was a no-brainer for me after spending so much time with Leo. For the past year, I have been either here at home with my family or at school in lectures, and now, I am well on my way to becoming a fully qualified teacher. Every three months, Dante takes me to see Doctor Wakeford for a scan of my breasts and blood tests. It isn't medically necessary, but he is being cautious and protective, so I let him. After everything we've been through, we have no secrets and tell each other everything. We both trust Doctor Wakeford with our lives, but unfortunately, she is moving down to Philly. She was a bit cagey when I asked her about it, so I didn't pry, but I will miss her. She has become a wonderful friend.

I sit back, stretching my arms high above my head, trying to remove the pain in my upper shoulders as Maria comes by and places another plate of food in front of me.

"Oh, Maria, really, I am okay. You don't need to look after me." She is no longer the housekeeper, but our full time Nona, taking on a grandparent role and spending time with us all at home with no expectation of her having to cook or clean, even though she still does.

"Hush, Bella. If I don't feed you, you don't eat!" she huffs out at me, before kissing the top of my head and walking back out to the kitchen. I love her, I really do.

I grab a cookie from the plate in front of me and look at the mess I have created. I have books and notebooks, along with highlighters and pens, all strewn from one end of the dining table to the other. You cannot see the table from the mess.

I put my head back down and after another 30 minutes, I am done. Proud of my efforts, I save my document and smile.

I did it!

Dante believed in me every step of the way, knowing that I really wanted to make something of myself. He has supported me through it all. Ensuring I have everything I need; I get driven to and from the university, he lets me use Leo for case studies, and provides many stress relievers along the way.

As I close my laptop and tidy up the papers, I look around the house and am puzzled with how quiet it is. No Maria. No Leo. And Dante is nowhere to be seen. In fact, I haven't seen him for hours, yet I thought he said he would be home all day today.

I decide to leave the rest of the packing up for later and stand, stretching my legs.

"Leo?" I call out, to no response.

"Dante?" I yell, but hear nothing.

I pad down the hallway, admiring our beautiful home. It took most of the year to renovate, but we are now back into the original space in the compound; however, it has an entirely different floor plan, a new color scheme, and new decor. Dante asked Leo and I to make the decisions, as he wanted the space to feel safe for us both after Angelina came here, and we had so much fun with it. I even had our bathroom painted bright blue, like the waters of Sicily. An artist from Maddison's gallery connections came in and painted his boat on the water to remind Dante of his love of his home country—a place he says he will take me to again as soon as all my exams are over, and I can't wait. Sicily is now our frequent holiday destination. I reach his office and look inside, expecting him to be behind his desk, his head buried in papers, but it is also empty.

"That's odd," I murmur to myself, because I am sure he didn't leave the house this morning.

I walk back through the dining room again, to the other side of the house toward our bedrooms, figuring Leo is probably in his room, playing. I stop by his room and poke my head in. "Leo?" I call out, and there is no answer. The room is spotless, and he is not here.

Feeling a little uneasy, because it is so quiet, I spin

quickly and walk down the hall to our room. I open the door and push through, stopping dead in my tracks.

"Dante?" I say quietly, as shock stills my body and the blood drains from my face.

Dante clears his throat, before my eyes sweep around the room.

Rose petals are on nearly every surface, candles are lit around the room, and Dante and Leo are standing side by side in matching black tuxedos, their hands clasped in front of them like soldiers. Only Leo is grinning from ear to ear and elbowing his father.

I look back to Dante, and my gaze softens.

"Little Red. Annie. My Bella," he starts, before clearing his throat again, and I realize he is nervous. I have never seen Dante nervous before; he is usually so stoic. My chest warms as I watch him squirm a little. I take a few steps closer, my heart pounding, and my lips are dry as I watch him, waiting for his next words.

"It has been over a year since I slammed you into the pavement on your first morning here in New York, and I have no idea how I ever lived without you. I knew from that moment, you were different, and I never wanted to let you go. We have been through so much, and I want you more and more every day. I can't stand the thought of never being together. I love you. You are my everything. You have given me life. Us life," he says, taking a quick look down at Leo who is standing by his side, his grin now even wider. "So.." He stops for a moment as both he and Leo bend down on one knee, both presenting me with black velvet boxes. They open them at the same time. In Leo's is a sparkling diamond heart necklace that shimmers in the lights. Dante's box holds a ring, a large bright solitaire diamond, bigger and more sparkly than I ever thought possible, and I lose my breath.

"Will you give us the honor of being our everything, always?" he proposes, looking directly at me. "Be my wife, Annie, let's have forever together?"

I never thought this would happen. I never thought I would have anyone other than myself.

"Yes. Yes, I will forever be yours," I say as my eyes start to water. "Both of yours." I look at Leo, who fist bumps the air and rushes to me, slamming his little body into me. Dante slips the ring on my finger, standing and kissing me before hugging us both.

"Forever mine," Dante whispers into my neck as he pulls me close, and the three of us stand together. My life is now finally complete.

GRAB a **bonus scene** to get Dante's point of view on what his life is like with Little Red one year on.

Bonus Scene

DO YOU WANT MORE?

My Fight

Carter Grange has had to fight for everything, the struggles of life sticking to him from a young age. In contrast Doctor Catherine Wakeford grew up with a silver spoon, not a feather ruffled, her perfect life and her perfect body not something Carter needs to get involved with...or touch.

But he does and now he can't get enough.

Grab a copy of My Fight now!
https://books2read.com/My-Fight-Samantha-Skye

ALSO BY SAMANTHA SKYE

Boston Billionaires Series

Coming Home - Now **FREE**

Finding Home

Leaving Home

Building Home

Men of New York Series

My Legacy

My Destiny

My Fight

My Chance

ABOUT THE AUTHOR

Samantha Skye is a contemporary romance author from Melbourne, Australia. A country kid turned city slicker, Samantha writes characters that are as diverse as they are devilishly handsome. Her unique brand of suspenseful spice deftly combines the risky and the risqué, setting hearts pounding for more than one reason! When she's not plotting her next novel, Samantha can be found chatting on podcasts, or anywhere there's sunshine. An avid traveler, Samantha is just as comfortable in gumboots as she is in Christian Louboutins...but she's usually having more fun in the latter.

To learn more about her and what comes next in her author journey you can find her on;

WEB: samanthaskyeauthor.com